COYOTE

A JESSICA JAMES MYSTERY

BY

KELLY OLIVER

Please review it on Amazon

and rate it and vote for it on Goodreads

I appreciate your support!!

Thanks, Kelly

www.kellyoliverbooks.com

Formatting performed by Damonza.com

Print ISBN number 978-0-9975836-0-1
Ebook ISBN number 978-0-9975836-1-8

Praise for COYOTE

"**A splendid mystery** *involving one of the most resonant issues of our dangerous times.* **Jessica James is a new American original.** "

—Jason Miller, author of *Down Don't Bother Me*

Praise for WOLF

Jessica James, Cowgirl Philosopher Mysteries, Book One

"**...a gripping mystery and humorous read.** "

— Samuel Marquis, author of *The Coalition* and *Bodyguard of Deception*

"**...a rollercoaster of a ride. Exquisitely not put downable!** "

—Tracy Whiting, author of *The Thirteenth Fellow*

"**Jessica James is a...unique combination of smart and witty.** "

— Charles Salzberg, author of *Swann's Lake of Despair*

"**... a suspenseful, well-paced debut novel.** "

— Debra H. Goldstein, author of *Should Have Played Poker*

CHAPTER ONE

JESSICA JAMES HAD only been home for two hours, and already Whitefish was a couple of sizes too small. She waited until everyone else cleared out, then loaded a flimsy paper plate with crusty potato salad and the last piece of huckleberry coffeecake. Standing alone under the shade of a hemlock tree, she was just digging in when she heard a ruckus coming from the waterfront in the direction of Specht Mill. Stopping mid-bite, fork still in her mouth, she turned toward the river. Squinting against the sun's glare behind the jagged peaks of the Whitefish Mountains, all she could make out were four silhouettes, arms flapping. Shading her eyes with one hand, and balancing her plate on the other, Jessica peered in the direction of the commotion. To her surprise, she recognized her cousin Mike shaking his finger at a tall overdressed woman who stood out amongst the lumberjacks like a rattlesnake at a square dance. Usually so laid-back he was prone, she'd never seen Mike this agitated. Jessica narrowed her brows, retracted the fork from her mouth, and stabbed it into a fat chunk of greasy potato. Grabbing her sweaty beer bottle off the picnic table, then gripping her precarious plate by its sticky edge, she strode across the park grounds to investigate.

As she wove her way through the jumble of lumberjacks, mill workers, forest service hacks, and timberland owners (and their wives and girlfriends), their unforgiving stares burned through her freckled skin; suddenly she was an alien visiting from another planet. Except for the woman in the navy blue sheath and pearls down by the river, she was the only one wearing a dress, albeit a wrinkly gabardine vintage number with faded black velvet embroidery. And for all the cowboy boots in the crowd, hers were the only ones painted bright red with model paint.

But it wasn't just her funky mismatched clothes or tangled mop of blonde hair that made folks shake their heads and tut with their tongues as she passed by. Even before she left Montana to go "back East" and study philosophy, she'd never been able to meet their expectations of a proper young lady. A "klutzy tomboy" constantly getting into scrapes and a "trouble maker" constitutionally unable to play by the rules, growing up she'd always run afoul of the "natives." Still, she hadn't expected kids she'd known since kindergarten to turn up their noses and snub her attempted greetings. On the way from the airport, her cousin Mike had warned her that some of the old crowd thought she'd gotten "too big for her britches," coming back and flaunting her fancy degree and "book learning." But she could no more resist philosophy than they could resist reproducing. Just as their new babies sprouted every spring following a cold harsh winter, her perpetual soul-searching was the natural consequence of the cold harsh reality of her child-hood, starting with her birth.

Her mom loved to tell Jessica she'd been born rolling her eyes and sucking her thumb, "only a few seconds old and already bored with life." If it was true she'd emerged from her mother's womb sucking her thumb, she'd prob-ably just been biding her time, waiting until she could escape from the constricting grip of her maternal confines and get on with life. Even in utero she'd been pensive and brooding, a natural born philosopher, and the perfect fit between her tiny thumb and the roof of her mouth con-firmed her contemplative character. It also meant she'd wear braces for most of her adolescence. The braces may have straightened her teeth, but nothing could straighten her temperament as meandering as a Montana stream.

Concentrating on her plate and avoiding eye contract with the disapproving Specht Mill picnic crowd, she snaked her way toward the shore. By the time she approached her cousin, the well-heeled woman he'd been gesturing towards had taken cover behind one of two gray suits and was shak-ing her head "no." When Jessica was within earshot, she heard her cousin say, "I *know* it was you."

She sidled up to Mike, then, glancing back and forth between the attractive well-dressed trio and her shaggy shabby cousin, she took another bite of coffeecake and watched for his next move. Mike snorted, crossed his arms over his broad chest, and just stared across the river at the mill. Mouth full, she shrugged her shoulders at the suited trio now gawking at her. After several awkward seconds, the younger of the two gray suits extended his hand to her. "Hi, I'm David and this is my brother, Richard, and his wife, Maggie...er, Margaret." David's angular jaw and full lower lip reminded her of a twenty-something Johnny Depp, and his smoky voice went down like a barrel aged Kentucky bourbon.

With both hands full, she waved her beer bottle in acknowledgment, swallowed her cake, and said, "I'm Jess..." But before she could finish, her cousin grabbed her by the arm and whisked her away food first. "What the hell are you doing, Mike?" she demanded as he pulled her along.

"I'll tell you in the rig," Mike said, still tugging at her arm as he marched across the dry grass toward the parking lot.

Trying to keep up, she stumbled over her own feet, and the paper plate slipped from her hands, slid down her front, and skidded across the dry grass, sending mayonnaise drooling down her leggings and spitting chunks of pickle into her boots. She barely managed to hang on to her beer bottle and keep from falling flat on her face.

"Now look what you made me do!"

"Sorry," he said as he opened the passenger door to his beat-up Ford King Ranch. "Get in. I'll take you home."

Jessica grabbed the handhold and hauled herself up into the passenger's seat. She remembered back five years ago when Mike had finally saved enough from working at the Mill to buy the shiny black pickup, his pride and joy. He'd driven through town every chance he got just to show off his fancy ride, especially during hunting season when he could tie a buck's antlers to the rack behind the back window. The rusty concave fender suggested he'd hit something bigger than a deer though, a moose maybe, or a grizzly bear.

"You made me dump a perfectly good plate of grub." She glared at her cousin, pulled some Kleenex from her backpack, wiped at a glob of potato salad on her favorite dress, and then started picking crumbs out of the fringe of her buckskin jacket.

"What was going on back there? Why were you yelling at that woman?"

Mike shifted in his seat. "She's the wife of that damned business mogul Knight. He's trying to buy Specht Mill, along with half of Montana."

"Never heard of him."

"Richard Knight, one of the richest men in the country."

"What's he doing in backwater Whitefish?"

"Let's just say, a lot has changed since you left, Jesse."

"I bet nothing has changed at the trailer park. Ten bucks says my mom's probably not even out of bed yet." After almost a year in Chicago, her mother and Alpine Vista had become a bog of soggy depression and sappy expectations. She shuddered, imagining herself in a trailer next door to her mom, married to a beer swilling lumberjack, changing diapers and wiping up baby puke, a stash of Xanax in her nightstand and a bottle of Jack in her pantry to counteract the mind numbing domestic routine.

"So what's up, Mike?" Jessica reached across the center console and put her hand on her cousin's shoulder.

"Somethin' weird's going on at the mill." Mike

narrowed his brows as he stretched the seatbelt around his doughy belly.

"Weird? Are they downsizing or something? Or, did Mr. Swanson run off with that transvestite you tried to set him up with at the Christmas party?" Jessica poked him in the shoulder and laughed.

"I wish." Mike slammed on the brakes to avoid hitting a deer and her fawn leaping up from the underbrush across the road.

Jessica white knuckled the handhold and let out a little squeak as she watched the mother and baby disappear into the forest. The view of the rugged snowcapped peaks up ahead hit her harder than a shot of whiskey. She may be a nerdy alien among the shaggy old hippies, neo-Nazi skinheads, redneck cattle ranchers, and gun-toting Libertarians, but damn how she loved this place. She had a visceral connection to the land itself; the blood, sweat, and tears of her ancestors were part of her DNA, and her sinews and tendons were rooted deep in the dry Montana soil. Surrounded by these fierce mountains, she felt safe in the earth's strong arms, but the smoky haze encroaching on the horizon suggested otherwise.

"There was an accident at the mill last week," Mike said, interrupting her reveries. "Johnny Dickerson, right after his promotion."

"Oh my god. I remember Johnny. I met his sister, Little Eagle, once at Glacier Lodge. Is he okay?" she asked, dreading the answer.

"He's dead," Mike said as he pulled into the driveway. "And I don't think it was an accident."

"What?" she asked, distracted by the dilapidated doublewide's decrepit front porch and an overstuffed armchair oozing filthy stuffing that was swallowing up her tiny mom. Smoking a cigarette and petting an orange tabby cat on her lap, her mom sat at attention, shaded her eyes, and looked in their direction. The ramshackled scene brought back the pain and loneliness of her childhood: Her dad's senseless death, her mom's melancholic drinking, her own introspective isolation, all one sharp slap in the face named Alpine Frigging Vista. How could the grass be both overgrown and dead? Her mom dropped the cat, then the smoke, and bounced across the brittle lawn, waving her spindly arms in the air. Jessica steeled herself for a sloppy reunion. Twisting a piece of leather fringe between her thumb and forefinger, now she regretted ever coming back home.

Jessica waved back to her mom. When she reached over to hug her cousin goodbye, she noticed tears in his eyes. "I'm so sorry about your friend, Mike." She sighed and pulled Mike closer, inhaling his cinnamon roll scent, remembering all the times he'd gotten her out of scrapes: pulling her out of playground fights, bandaging her bloody knees, doing her chores so she could ride Mayhem, even covering for her when she'd sneaked home in the middle of the night from high school parties. Mike had been her only friend, at least her only human friend.

"Johnny killed himself?"

"No, he wouldn't do that. I mean….I mean…it was foul play."

"You think someone killed him? Why?"

"I don't know, Detective Clue Slow. You tell me." He

smiled knowingly. Once, during recess in grade school, Mike had found her crouched inside a box. Instead of going outside to play, she'd hidden in the ball box pretending to be a detective, peeking up over the edge, stealthily spying on the other kids, looking for something to pin on them. Since then, Mike had called her "Detective Clue Slow."

It was true. She'd spent most of her childhood wandering off to explore bear caves, abandoned hay barns, or hunter's tree stands. She pretended the school bus was the starship Enterprise taking her to rendezvous with intelligent life on other planets to collect evidence of crimes committed by humans towards other species. Now, instead of creeping around secret caves and spooky barns, she haunted libraries and museums; and instead of wielding a special gadget lodged in the tip of a ballpoint to unlock secret passageways, she used a pen and notebook to unravel the existential quandaries of life, and searched for clues to the meaning of life in dusty old books. She was becoming a detective alright, just not the sort she'd imagined as a kid.

"If there's foul play at the mill, we'll get to the bottom of it." She shuddered, thinking about Johnny chewed up by a saw at the mill. "You can count on Detective Clue Slow." She forced a smile as the wild woman closed in on them from the sunburned yard. At least her mom zooming toward the truck pushed thoughts of dead bodies and gruesome mill accidents out of her mind. Just two weeks ago, she'd seen the dead body of her thesis advisor lying in his bathtub, killed by a deranged student. She'd solved the murder, but she much preferred contemplating the mysteries of life to the mysteries of death.

"Wanna come in for a drink and save me from my mom?" she asked, rolling her eyes at the spray tanned, bottle blonde, sinewy snip of a woman flying towards the pickup. She'd kicked off her shoes and was picking up speed. From a distance she looked like a young girl in her tight jeans and tube-top, but as she got closer, Jessica could see the deep lines in her leathery face. Since her dad died, her mother had started drinking hard. And gambling even harder.

"I'm afraid you're on your own. I've got to be at work first thing in the morning. I'm subbing for my friend Kyo Kosi, Johnny's brother."

"Is that a Blackfoot name?" Jessica tugged on her backpack trying to free it from the tumble of stuff in the backseat—old tools, greasy rags, and candy wrappers.

"Means Bear Child in Blackfoot." Mike's burly body slumped in his seat and he sighed. "Johnny and Kyo Kosi are, were, my best friends at the mill." He unbuckled his seatbelt, leaned across to wrap his arms around her and squeezed her so hard she could hardly breathe. Still holding her tight, he asked, "Jesse, can I tell you something? That woman back there. She's the one that took the baby. I'm sure of it."

Confused, Jessica pulled free of her cousin's embrace and scrutinized his sorrowful eyes. "What baby?"

"She's the woman from the bus wreck, the one with the baby," he repeated. "They were at the Snow Slip Inn that night. I'm sure of it."

"The bus wreck? You mean my dad's…" Just then, her mom rapped on the window, jumping up and down and waving. Jessica inhaled deeply, gave her cousin an apologetic shrug, and opened the passenger door, wishing like hell she'd cashed in her plane ticket to hole up in the Philosophy Department for the summer, smoking dope, drinking whiskey, and arguing about the liar's paradox or brains in vats with the other graduate students.

"I'll be back on Saturday to drive you over to East Glacier," Mike said as she tugged on her duffle bag to free it from the bed of the pickup. "I have a hunch about that baby and I'm going over to North Valley hospital. I'll tell you what I find out."

She blew her cousin a kiss, and then turned to face the flurry of maternal affection coming at her.

Still jetlagged even after twelve hours of sleep, Jessica spent the next afternoon sitting cross-legged on the tatty plaid Lazyboy in her mom's dingy living room watching television and petting the cat. Her jaw dropped and her eyes widened when she saw Mike's graduation photo flash onto the boxy set. She turned up the volume as she stared at the caption "second mill accident in two weeks." She could barely breathe, glued to the television, waiting for more details.

A woman reporter held a microphone up in front of the mayor's face. "It's tragic. Our hearts go out to the friends and family of Mike James. It's just terrible." A group of local officials touring the mill had found the body, what was left of it. A picture of Johnny Dickerson appeared in the corner of the screen while the camera panned the mill in the background. The reporter came back on and introduced "City Councilman William Silverton of Whitefish." She uncrossed her legs and scooted to the edge of the easy chair, holding her breath and gripping the armrests as her childhood crush (now with more girth and less hair) described the grizzly scene: "The City Council was touring the facility when we heard yelling and I ran into the saw room. One of the workers, I think it was Tom Dalton, had already stopped the machinery, but it was too late. Apparently, Mike James had gone inside the debarking machine to clear a jam and somehow the large rotating drum used to strip bark off the trees had gotten turned back on, and he was... he was killed." Her stomach flipped, and she fought off a wave of nausea, then buried her head in her hands. It couldn't be true. Mike was dead. Last year she'd been afraid to leave Whitefish, now she was afraid to be back.

Tears streaming down her face, Jessica heard the news anchor conclude, "The mill will be closed until further notice." She staggered outside to find her mom lounging in the recliner on the porch playing online poker and drinking a vodka Collins, a burning cigarette dangling from her thin lips. Choking back her tears, the brutal words stuck in Jessica's throat. She should have paid more attention when Mike told her something sinister was happening out at the mill. Two accidents in two weeks couldn't be a coincidence. Now she realized what Mike had been trying to tell her: Johnny had been murdered, and so had her cousin. Bile pooled at the back of her tongue. She'd expected her homecoming to be rough, but not gutting.

CHAPTER TWO

JESSICA JAMES HAD been biting her nails in her sleep again, struggling through a recurring nightmare of riding her horse through a field, surrounded by fire, gasping for air, looking for an escape route. Sweating and thrashing, she rolled off the sofa bed and onto the shag carpet, then she woke up and realized she was at Alpine Vista, her ancestral home. Her mom was probably still in bed, sleeping off an all-nighter of booze, cigarettes, and online poker. The trailer smelled like a Montana bar after a rodeo, and Jessica was chomping at the bit to get out of there. Still half asleep, she dialed Mike to ask when he was coming to pick her up to take her to Glacier to start her job; the park service provided room and board, and just enough cash for the essentials: books and whiskey.

"This is Mike James, I'm either not home or in bed with a beautiful woman, so please leave a message, and I'll get back to you when I can." Mike's voice on his answering machine punched her in the gut. He was never coming back. His funeral was this afternoon. She'd never hear his buttery voice call her "Bug," or smell his cinnamon roll sawdust scent, or see his easy dimpled smile brighten his pale baby face. Never, ever again. He was dead forever. Jessica wiped tears from her eyes with the backs of her hands.

She untangled herself from the moth-eaten wool blanket wrapped around her legs, pulled herself back onto the lumpy mattress where she'd been sleeping, then surveyed the dank depressing living room. Peeling paisley wallpaper bulged over swollen sheetrock, and stained ceiling tiles drooped, threatening to fall on her head. Heavy balding velvet curtains hung over the windows, sleepy eyelids closing over old eyes tired of looking without seeing. Jessica grabbed her jeans off the floor, tugged them on, then reached down the front of her pants to retrieve her stale socks, put them on, and jammed her feet into her boots. Using the scuffed glass coffee table as a mirror, she tousled her dirty blonde hair to increase the bedhead effect, administered Visine drops to decrease the redeye effect, and pinched her pale cheeks to counteract the corpse effect, then shuffled into the kitchen.

Scrounging around in the refrigerator and freezer to find something for breakfast, Jessica weighed her choices: a frozen waffle growing a full head of icy hair or Swiss cheese growing a furry green beard. She settled on a toasted waffle covered in Hersey's chocolate syrup, with a shot of frozen vodka chaser. After breakfast, she spent three hours tackling the overgrown dead grass with the push mower, then drove to Wal-Mart and bought thick pink rubber gloves to battle the black mold growing on the bathroom grout. She'd been so busy running back and forth for paper plates, cups, napkins, and various cleaning supplies, she'd almost forgotten the miserable reason for the party.

As a last ditch effort to tidy up the place, she dusted the picture frames on her mom's collection of Western art, taking special care with Cowboy Jesus, his long flowing hair streaming out of a Stetson as he sat on a mountaintop looking down at his father's creation. Growing up, Jessica had spent too many hours at "The Adventures and Mysteries" Bible Study escaping sappy sermons by retreating into imaginary adventures of her own. If God could see into her heart, he'd know she was a big fat liar. Even so, she wasn't about to admit her darkest secrets to some priest with bad breath hiding in the confession box. Her mom never made her go to confession again after Jessica "confessed" to playing with matches in the kitchen while her mom drank vodka and played poker on the porch. Jessica never had understood her mother's faith in God or her belief that everything happens for the best, especially after the accident. If it wasn't her dad's fault he'd died, surely she could blame an omnipotent God. And now she'd lost Mike, too. Who was to blame for that? After Mike's cryptic comments the day before his death, she planned to find out, even if it meant meeting her Maker and confronting Him.

The funeral home sat across the street from a lumber yard, and the pallets of lumber wrapped in white plastic taunted her as she wound her way toward the squat building through the cars parked in the crowded lot. Sitting behind the curtain partition at the funeral service, sobbing silently, Jessica listened to Mike's friends talk about what a great guy he was. "Mike James was like a brother to me and

Johnny," Kyo Kosi started the eulogies. The mill boss, Bob Swanson, went next, telling the funny story of how Mike tried to set him up at the Christmas party with Jacqueline Rogers, formerly Jack. "The next morning, I shouted down from my office, Mike James you sonofabitch, I should fire you! And Mike laughed like the dickens. He loved to laugh." Even Old Man Specht, the mill owner, talked about Mike's integrity and hard work. It was true, Mike wasn't afraid of hard work. Even as a kid, he'd mown lawns and sold huckleberries, saving his money to buy a bike so he could deliver newspapers. Jessica wanted to tell a story about the time he'd used his hard earned cash to buy her a new saddle before her first barrel race at the Flathead county fair, but she was too choked up. She kicked herself all the way back to Alpine Vista for not pulling herself together enough to say something at the funeral.

The party on her mom's front lawn was more like a high school reunion than a wake. Jessica saw kids she hadn't seen since graduation. Most of her class hadn't left Whitefish and Mike was always popular, so the turnout was good. She'd spread the buffet out on folding card tables she'd found in her old bedroom, now cluttered with discarded junk. Back in the day, her dad had hosted raucous poker games with his friends from the mill on those rickety tables. For the party, she'd spruced them up with colorful paisley plastic tablecloths from Wal-Mart.

"Hey, JJ, too bad 'bout Mike." Tommy Dalton sidled up to her at the buffet tables. "If only he ain't switched shifts with that Injun, he'd…."

Jessica did a double take and blinked. "What?" She

stared into Tommy's broad face and wondered why she'd ever kissed that crooked mouth. He'd been her first steady boyfriend back in ninth grade, before he'd dropped out to work with his father at the mill. She hadn't really liked him, but her mom insisted she "be polite," and go out with him. Her heavily padded push-up bra wasn't the only reason she never let him get to second base. But the skinny kid with an infectious smile had become a muscular man with a hard demeanor, a tomcat with a head too big for his body.

"Then that Injun woulda been kilt 'stead of Mike." He spit disgusting tobacco juice into a red plastic cup.

Jessica screwed up her face. "Tommy, surely, it's not an either/or proposition…"

"Just Tom," he interrupted.

"What?"

"Just Tom."

"Okay, just-Tom." Jessica looked over her shoulder to see if any of her friends were nearby.

"Hey, Jesse, what did the Injun say when his wife tied his dick in a knot for cheatin on her?" He held up one hand like in a Western, "How come." Cracking up, he repeated, "*How* come." She flinched when he poked her shoulder with a sharp finger.

"I guess your dick's in a knot now you're out of a job." She gave him a fake smile.

"You ain't heard?" Tommy asked, stifling his crazed laughter. "Old Specht is selling out to Knight Industries, so I'm goin' back to work soon as the ink's dry and gettin' promoted, too. 'Course, I got other irons in the fire, ya know. I ain't gonna work at the mill all my life. I'm gonna..."

"Knight Industries?" Jessica asked before he could finish. *Richard Knight, the suit from the mill picnic?*

"Yeah, you know, the big company that's runnin' all them oil rigs east of the mountains?"

"Really." Jessica's mind was racing.

"Knight's been tryin' to buy, but old man Specht wouldn't sell. He's a stubborn S.O.B." When Tommy chuckled his mouth was so twisted he could swallow nails and spit out corkscrews. "Now with the...er...accidents, he ain't got no choice."

"Accidents..." The word was a sledgehammer crashing against an anvil and it made her head hurt. She closed her eyes tight to keep from crying.

"Ain't you heard? Last week, one a them Injuns is repairing the planer when it flattens him." Tommy smirked and took a swig from a second plastic cup in his other hand. "By the time anybody notices he's gone, he's already bundled and loaded on trucks to Home Depot, lumber for them do-it-yourselfers."

Jessica cringed and dumped her half-eaten lunch in the garbage can. She pulled Tommy away from the line of black clad mourners, crows cawing around the buffet table. "Two accidents in two weeks, doesn't that seem suspicious?"

"Yeah, I guess so." Tommy scooped a soggy wad of chewing tobacco out of his lower lip, flung it in the trash, and gawped at his shoes. Jessica's eyes followed his, and when she saw what looked like a bloodstain on his worn work boots, her pulse quickened. She looked around. He wasn't the only dude wearing work boots. Others were wearing tennis shoes with holes in them and some were wearing hiking boots held together with duct tape. She stared down at her Ropers and heard her dad's voice echoing in her head: "Don't judge others, Jess, until you've ridden a mile in their saddle." A homegrown philosopher, her dad also used to say, "The answer's not in the bottom of a glass," but she definitely needed another drink—or five—to get through this dreadful day.

"I'm parched," she said, waving her empty glass. "I'm going to go get another. See ya later, Tommy."

"Tom. Just Tom. Say JJ, wanna get dinner sometime?" Tommy asked glancing up, as he dipped a furry mound of fresh tobacco from the round tin he'd taken from his back pocket, and then stuffed the wad into his lower lip.

"Um, thanks, but I'm heading back to East Glacier as soon as I can." Jessica did an about-face towards the drinks table and left Tommy Just-Tom Dalton sputtering something about driving over to visit her. Her stomach soured at the prospect of seeing him again.

She darted across the brown stubble yard, made a beeline for the back door, then ducked into the kitchen. Her mom, aunt, and some other ladies from town were sitting around the small Formica table, smoking cigarettes and drinking cocktails. She tip toed to the hutch in the alcove, what her mom called the "dining room," and found the car keys in the top drawer where her mom had always kept them. Seeing her mom deep in conversation, she scratched out a note and tucked it under one of the dozen cat shaped magnets attached to the refrigerator. She sneaked out the back door, scooted around the side of the trailer, then jumped into the mustard Subaru Forester; the rattletrap was almost as old as she was. She rolled out of the drive-way so no one would notice her leave. She couldn't stand around making small talk with jerks from her childhood while Mike's killer was on the loose. She drove halfway to the highway before she took a breath, and white-knuckled the steering wheel the rest of the way to town. Detective Clue Slow was on a mission.

CHAPTER THREE

STOPPING FOR SOME liquid courage, Jessica James pulled up in front of a familiar washed-out wooden building sporting a faded mural of a muscular Bulldog in boxing shorts and gloves ready to fight. The place was at least a hundred years old. It had been everything from a doctor's office to a boxing ring, but it had been the Bulldog Saloon for all of Jessica's twenty-one years. When she opened the front door, the smell of stale beer, burger grease, and Alpo dog food hit her in the face, and brought back memories of fake IDs and high school dates gone wrong. A pudgy white and brown bulldog was snoring next to the woodstove—even in June, they had a fire going. A sign above the bar read, "Find us online at WWW.Fart-SLOBBER.COM." With his jowls and bald-head, the bartender-slash-owner resembled the chubby bulldog. Some things never change.

She went to the wooden bar, sat on an antique barstool, and swiveled back and forth in time to the 80's rock blasting from the jukebox. When the bartender saw her, he tapped a glass of beer, slopping Coors Light onto the floor as he delivered it. He tossed out a fart-slobber bull-dog coaster onto the bar in front of her, and sat the frosty mug on top of it. "On the house. Welcome back, Jesse." His jowls wobbled as he leaned over the bar to kiss her on the cheek.

"Thanks, Boomer. Beer, it's not just for breakfast any-more." Picking up the overflowing glass, she tried not to spill as she sipped. "Hey, Boomer, do you know what's going on out at the mill?" she asked, distracted by the collection of antique jockstraps hanging from the wall. Glancing around her old haunts, she saw Tommy Dalton's older brother, Jimmy, sitting at the other end of the dark bar. Illuminated by flashing neon signs, his fat face was pointed right at her, and it was too late to duck back out of the tavern. Why was it, everywhere she turned there was a cursed Dalton brother?

Jimmy shouted down the bar, "Why if it isn't Miss Jesse James. Get your butt over here, girl." He patted the stool next to him. He was the last person she wanted as company. She'd left the reception to get away from his idiot brother Tommy, but now she was trapped. Growing up, Tommy Dalton was the nice one, Jimmy Dalton was the obnoxious one, and Frank Dalton was the responsible one. Reluctantly, she scooted to the other end of the bar and pulled up a stool next to Jimmy. In the sickly green light, his dark glassy eyes peering out of his round, flushed face had a sinister glow. She prayed somehow he'd become the nice one. You never knew with the Dalton brothers. She'd heard rumor they all still lived together in some shack out in the hills near Hungry Horse.

"You don't need to buy me a drink, Jimmy," she said.

"Jim," he corrected. "Honey, I'm loaded."

She was puzzled. "You're loaded? Are you sure you want to have another drink?"

Spittle formed around the corners of his mouth when he laughed. "No stupid. I'm loaded in coin. Just sittin' here on my ass, I'm makin' $500 a day." When Jimmy leaned towards her, she was assaulted by the rank smell of booze emanating from every pore of his body. She blinked and stepped off her stool.

"Best investment I ever made. That old dozer paid for itself in the last week just sittin' up there on a lightning fire in Flathead National Forest. From here on, it's all gravy." Jimmy slapped the bar and sent pretzels flying in all directions.

Jessica downed her beer. "Thanks, Jimmy, er Jim. Gotta run." She'd heard the Forest Service paid loggers to keep their equipment on fires to build fire lines and trenches, but she had no idea it was that much. The high pay explained the two-hundred-dollar Stetson on Jimmy's ten-cent head.

"Wait, JJ. Boomer, get Miss Jesse here a whiskey."

"No really, I have to go. But thanks anyway." When she turned to go, Jimmy grabbed her sleeve. "Sit down here and have a drink with me. What? Are you too stuck up now? Too good to have a drink with old Jim? I remember when you wasn't above snugglin' up with my little brother Tommy." Jimmy gave her a lecherous look and a menacing drop of saliva fell from one side of his mouth.

Jessica grimaced and pulled her shirt loose from his grasp. "That's not it. I just...."

Jimmy interrupted. "Sit back down here, girl." He slapped the barstool. "I wanna tell you something about your cousin Mike. Yeah, good ol' Mike." His head bobbed and swayed to some inaudible music. Suddenly, he slammed his beer down on the bar. "Sit!"

Jessica dropped back onto the stool, sipped her whiskey, and waited. Jimmy stared into space as if she weren't there. After a few minutes of silence, she turned to him and asked, "What about Mike?"

"What?" Jimmy gaped at her. "Mike?" He swiveled his stool to face her and put one foot on the bottom rung of her stool in between her feet. "Mike was a heluva guy. Let's drink to Mike." Jimmy missed his mouth and spilled his beer down his shirt. "Fuck! Get me another barkeep!" he yelled. His maniacal laughter clawed at Jessica's skin. He put his hands on either side of her stool and like a caged wildcat she was desperate to get out.

"Please Jim, I need to go. Thanks for the drink. But let me go." She tried to stand up, but Jimmy still had one foot and two hands on her stool.

"Yeah, Mike was a heluva guy. Too bad he was an Injun lover. What about you? You an Injun lover too?" Jimmy narrowed his watery eyes and bared his teeth at her. Jessica pushed his arms away with both hands, knocking the nasty Dalton off his stool and onto the floor, then she stepped over his spread eagled legs and marched out of the bar.

CHAPTER FOUR

RAZZLED FROM AN overdose of Daltons, Jessica James drove to the junction of Whitefish River and Hellroaring Creek to clear her mind. When she was a kid, she and her dad would wade up the crystal clear stream in their felt-bottomed boots and waders fly-fishing for cutthroat trout. Her dad was gone, so were the trout. Sitting beside the creek, Jessica lost herself in the reassuring sounds of water rushing over rocks. No matter what else changed, this place was forever. As she marveled at the rhapsody before her—river, stream, and sky—time stood still. She watched the sun burn its way to the horizon, a blazing reflection on the water chasing after it. The approaching darkness forced her out of her dream state, and she brushed the dirt off her black pants and headed back to the Subaru.

Still not ready to go back home to face the stragglers and leftovers from the funeral party (or risk running into another Dalton brother), Jessica continued driving up the river. She could have followed the Whitefish River all the way to where it joined the Flathead River. But when she passed the road to Half Moon Bridge, she turned around and parked near a picnic area. The bridge was one of Mike's favorite spots on the river. Just up the bank was one of the places they used to come to pick wild huckleberries. She'd always admired the mysterious little berries for resisting domestication. She intended to do the same.

For as far back as she could remember, every August her grandfather would drive her and Mike up the windy roads to his secret huckleberry patch. To distract her from her car sickness, Mike would teach her silly songs to the tune of John Philip Sousa marches: "The worms crawl in, the worms crawl out, the ants play pinochle on your snout...." Her grandmother would demand a full gallon Crisco can full of berries before they could go home. They'd sing as they picked. "Comet, it makes you vomit, it makes your teeth turn green...." By the time they finished, they had purple stains on their hands, tongues, and pants from picking, eating, and sitting amongst the berries. On the way home, they'd start singing again. "Don't ever laugh when a hearse goes by, 'cause one of these days, you're gonna die...." And now Mike was dead.

A flickering light in the distance ignited a startling realization: she was just across the river from the Specht Lumber Mill where Mike had been killed. She'd returned to the scene of the crime. She narrowed her eyes and tried to process what she was seeing, a light in the office at the closed down mill. Jessica gazed across the river at the abandoned mill, wondering who was over there at this time of night. Mike had tried to tell her something wasn't right at the mill, and she planned to find out what. She couldn't bring Mike back, but if it wasn't an accident she was going to determine who killed him and why. Growing up, he'd always been there for her, driving her to the hospital to get broken bones mended when she was bucked off a horse, fell out of a tree, or skated off the roof. Now, it was her turn to do something for him.

She headed for the wooden bridge to cross the river toward the mill. But as she grasped its rickety railing, the buzz of her cell phone knocked her off balance.

"Hi Mom, what's up?" she whispered, and then switched the phone to her left hand to get a better grip on the rail with her right.

"Why didn't you ask before you took my car? Where are you? It's almost midnight." Her mom sounded tired.

"Sorry, Mom. I can't really talk now. I'm driving"

"When will you be home?" her mom asked.

"Don't worry, Mom," Jessica said. She could hear her mom tapping on her computer in the background. Online poker.

"Okay, be careful, Sweetie," her mom said. Tap, tap, tap.

"I'll be home soon," Jessica said, then whispered under her breath, "and if I'm not, call the police."

CHAPTER FIVE

SPECHT LUMBER MILL was dark and deserted except for the one light in the main office. Jessica James inhaled the scent of pine bark and sawdust, a smell familiar from her childhood, the smell of her father returning from work at the mill, metal lunchbox swinging in one hand and a big hug for her waiting in the other. Mike was right: a lot had changed. Now the smell of sawdust made her think of death and the abandoned mill was a grizzly reminder of Mike's dismemberment.

Illuminated by the ominous full moon, the massive gate blocking the entrance to the mill was dead ahead. When she yanked on the heavy chain link, she discovered it wasn't locked, and it squealed as she heaved it open. She cringed and glanced around the mill, then tiptoed through the gate onto the grounds, hoping whoever was inside didn't hear her trespassing. Across from the office building, a lone train car sat empty next to a gigantic rusty warehouse; the bunching grapple on a knuckleboom loader menaced with its monstrous claw dangling overhead; and stacks of logs awaited their mutilation. On the other side of the warehouse, packages of lumber wrapped in white plastic suffocated waiting to be hauled to Home Depot.

Still dressed in all black from the funeral, a stealthy avenger, she crept around a pile of empty pallets to the side of the office building and squeezed behind the shrubbery, then crouched down under an open window. Voices were coming from inside the office. She soundlessly stretched out on the cold ground under the prickly ornamental bushes, and lay on her stomach straining to hear what the voices were saying.

A smoky voice boomed, "I ordered you to slow down operations, not kill people for God's sake."

"But, but, Sir. Them was accidents," a high pitched voice responded.

"I sincerely hope so for your sake. There are thousands of wines that can take over the mind. Don't think all hell is the same."

"What?"

"Never mind. If I'm going to get this mill up and running again, unfortunately, I'm going to need your help."

That voice, it sounded familiar.

"Yes, Sir. Whatever it takes."

Where had she heard that voice before?

"Maybe you should lay low and get out of the country for a while until this investigation dies down," Smoky Voice said.

Jessica clasped her hands over her mouth and almost choked on a clump of grass she'd pulled along by accident.

"Do you have a passport?" Smoky asked.

"A what?"

"Never mind. I'll make sure you get an identification card to cross the border under an alias."

"A what?"

"Never mind," Smoky said. Jessica involuntarily gasped when she recognized the raspy voice. She propped herself up on her elbows, straining to hear.

"I don't want anyone else at the mill or Knight Industries to know about these arrangements. That's why I came to meet you myself. There'll be hell to pay if anyone finds out," Smoky said.

"Don't worry none, my lips are sealed."

"They'd better be or I can make you disappear faster than a bottle of Thunderbird at a homeless shelter."

Jessica couldn't believe what she was hearing. *The smooth voiced businessman from the picnic?* She was sure she recognized his sultry voice.

Jessica heard the office door creak open and then a truck door slam shut. She burrowed further into the bushes. As she peeked out, she saw a pickup pass by. Her heart was galloping. She tried yogic breathing exercises to calm down and get ready to make her escape. She had to flee before they left and locked the gate behind them. She didn't want to be trapped inside this eerie place. Even if Mike hadn't died here, the full moon looming over the empty warehouse and the coyotes howling in the distance gave her the creeps. After the truck was out of earshot, she counted to three, and then lifted herself off the ground. She was about to make a dash for the gate when a shiny Cadillac sedan rolled into the driveway, its gold paint job reflecting the moonlight. She dropped back down behind the bushes. The Caddy stopped on the other side of the office building, gravel crunched when someone got out, and then she heard knocking on the office door.

"Come in, my friend, come in," Smoky voice said.

"Good to see you again, *Napekwin*." The Cadillac driver's voice was deep and sonorous.

"*Napekwin*?" Smoky asked.

"*Napekwin* means… it means, honored Friend," the baritone laughed. "An enemy of my enemy is always my friend."

"And do we have a common enemy?" Smoky asked.

"The Eco-terrorists who want to kill our livelihood and stop progress. Oil operations are good for the Blackfeet. Fracking is the best thing to happen to us. It's even more lucrative than gaming. Sovereignty by the barrel, my friend. That's what fracking is to us. Sovereignty by the barrel."

"In the Bakken, they have huge housing developments for the men working in the oil fields, and even so, there's still a housing shortage. Here, we simply don't have the infrastructure to support the operations we have planned. We need to build cheap housing for the men to attract workers to Western Montana. I'm going to supply the lumber to build that housing, boards from this very mill."

"You know you can't build houses on the Reservation without a Blackfeet business associate," the baritone said with a chuckle.

"Exactly! That's why I need your help. Do you know where I might find such a business associate, Mr. Rowtag? I was hoping it might be you. You have a reputation for being a very shrewd businessman."

"You've come to the right person." The baritone laughed. "You're looking at your new business partner,

Napekwin. What's good for you will be good for all of us. And what's good for the Blackfeet will be good for you."

Jessica was listening so intently that when her phone buzzed in her back pocket, startled, she instinctively flipped over on her stomach and lay on top of it.

"What was that?" the deep voiced asked.

"What?"

"Didn't you hear that rustling outside the window?" he asked.

"Probably a skunk or opossum," Smoky said. After a brief silence, he continued, "If those damned environmentalists would quit whining about the Grizzly Bears, I could cut timber in the Stillwater. Mr. Rowtag, perhaps we could make arrangements to cut timber on the Reservation, too?"

"That's a possibility," said Rowtag. "For the right price."

"Montana is covered in forest but the government owns thirty percent. Talk about Socialism. And now those tree-hugging, grizzly-loving, greenies have the lobbying power to close the public forests. It's absurd."

"That's the beauty of our partnership, *Napekwin*. We don't have to worry about the Forest Service or the EPA. As I said, the enemy of my enemy is my friend."

Lying on the cold damp ground, Jessica tried to fathom the connection between Specht Lumber Mill, fracking, and the well-dressed businessman's part in this scheme to exploit Blackfeet land, but she didn't have time to ponder what she'd overheard. She had to get back to her car before she was locked in, or worse, discovered. She needed to make a break for it before the smoky-voiced corrupt businessman and Mr. Rowtag left the office.

In the chilly night air, she did a down-dog to a standing position stood perfectly still in mountain pose, and forced herself to breathe. She held her breath, counted to three again, then glancing right and left, took off running full force towards the fence. Almost there, she slipped on a patch of dewy grass, slid face first into the chain link, and felt a piece of wire rip her cheek. She wiped at the tears and blood with her shirtsleeve, and then hauled herself up the paling. Another sharp wire tore her shirt. Heart pounding, she stumbled toward the gate.

She heard the office door slam shut, followed by a car door, and she immediately dropped back to the ground, panting. Still watching the office, Jessica scurried backwards away from the gate as fast as she could. When the Cadillac came into view, she froze as she watched the car drive through the gate. She had to make a break for it before Smoky left too and locked her in. Once the Caddy was out of sight, she crawled back along the fence towards the entrance gate. She stiffened when she saw another set of headlights approaching from the office driveway. Blinded by the glare, she crawled straight into the wire fence. The impact gashed her outstretched hand. She clutched her injured hand in the other and knelt beside the fence. She tucked herself into child's pose, hoping she'd be hidden in the tall grass along the fence. As she listened to someone get out of the vehicle and close the gate behind him, she held her breath. He spent some time rattling the lock. When she peeked up above the grass, she saw his silhouette in the distance peering in her direction. When he started walking towards her, she panicked. *She was a friggin' goner.*

The dark figure was a dilated black pupil in the center of the eyeball of light shining from his SUV.

Jessica stole another glance and saw the shadow bend down to pick something off of the fence. Her heart sank as she realized it was the blood soaked fabric from her shirt.

"What might this be?" Smoky asked, turning the cloth over in his palms. "A spy? Looks like another job for the Dalton brothers." The shadow got in his vehicle and drove slowly up the highway like he was looking for something… or someone.

Jessica waited until he was out of sight then dragged herself to her feet. Glad she'd worn her pointy toed boots instead of her high tops, she climbed up to the top of the fence, white-knuckled the thick chain link, and swung her left leg over, hooking her toe into another loop. Three feet from the ground, she jumped, squatted, and then glanced around. Her hands hurt from holding onto the wire and she rubbed her palms. Sticky liquid trickled down her arm, and she knew it must be her own blood. She peered across the river toward the picnic area where she'd left her mom's car. In the first light of dawn, she saw the outline of a pickup truck parked next to the car. As nervous as a long tailed cat in a revolving door, she rolled into the ditch by the side of the road, panting. Someone was waiting for her across the highway.

CHAPTER SIX

USING HER ELBOWS, Jessica James crawled up the bank then peered over the berm. She had to force herself to focus in the dim light of dawn. Across the river, the truck parked next to her mom's car was too far away to make out. She inhaled sharply when the dark outline of a man with a beaming flashlight came around the truck. She inched further into the bushes alongside the highway and hid.

Her mind was racing. She had to call for help. She removed her cell phone from her pocket. Five messages from her mom. *Shit*. She must be freaking out. Desperate to get away before the ominous shadow across the river captured her, hand shaking, Jessica called her back.

"Where are you?" her mom shouted down the phone. "I've been worried sick. Are you okay? It's nearly dawn. What have you been doing? I was afraid something happened to you. I imagined the car overturned in a ditch somewhere, or worse. Has something happened? Are you all right? Why didn't you call me? Why didn't you answer your phone? I'm a nervous wreck."

Jessica waited for her mom to take a breath. Maybe calling her wasn't such a good idea.

"Mom, I'm okay. But I need you to have someone come get me. Uhhh....your car broke down on the highway," Jessica whispered, craning her head to see over the brush.

"Where are you? Why are you whispering? I knew I should've had that damned car serviced. Hold on a second. I have another call."

WTF. Jessica couldn't believe her mom was answering call waiting in the middle of a crisis. She felt like hanging up, but she knew better than to give up her only lifeline.

"That was Councilman Bill Silverton. He said he just found my car out on Highway 2. What are you doing out there? Where are you? He said he didn't see you. He's still on the other line. Should I ask him to go get you?"

"Cannon is out here! Why?" Jessica asked in amazement. "You called the friggin' City Councilman?" At twenty-eight, Cannon Silverton was the youngest city councilman ever elected in the state of Montana.

"It was the middle of the night. You weren't answering your phone. I was scared so I called Bill. He said he'd find you, and apparently he did. Why aren't you with the car? Where are you? I'm going to ask him to get you. Tell me where you are," her mother demanded.

Cannon was *almost* like an older brother to Jessica. After her father died, he came by every weekend and did chores around her mom's place. He mowed the lawn, clipped horse hoofs, fixed the fence, repaired toilets, and whatever else needed to be done. The only thing he couldn't mend was Jessica's broken heart, although he did come pretty darn close. She'd had a secret crush on him since she was a kid. Once, when she was sixteen, he'd kissed her. They were in the barn at Alpine Vista. He was shoveling horse manure and she was grooming Mayhem. She'd brushed past Cannon on her way to get some ointment for a spot where Mischief had bitten Mayhem. As she was passing by him, Cannon reached out and seized her arm, turned her to face him, and kissed her full on the mouth. It was the first time she'd ever been properly kissed. She was stunned, even scared. Red faced, she jerked away and hurried towards the storeroom to fetch the medicine. Why'd she have to call Cannon Silverton, of all people?

"Mom, calm down. I'm fine. Okay, ask Cannon, er Bill, to wait and I'll meet him at the car." Jessica could hear her mom crying on the other end. "Please, don't cry mom. I'll be home soon. If it will make you feel better, I'll ask Bill to follow me home. Okay?"

"Follow you home? I thought the car was broken down. What's going on out there?" Her mom sniffled.

"Right. I'll ask Cannon to fix it. He's very mechanical. I'm sure we can get it going. Probably just a dead battery or something...."

Her mom interrupted, "Bill Silverton is a councilman, not a car repairman."

"Yeah, so why did you call him in the middle of the night?" Jessica sat up in the grass and kicked the ground. Cannon Silverton could have been a mechanic. He had a way with machines. He might have been a math whiz and valedictorian of his class, but he wasn't just an egghead; he could tell a glowplug from a gudgeon pin. He could fix just about anything mechanical…. Human beings were another story.

"I've known Billy Silverton since he was in diapers…." Her mom was on a rant. Jessica stood up and held the phone away from her ear. She imagined Cannon in diapers and smiled.

Without letting her mom finish, Jessica said, "I'll explain everything when I get home. Bye Mom, and thanks."

Cannon was approaching from across the bridge, shining his flashlight across and up and down the river. She wiped her hands on her pants and headed towards the beam of light. As she got closer, the beam blinded her and she waved into the brightness. She had only a few seconds to decide whether to tell Cannon the truth or come up with a whopping good story. She ripped off her bloody tattered shirt and threw it into the river.

It wasn't just the lie she was about to tell Cannon Silverton that made her heart pound. The anticipation of seeing him again after all these years brought back teenage butterflies. She wondered, as she often did, what might have been if they'd ever gotten together. She'd heard Cannon had married Annie Davies, which surprised her. Annie was pretty enough, and the second smartest girl in their class, but she was so reserved, and she wasn't one of the popular girls Cannon usually dated…. Annie Davies didn't even play an instrument. What if Jessica had just kissed him back instead of staring at him like an idiot and running away? Maybe she'd be living in Whitefish, a stay-at-home mom with two kids, married to a city councilman. Maybe in some alternative universe, she was. She thought of the

Star Trek episode, "Mirror Mirror," where in an alternate universe, Captain Kirk and his crew were bad guys instead of good guys, and Spock had a wicked sexy goatee.

"Hey Cannon." A chipped-tooth smile flashed across Jessica's flushed face when she saw her old friend. "Sorry my mom called you in the middle of the night to come to my rescue." Cannon had been muscular and strong even as a teenager. He'd filled out into a sturdy man with an attractive enough everyman kind face that didn't call attention to itself. In high school he'd worn his dark brown hair as long as the wrestling coach would allow. Her lips stretched into a grin as she remembered when he tried to grow a soul patch on his chin. Now, his closely shaven hair accentuated his sad eyes and dimpled chin.

"Gosh, haven't heard that in a while," he said. "Everyone calls me Bill now, or Councilman Silverton." In school, everyone thought he'd become a professional jazz musician. That's how he got his nickname, "Cannon," after saxophonist Julian "Cannonball" Adderley, his idol.

"Give me a hug. Man, it's been forever, Jesse James." He held her at arm's length. "You haven't changed a bit. You're as pretty as ever. Little Jesse James." He let go of her shoulders. As rays of orange burst over the mountains, the sheer magnitude of the towering Rockies rendered them two-dimensional, dusky rose painted against an emerging pale sky, as magnificent as they were threatening.

"So, your mom says your car broke down. I'll take a look and see if I can fix it." Cannon clicked off the flashlight. "But first tell me why were you snooping around at the mill in the middle of the night?"

CHAPTER SEVEN

"UH, WELL, I was just out for a drive." Jessica James blew at her bangs.

"You were just driving in the middle of nowhere in the middle of the night? What were you doing over at the old Specht mill? You know it's closed down." Cannon's broad face and gentle sad eyes were disarming.

"I was driving out to watch the sun rise over the mountains." Jessica gestured towards the mountains. "It's gorgeous." She stood silently watching the sunrise from the bridge for several seconds before continuing to her mom's car. There was something brutal and fierce about those jagged peaks, jutting above the tree line, clawing their way toward heaven. Perched above the river, looking up at those mammoths, there was no denying the earth's violent birth.

"You really shouldn't be out here alone in the dark." Cannon shook his head. "These mountain roads can be dangerous, especially at night."

He should know. He'd survived the deadliest automobile accident in Montana history. THE accident. That was eleven years ago, when Cannon was a junior in high school.

The wrestling team and the cheerleaders had been on a school bus slowly winding its way home along Highway US 2 through a blinding blizzard when it smashed head-on into a jack-knifed tractor trailer, a logging truck. Jessica's dad was driving that truck. He should have been home safe and warm with his family, but on his way back from work, he'd spotted a hitchhiker with a baby and stopped to pick them up. He was driving them back to Browning, miles out of his way, when within seconds, his truck skidded on the ice, the trailer jack-knifed, and was slammed by the bus. Everyone in the truck died. After the accident, Cannon started coming over to the house. At first, she'd hated him, wondering why he'd saved all those other people and didn't save her dad. Eventually, she couldn't help notice his gentle kindness and lush lips.

That night eleven years ago, Cannon had become a hero. He'd made several trips carrying injured cheerleaders and fellow wrestlers to the Snow Slip Inn, a quarter-mile away from the wreck. The story was that once he finally sat down near the wood stove at the Inn where his teammates had gathered, he couldn't stand up again. He'd fractured a hip. But being in shock, it wasn't until he'd gotten all of the survivors to safety that he felt the searing pain. He got his picture on the front page of the *Whitefish Pilot*, with the headline, "Hero saves Teammates." Everyone in the first three rows of the bus died on impact. Minutes before the accident, the volunteer coach's five year old daughter, who'd gone along for the ride, skipped to the back of the bus. Her childish whim had saved her life, and that of her mother, the school nurse. Jessica pondered the precariousness of life and the randomness of fate. Nietzsche claimed the test of a life well lived was *Amor Fati*, Love Your Fate. Right now, she loved that fate had brought Cannon to her side.

"Come on, let's get you home," he said, and then led her by the elbow to the other side of the bridge and back to the picnic area where they were parked.

"Maybe I should try the car one more time to see if it starts." Jessica pulled her mom's car key out of her back pocket, unlocked the door, and slid into the driver's seat. The car started right up. She rolled down the window and Cannon leaned in so far she wondered if he was going to kiss her again.

"Thanks for coming to my rescue Cannon, I mean Bill, er, Councilman Silverton." Jessica smiled up at him.

"I like it when you call me Cannon. Reminds me of when we were kids. You know, I never told you, but I had a terrible crush on you back then." He laughed softly.

"Aha! Is that why you kissed me in the barn that time?" Jessica asked playfully.

"I never kissed you," Cannon said.

"Did too. Don't you remember? I'll never forget it. I was stunned."

"I think you're pulling my leg. I'd remember if I kissed you."

"My first kiss ever and you don't even remember it." Jessica laughed.

After an awkward silence, Cannon stood up and patted the car door.

"I guess you're good to go."

"Can I ask you something?" She looked up at his

kind face. "What's going on at Mill? You were there when Mike died."

Cannon coughed and when the coughing fit died down, he said, "I'm really sorry about your cousin."

"Thanks," she said. "Was anything strange going on out here?"

"Strange?" he asked. "Two major accidents, followed by Specht's announcement that the mill is indefinitely closed due to inadequate supply. Yeah, that counts as strange. Believe me, the city is investigating."

"Cannon, could you do me a favor and let me know if you find out anything?" she asked. "I'm haunted by Mike's last words. He warned me there was something weird going on at the mill. He was really scared."

"Scared of what?" Cannon bent down towards the car window.

"How about I buy you breakfast and we can tell each other what we know." Jessica raised her eyebrows at him.

"Well, I'll take you up on breakfast and *you* can tell *me* everything *you* know. How's that? Only place open is the nasty ole Pin & Que."

"Nasty ole Pin & Que it is. Meet you there." Jessica cranked up the window, put the car in gear, stepped on the gas, and headed into town. The Pin & Que was the local bowling alley, hang out for wayward teens and drug dealers, and the only place in town with breakfast all night.

"So what's up with Specht mill?" Jessica asked as soon as they'd ordered.

"Well, obviously you know about the accidents. Management claims they closed down because of lack of supply.

Environmental pressures have closed most public land around here to logging, so the mills rely on private logging. Specht just can't compete with other outfits like Plum Creek and Stimson that own hundreds of thousands of acres of timberland. It's sad really. Like everything else, the small family run mills are going out of business. Good thing tourism is taking off again." Cannon dumped two packets of sugar into his coffee.

"I guess I owe my summer employment to tourism, but I hate to think of this area ruined by people," Jessica said.

"We're damned if we do and damned if we don't," Cannon said. "Either no one can live here because there's no jobs, or we embrace logging and tourism."

"But logging and tourism could ruin the very reason we *want* to live here." Jessica smiled when the waitress delivered her huckleberry pancakes.

"Well, we have to keep the economy going somehow." Cannon took a grizzly sized bite of his rare breakfast steak. "They don't call Whitefish 'Stumptown' for nothin'."

"That's right. I forgot. You're a politician now." She stared at the bloody piece of cow on his plate. Cannon doused his pancakes with maple syrup and put on the nose-bag.

"Hopefully, next year I'll be in the State House. I think we can do a lot of good for Flathead County, and for the rest of Montana. We need to balance growth with preservation of natural resources. We don't want to alienate big business or stop tourism, but we want to keep Montana beautiful...."

Jessica interrupted. "Spoken like a true diplomat.

But you know, you won't break any horses by sittin' on the fence."

Staring out the window, she wondered if she should tell Cannon about what she overheard at the mill. She needed to find out what was going on before she told anybody, especially a city councilman with aspirations to become Governor.

"What's on your mind, Jesse?" Cannon asked. "You never were good at hiding your feelings."

She twirled a strand of her hair between her fingers. "Can I ask you something about the accident?"

"I don't want to talk about it. I wish I could erase it from my memory. And you don't need to hear the details. All you need to know is it was quick. Mike died instantly."

"Not the mill accident. The bus accident eleven years ago. When my dad died."

Cannon put his hands in his lap and stared across the table at her with his sad brown eyes.

"Was there a woman with a baby?" she asked.

"Don't you remember?" he asked. "The hitchhiker who died, she had a baby. It died too." Cannon stared down at his hands, and his eyes welled with tears. "I couldn't...."

Jessica interrupted. "Cannon, you saved so many people. You did everything you could and more." She waited while he blew his nose on his napkin and then sipped some water.

"Mike said something about the Snow Slip Inn. A woman with a baby. He'd stopped there for a bowl of chili after cross-country skiing. He saw you all come in after the accident. Remember?"

"I wish I could forget. It was the worst day of my life," Cannon said.

"Was there a woman with a baby at Snow Slip?"

"Do we have to talk about this Jesse?" he asked.

"Just tell me about the woman and I'll never ask you again."

Bill's sad eyes welled with tears. "I can still see her face, the Native American woman. She'd been thrown from the truck and was laying on the highway screaming about her baby." He put his head in his hands. "Then all of a sudden, she went quiet. Her silence was worse than her screaming." His voice was muffled. "I never saw any baby."

"If she died at the scene, then who was the woman Mike saw at Snow Slip?"

CHAPTER EIGHT

AFTER NEARLY TWO hours on the sick smelling Greyhound bus, Jessica James drank in the brisk June breeze coming off the mountains at Glacier Lodge. The ride had been depressing. With no car and now no cousin, she'd had to buy a one-way bus ticket. On the ride over the Rocky Mountains, she couldn't quit thinking about Mike, mutilated by the debarking machine. It made her want to puke. She should've paid more attention when he'd tried to tell her about foul play at the mill. She thought of the Butterfly Effect, how a tiny action like the fluttering of a butterfly in New Zealand could have a huge impact across the globe. She wondered if she was the butterfly, mindlessly flapping, not realizing the deadly effects of her actions on others. Seemed like wherever she went, death followed. Wiping the tears from her eyes with the back of one hand, Jessica grabbed her duffle bag with the other, then headed for the office to get her room key and uniform. Conjuring all the stoicism of her Swedish ancestors, she pulled herself together and marched through the office door to get her work assignment.

During the summers of her college years she'd done everything from maid duty to gopher work in the mechanic shop. As she ambled across the grounds from bunkhouse to garage, Jessica filled her lungs, savoring the spicy pine scent and crisp cool air. Taking the long way around toward the bunkhouse, she meandered across the grounds, admiring the rugged mountain views. The usually lush lawn wore crispy draught burnt fringe. The bunkhouse was at the back of the compound, tucked away from view. She dragged her heels as she crossed the threshold from the bright, fresh, vibrant world outside to the dimly lit, mildewed world inside.

When she got to her assigned room, a curvy girl in tight jeans was already there unpacking. Without a word, the mahogany skinned girl continued moving clothes from her suitcase into the dresser. She'd already claimed the twin bed closest to the bathroom. Jessica put her backpack on the second twin and surreptitiously assessed her roommate. Mournful almond eyes, high arched brows, full pale pink lips, and shiny frame of black hair curving around her oval face were at war with her grubby t-shirt and ripped jeans, she looked like an Egyptian princess passing as a peasant girl.

"Are you from around here?" Jessica asked. Students came from all over the world to work at Glacier National Park.

"Do you consider the Blackfeet Reservation 'around here'?" The unkempt girl made air quotes.

"Why are you staying at the bunkhouse if you only live fifteen minutes away?" Jessica unzipped her bag and stood waiting for her roommate to finish with the dresser.

"You ask too many questions." Her roommate's wide-set dark eyes pierced Jessica's soul. There was something calm yet fierce about her. Still, she looked tired….No, more than tired, exhausted. Her roommate's fine features and severe bangs along with her slow and deliberate demeanor tinged her beauty with a sepia melancholy. Jessica thought of Nietzsche, "There are no beautiful surfaces without a terrible depth." Was that a tear staining her roommate's dusty cheek? Jessica winced and went back to unpacking.

After a long awkward silence, glancing up as she put her underwear in the bottom drawer of the dresser, Jessica said, "At the risk of asking another stupid question, what's your name?"

"Kimi." The bronze skinned girl glared at her. "Kimi RedFox. And yes, I grew up on the Reservation. And no, I don't wear black soled moccasins and eat Pemmican, if that's what you're thinking."

WTF? This girl has a serious chip on her shoulder. "Jessica James, glad to meet you." She extended her hand. "My friends call me Jesse." Kimi hesitated, and when she reluctantly stretched out her arm, her small fingers were cool against Jessica's warm palm.

"I don't have any friends, so everyone calls me Kimi RedFox."

"None?"

"Yeah, well, life's lonely, get used to it."

"Okay," Jessica sat on her bunk. "What's your work assignment friendless Kimi RedFox?"

"Maid," Kimi answered. "Of course they expect the Indian to clean up the white people's shit."

Jessica didn't envy her. She remembered all too well when she'd had maid duty and the nasty surprises that could lurk behind those locked doors, even in the family friendly National Park. She hated to think what maids found in places like Las Vegas. Drawers full of sticky used condoms. Broken glass and burned rugs. Men in bathtubs filled with ice, missing a kidney. At least in Glacier Park, the worst was usually stinky diapers and kid vomit, or occasionally honeymooners who forgot to bolt the door and put out the Do Not Disturb sign.

"Maid, that's the worst," Jessica said. "I'm late, so I'd better hoof it to the garage. I'm driving the red bus this year." Known as "Rubies of the Rockies," painted the color of the ripe Mountain Ash Berries native to the park, the vintage crimson and black caravans had shuttled back and forth between the railroad lodges for the last fifty years. The drivers were called "jammers" because back when the buses had standard transmissions, you could hear the gears jamming on the winding, precipitous, Going-to-the-Sun Highway. The steep, curvy, narrow road wasn't for the faint of heart. She'd seen many unsuspecting tourists stopping along the road to toss their cookies.

"Lucky you," her roommate replied, but didn't look up as Jessica left the room.

On her way to pick up the keys to the Ruby Red shuttle bus, Jessica gazed up at the snowcapped peaks, her whole being expanded, a bud opening into full bloom. Now she remembered why nature was her religion. She worshipped these mountains, trees, streams, and lakes. They were a tonic for her troubled soul.

As she crossed the parking lot, she recognized the

handsome businessman from the picnic sauntering up from the pool. When he saw her, he waved and trotted toward her.

"I was hoping to see again," he said, wrapping a towel around his waist.

"What are you doing here? Are you in Glacier on business or pleasure?" she asked, trying to avert her keen eyes from his toned abs and the fine hairs peaking up over the top of his swimming trunks.

"Both," he replied. "And you?"

"Neither. I've come home to the cave where I was hatched." The words sunk into her bones, and she sighed.

"Cave?" he asked.

"I joke that I was raised by wolves in Montana. I grew up here."

"Oh, lucky you. Beautiful country," he said. "You live in Glacier Park?"

"No. I grew up in Whitefish. I'm back from grad school for the summer to work in Glacier Park."

"I'm working near here, in Browning," the Johnny Depp look-alike said.

"Browning? What the hell are you gonna do in that shit hole?" She clasped her hand over her unfiltered tap of a mouth. Browning was the capital of the Blackfeet Reservation, a rundown excuse for a town on the edge of the Rocky Mountains. She'd only ever stopped there for gas. Red cheeked, Jessica looked away, then turned back and asked in a softer tone, "I mean, how long have you been working in Browning?"

"I just got here. My older brother, Richard, ordered me out to check on some investments. I was supposed to do it last January but didn't get any further than Big Mountain ski resort. Awesome snowboarding." His raspy voice made her wonder if he was a smoker.

"You wouldn't by chance be investing in lumber?" she asked, narrowing her brows. She knew she'd recognized that voice. "The old Specht mill to be exact?"

"Lumber? No. Have you heard of Hydraulic Fracturing for shale oil?" When he dried his wavy hair with the towel, she resisted staring at where the towel had been.

"Fracking? I thought that was in North Dakota."

"You're thinking of the Bakken Fields. We're drilling for smaller deposits in western Montana." He smiled. "I'd love to chat, but I promised my brother I'd read over some reports, and I've put it off until the very last minute.... They're deadly."

He smiled, wrapped his towel around his shoulders, and extended his hand. "David Knight, at your service. I should have introduced myself earlier. And you are?"

"Jesse, um, Jessica James." She noticed the giant Rolex on his wrist and hoped it was waterproof.

"An outlaw! Aha! That's your allure." David Knight held her hand a few seconds too long for a handshake.

Jessica blushed. "I've gotta saddle up or I'll be late."

"Are you always on the run?" David's teeth were white, straight, and expensive, like the rest of him.

"Were you at the Specht Mill a couple nights ago?" she blurted out.

"Where? Never heard of it."

"The old mill outside of Whitefish." She narrowed her eyes and stared into his boyish face.

"Last Saturday I hiked up to Sperry Chalet and spent the night. Why don't we talk about it over dinner tonight?"

Jessica twisted a lock of blonde hair behind her ear and glanced in the direction of the garage. She was supposed to have been there ten minutes ago. "I don't know."

"Dining room at seven. Be there, or be square." He winked and jogged toward a silver Cadillac Escalade with a Hertz bumper sticker. She was glued to that spot, watching him. Standing just inside the door of the SUV, with the towel still around his waist, he reached in and fetched his clothes, perfectly pressed designer jeans and a silky polo shirt. Probably a good thing he wasn't staying in Browning. With that expensive car and those designer clothes, he'd be a walking target.

In the parking lot, with his wild wet hair and board shorts, he was more carefree surfer dude than serious businessman. Probably what her mom would call a "flannel mouthed four flusher." In any case, after what she'd overheard at the mill, she didn't want to dine alone with David Knight.

On her lunch break, Jessica returned to the bunkhouse to change into her uniform, an unflattering but still cool black polo shirt with the Glacier Park logo: a majestic white mountain goat atop a red caboose. Kimi RedFox was lying on her back in her maid's outfit reading a math textbook. When Jessica asked what she was reading, her roommate scowled. "What? Don't you think I could be in college?"

The front of the black dress stretched across Kimi's breasts and narrowed to the white apron tied around her waist. She was the sexiest maid Jessica had ever seen, besides the stupid sorority sisters who dressed up as maids for the "hot maids" frat parties on campus. Actually some of those girls were the best students in the classes she taught at Northwestern. How could such smart girls be so stupid when it came to boys? She thought of her own experience with men. More vintage cowgirl than hot maid, she'd made her fair share of mistakes when it came to the less fair sex. She was probably about to make another, but she'd decided to take the risk.

"Wanna meet me for dinner after work?"

"No," Kimi replied, and continued reading.

"My treat."

Kimi glanced up from her book. "I don't need your charity."

"To tell the truth. You'd be doing me a favor." Jessica sat on the opposite bunk, wrapping the end of her pony-tail around her finger. "I met this guy on the plane, and I don't want to go out with him by myself. His name is David Knight and…."

Kimi cut her off. "Did you say David Knight? As in Knight Industries?" She dropped her book, abruptly sat up, and threw her legs over the side of the bed.

"That's right. Do you know him?"

"No, but I know Knight Industries are poisoning and prostituting the land and our girls." That was the most Kimi had said since she'd met her.

"Knight Industries. They bought the old mill right after Mike's accident," Jessica said under her breath.

CHAPTER NINE

KIMI REDFOX HATED Knight Industries and everything they stood for, including profiting from the exploitation of native peoples. What Knight Industries was doing to her family was no different from what the American Fur Company had done to so many Blackfeet when it introduced whiskey, not to mention smallpox, in the nineteenth century. Only now, instead of whiskey it was meth and crack, and instead of smallpox, it was STDs and AIDS. Unlike her ancestors, she didn't plan on taking it lying down. She was going to fight back.

Just walking into the sprawling dining room of the huge railroad lodge had put her on edge. She thought of the thousands of Mayflowers who trekked across the country by rail to trample on Blackfeet land, never giving a second thought to who was really first in their stupid "See America First." She wished the roaring blaze in the giant stone fireplace at the center of the restaurant would escape its confines and burn the place to the ground. Reflections of forked flame tongues bounced off the glasses and danced wickedly across the knives and the spoons. Stuffed animal heads, moose, elk, sheep, wreathed the walls, more resources taken from Blackfeet land. The rafters of the cathedral ceiling loomed overhead, giant scaffoldings to the gallows below. An iron chandelier suspended above between two beams was a giant manacle threatening to fall, imprisoning her in its steely vice.

She was ready to bolt when Jessica James asked in her annoying little girl voice, "Aren't you eating, Kimi?"

"I've lost my appetite," Kimi replied, eyeing her room-mate's loud purple cowgirl shirt. She sat on her hands, wordlessly watching Miss Priss eat her side salad. She couldn't stand it any longer. She tossed her napkin on the table, stood up, and stamped her foot.

"You are as thoughtless as they come." Kimi's high cheeks turned a burnished bronze. She was determined not to cry.

"What do you mean?" Jessica asked.

"Look at him devouring that Bison steak. It's disgust-ing." Knowing full well her rage wasn't really about his din-ner, Kimi pointed at the hunk of meat and pool of bloody juice on David's plate. He stopped eating and gave her an apologetic look.

"Why didn't you tell me you were a vegetarian too?" Jessica asked. "Want some of my salad?" Jessica shoved her half-eaten salad across the table. "Maybe we should have gone some place else. The only thing I could order was this cursed side salad. Reminds me of my mom opening an extra can of green beans and calling it a vegetarian dinner." Jessica chuckled.

"I'm not a vegetarian. I'm a Blackfeet Indian. And

watching Mr. Knight Industries eat Blackfeet buffalo *reminds me* of when my mom stole ketchup packets from Subway and called it dinner because we were starving." Kimi had spent her entire life, all twenty-four years of it, on the Reservation hearing her grandmother's stories about "our people." Even when her belly was empty and she and her sisters went hungry, she'd been fed a steady diet of stories. Stories wouldn't fill her belly and provide the nutrients she needed to grow. Stories wouldn't put clothes on her back or a roof over her head. Stories wouldn't get her an education and a job. She wanted something more than the misery the Reservation had to offer. But escaping was another matter.

Kimi balled up her fist and punched the palm of her other hand. Unlike her grandmother, she regarded Blackfeet traditions and myths as fairytales on par with Walt Disney, different moralities maybe but the same brainwashing. She had factual reasons to believe rich white people and their corporations shouldn't be allowed to exploit the land and its people. She didn't need myths. The problem wasn't spiritual but political. Because of confusion over jurisdiction, lack of enforcement of tribal law, and a corrupt tribal council, not to mention outright racism, the *Napekwin* could get away with anything, even murder. And she didn't intend to sit around and do nothing while the rich bastards raped the land and her sisters.

Kimi bent over, looked him straight in the eyes, and pounded her fist on the table. "You're killing us!"

David Knight coughed into his napkin and continued to hold the cloth over his mouth. Rich *Napekwin* like

David Knight were the enemy. She could barely stand to look at him with his wrinkled blazer, khaki pants, and pink polo shirt, obviously the son of great privilege and wealth bought on the backs of others. She'd just as soon spit on him as look at him. Yes, Kimi RedFox hated the young upstart chief of Knight Industries. From his expensive loafers to his posh haircut, he represented everything wrong with her life. She wished she could wipe that smug grin off his arrogant face. She jerked her head towards the windows so the privileged white kids wouldn't see her tears of anger. She shouldn't have come. These people couldn't understand what it was like to grow up on the Reservation.

"Calm down, Kimi," Jessica said, shaking her head. She cupped Kimi's balled up fist. "Sit down and let's talk it over."

Kimi retracted her hand from her roommate's clammy grip. "There's nothing to talk over! Our water is so polluted it catches fire. The landscape is scarred by oilrigs and littered with radioactive Fracking socks. And now, both of my little sisters are gone, maybe even dead, thanks to this pig and his swine company!"

"Please Kimi, sit down. Have some water. Here." Jessica poured some water into Kimi's glass, and gave her a sour look. "Tell us what's going on," she ordered, then softened her tone, "Please?"

"Of course, yes, right," David sputtered and finally lowered the napkin to his lap. "I mean, yes, I assure you that Knight Industries cares about the environment and uses only approved methods...." When Kimi glared at him, he clapped his mouth shut mid-sentence. After flapping his gullet a few times, a fish out of water, he grabbed his glass and gulped his wine, then he tightened his lips, nervously running his fingers through his hair.

Eventually, Jessica broke the awkward silence. "What is Knight Industries doing in Montana? Why did you buy Specht lumber mill after the accidents?"

"I thought this was dinner, not an inquisition," David said. "I just got here. All I know is my brother's oil interests extend into Montana. I've never heard of any lumber mill. And I don't know what Knight Industries has to do with Ms. Redfox and her sisters."

"I'll tell you Mr. Knight. Someone working for your company lured both of my younger sisters off the playground and into crack cocaine. He took them to the man-camps in your oil fields where he prostituted them in exchange for drugs." Kimi's silent tears hit the tablecloth and soaked into its fibers. She realized she was helpless. She hadn't been able to protect her little sisters.

"An employee of Knight Industries kidnapped your sisters?" David asked. "Who?"

"How the hell should I know? I don't know your employees. All I know is his truck had your logo on it. Some guy called Big Mack would pick them up after school on Fridays and take them to the camps. He always brought them back Sunday night, completely strung out and sick. But over three weeks ago, the filthy *Imitáá* dog picked them up and hasn't been back since." Kimi fell back into her chair, exhausted from the worn out rage she relied on to get her through life since her mother's death.

"Oh my god." Jessica's beak opened wide. "Your sisters are being prostituted in the oil fields? I'd heard it was going on, but I can't believe there's human trafficking happening here in this day and age. It's slavery!"

"Welcome to my world. Believe me, my sisters aren't the only ones. Girls as young as eight are being taken from school, plied with drugs, and prostituted out by these supposed oil workers. Like they don't make enough money raping the land, they have to rape girls too." Kimi cringed thinking about the torture her little sisters were suffering.

"Probably more profitable and less dangerous than working on the oil rigs," Jessica said, almost to herself.

"Yeah, well, I wish all the rigs would burst into flames and take those filthy dogs to hell where they belong." Kimi was yelling again.

"Please Ms. RedFox, please don't shout. We'll find...."

Kimi interrupted, "What? Mr. Big Shot is embarrassed because the little Indian girl is making a scene? Go to hell!"

"Please, I know you're upset, and with good reason. But truly, I want to help." David's voice caught. "I had no idea this sort of thing could happen...."

"Yeah, right. Mr. & Mrs. Naïve over there." Kimi squinted and shook her index finger at the rich white dog. "Just because you don't want to know something, doesn't mean it doesn't exist."

"Look, Kimi, we're on your side. Only a buzzard feeds on her friends." Jessica's freckled face turned blotchy and her buggy eyes widened.

"You're not my friends and if anyone's a buzzard, it's him!" When Kimi waved her towards David, she knocked over her water glass. Ice cubes slid off the table onto the floor, and a cascade of water spilled onto the carpet. Using her napkin, Jessica dapped at the puddle forming on the tablecloth.

"Ms. RedFox, Kimi, please believe me. I promise to get to the bottom of this." David reached toward her hand and Kimi pulled it away. "If he works for Knight Industries, I'll find him. Can you describe the man who stole your sisters?"

"Please, let us help you." When Jessica's cold fingers stroked her arm, every muscle in Kimi's body tightened. She wished she could believe these people. She wished they really could help her. But her experience, and that of her ancestors, had taught her not to trust *Napekwin*.

"Help me? Yeah, like Lewis and Clark when they promised peace but gut-shot my seventeen year old ancestor in front of his father and brothers?" Rage filled her throat threatening to choke her, and she felt like she'd been gut-shot.

"Look, Kimi, that's not fair. Right now you're mad enough to eat the devil with horns on. I understand that. Obviously, we can't undo all the injustices done to your people, but we want to help you find your sisters."

"I'm so sick of hearing about 'your people' I could scream!" She made air quotes and mocked Jessica's high voice. She didn't know why she was attacking her roommate when it was obvious she meant well, but she couldn't help herself. Her anger had always been the only thing between her and overwhelming sadness.

"If Knight Industries has in any way contributed to your suffering, I personally want to make it right." David took out his cell phone and started tapping. "I'm writing to headquarters to get a list of every worker we've assigned to the Blackfeet Reservation oil drilling operation. We'll go down the list one by one if we have to."

"Oh, you're smooth, really smooth." Kimi stood up again and kicked her chair away from the table. She knew better than to behave like a spoiled child, but she was on the verge of breaking down completely.

"Can I help you?" the waitress appeared from nowhere. "Would you like another glass of wine, some coffee, or maybe dessert?"

"Give me wine to wash me clean of my sins," David said. "I'll have another glass of Cabernet." The waitress surveyed the scene and scurried away.

"Ms. RedFox, yes, I'm probably naïve," he said, turning back to Kimi. "I admit it. This is my first week on the job. To tell the truth, I'm only here because my brother gave me an ultimatum, either start work in earnest or I'm cut off. I have no idea what goes on at Knight Industries except that my dad made a mountain of coin, and now my brother's rolling in it. True, he's an arrogant ass. He's actually just my half-brother. I didn't really even grow up with him. For all I know, he's pimping and dealing drugs, but I sincerely hope not."

"He *is* pimping and dealing drugs, Mr. Knight. That's the effect of drilling for oil in Blackfeet country shale. It's not enough you take our land, you have to take our children too." Fighting back tears, Kimi fell back into her chair and buried her face in her hands.

"Look, Kimi, I know you're upset," Jessica said. "And you have a right to be. But come on, you can't blame David for your sisters' disappearance. Even if his father or brother are involved in something so reprehensible, the son isn't guilty for the father's sins if he didn't even know about them."

"If the son benefits from them, then yes he is." Kimi's head jerked up and with tears in her eyes, she glowered at David. Even if her roommate was right, she wasn't about to admit it now.

"Fair enough," David said. "It's true. I've had a privileged life and I've pretty much taken it for granted and coasted through school, and not just school, but everything. When I went to work for my father two years ago, I promised him that I'd turn over a new leaf. I guess I broke that promise. I know I let him down. But on my dad's deathbed last year, I swore to him that I'd do better. My older brother is running the company now and I'm trying my best to live up to their expectations, my dad's and my brother's. Still, I promise you, Ms. RedFox, I'll do everything in my power to help you find your sisters. I'll scour the man-camps myself if I have to."

"What do you know of the man-camps, Mr. Knight?" Kimi challenged. "I bet you've never set foot in one." Her stomach turned as she imagined what was happening to her sisters in those camps.

"There you'd be wrong. Why, I drove out to one this afternoon. Truth be told, I was looking for someone to have a beer with. At first, the camp was deserted. But just after two o'clock, guys came pouring out of trailers on their way to start the afternoon shift. They instructed me to go to Warbonnet Lounge if I wanted to find the guys just

coming off the morning shift. Now that was a rough looking place!" David's grin made her want to punch him.

"You're lucky someone didn't take a notion to kill you,"
Kimi said. "Happens every weekend at all the bars around
the oil boom."

"I'll remember that." David's smile faded.

"What's a man-camp?" Miss Naive asked.

"Man-camps are what they call the barracks where oil
field workers, all men, live. Some are bunkhouses, some
trailer parks, usually cheap temporary housing, filled with
Roughnecks, Roustabouts, Toolpushers, Derrickhands,
Motormen, and everything from electricians to rig opera-
tors," David answered, looking a little too proud of himself.

"I don't think that trailer park outside Browning really
counts as a man-camp," Kimi said. "You have to go to Sidney or into North Dakota to see the real deal. That's probably where that filthy dog took my sisters. Feral packs of
vicious men attack each other and rape any girl they find.
Man-camps are lawless pits of filth!"

"You've been?" Jessica asked.

"I've driven all over Montana and North Dakota
looking for Hurit and Nadie. You wouldn't believe what
I've seen."

"Hurit and Nadie? Those are your sisters?" David asked.
"Interesting names."

"Yeah, Blackfeet names." Kimi smirked.

"What do they mean?" Miss Naive asked.

"If you must know, Hurit means beautiful. She's the
youngest, only fourteen. And, Nadie means wise. She's

eighteen." Kimi troubled the edge of the tablecloth between her thumb and forefinger.

"Do you have any pictures of them?" Jessica asked.

Kimi pulled her phone out of the back pocket of her jeans and searched her photos. "Here," she said. "This was at Nadie's birthday party last winter." She handed the phone to Jessica.

"Is that you holding the cake? Where are your parents?" Jessica asked.

Kimi narrowed her eyebrows. "They died in a car accident when I was young," she lied. Well, it was partially true. Her mom died in a terrible wreck, one written up in the papers because of all the nice white teenagers who'd also died. Not a word about her mom and her baby. No one cared when an Indian woman died, or an Indian baby went missing. She thought of her mom and the baby every single day. She wished her father had died in an accident. She hadn't seen him since just before her mom was killed, and she hoped to hell she never would.

"My dad died in an accident when I was ten. I'll never forgive him."

"Forgive him for what?"

"For leaving me and my mom alone."

"Was it his fault? Or was he killed through the idiocy and supreme negligence of others, like my mother?"

"He was generous to a fault." Jessica handed the cell phone to David, and looked away. "I guess that's why I blame him."

"Yeah, my father was overly generous too, especially with his prick." Kimi's dinner companions both looked up and stared at her, mouth's open, and then went back to studying the picture of her sisters. She regretted her outburst as soon as she'd said it, but she was overcome with rage. Her sisters were all she had left.

"Which one is Hurit and which is Nadie?" David asked, fussing with the phone.

"You can't tell a fourteen year old from an eighteen year old?" She said, summoning all the hatred she could for the yuppie boy sitting across from her. He looked more like a coyote pup than a business tycoon, but his company was responsible for her sisters' suffering.

"I try to avoid children if I can help it." David flashed a polished grin.

Kimi wiped tears from her cheeks with the backs of her hands, then leaned over the table and pointed. "This is Nadie, wearing the halter top and feather necklace. Hurit's in the white dress," she said in an apologetic tone.

"Ah, I see now. The older one is wearing less clothes and more make-up." Kimi glowered at him.

"Both very pretty and sweet," he said, and passed the phone back to Kimi.

"Let me see that again." Jessica gazed at the screen for a long time while they sat in silence. "What does Kimi mean in Blackfoot?" her roommate asked finally.

"Secret," Kimi whispered.

CHAPTER TEN

BEFORE DAWN THE next day, Kimi RedFox crawled out of her bunk fully dressed in holey jeans and a ripped T-shirt. She crept across the room glancing back at the motionless form in the other bunk. She shut the door as slowly as possible, cringing when the hinge creaked, and then she sat down on the hallway floor to slip on her tennis shoes. Looking around the employee bunkhouse entrance to make sure no one saw her, she bolted across the parking lot and raced full throttle across the grounds toward the train station. The predawn mountain air was frosty, and Kimi wished she'd thought to wear a sweatshirt. She ran faster to warm up. Within minutes, she was standing next to a beat-up beige Volkswagen Vanagon waiting in the drop-off area. Inside the van were four members of ELF, Earth Liberation Front. Kimi had met only one of them, Leon the group leader, and he'd convinced her to join the cause when they met in the Glacier Peaks Casino parking lot at a rally against fracking on Blackfeet land.

She'd attended protests against Knight Industries, but

this was the first time she'd joined ELF for some predawn ecotage, or "monkey wrenching" as they called it. The target was one of the new oilrigs just put into production outside Browning. Knight Industries was expanding beyond Elm Coulee in Eastern Montana, up to Toole and Liberty Counties in the northwestern part of the state. Now they were exploring the possibility of fracking on Blackfeet land in the plains adjacent to Glacier Park. Wildcatters had been drilling exploratory wells all over the Reservation ever since the tribal elders cut a deal giving Knight Industries a carte blanche lease allowing them to drill just about anywhere. The corrupt Chairman of the Tribal Council had a rig in his own backyard.

Kimi RedFox hopped into the front seat of the van and Leon sped across the train tracks and out of the parking lot. As they approached the oil field, off-gassing flames shot high up into the darkness. Above, the velvet sky was a shimmering bead studded robe, but below, the scorched earth was a ripped cloak of greed and corruption. The Vanagon approached a dimly lit trailer, the only structure for miles not counting oilrigs and toxic brine filled water tanks. The leaders of ELF had picked this small hour of the morning because workers were on the rigs for sixteen hours a day, in two shifts, running continuously from five A.M. until nine P.M. By the time everybody'd cleared out for the day, it was usually well after midnight. Earlier that day, Kimi had reluctantly delivered some marijuana cookies to her friend, Danny Hall who worked the graveyard shift as a guard. They'd been best buddies all through grade school.

staring at her. They all must know what she'd done. Their stares reminded her of when she was thirteen and she'd go out in public with her mom and the new baby. She called him Apisi, Coyote. Her mom called him Frankie, after his father. The cops said baby Apisi died in the accident along with Kimi's mom. But she knew better. She could feel it. He was still alive.

Before the oilfields and fracking, Two Medicine Grill welcomed both locals and tourists with its rainbow awning and cute little storefront. It was known for its fresh baked pies and cozy comfort foods. Now the tiny place was engorged with men in greasy coveralls and cork-soled boots. The cracked vinyl crinkled under her jeans as Kimi swiveled back and forth on a little blue stool at the counter. She stared into the heavy white porcelain of her teacup as she dunked a Lipton's teabag up and down. The waitress offered her three berry pie, "baked fresh this morning, with real butter crust, Hon."

Barely audible above the din of the men, the morning news was broadcasting from the radio. Kimi's teaspoon clattered on the countertop when the announcer mentioned an explosion near Red Hawk Elementary School: "Police suspect sabotage, and are looking for a light colored van. An unidentified employee of Tribal Oil suffered third degree burns and was life-flighted to Kalispell Hospital." Kimi gasped and covered her mouth with both hands. When the announcer reported that a grainy surveillance video showed the Volkswagen pulling up to the trailer and a young Indian woman getting out, Kimi dropped two dollars on the counter and bolted out of the diner. Once under the railroad overpass and out of sight of the diner, she raced towards Glacier Park Lodge.

From the hallway of the bunkhouse, she noticed the door to her room was ajar. She stopped in her tracks when she heard voices coming from inside. The voices stopped too. Then she heard Auntie Madge's distinctive lilt, "Kimi RedFox, I know you're out there. I can smell you. Get in here this instant young lady before I have to come after you." Madge Blackthorn was the chief of police on the Reservation. Her job mostly entailed corralling drunks and drying them out in the Blackfeet lockup—that is until the oil boom. Now, meth, crack, and heroin ran rampant, rape and prostitution were commonplace, and murder accompanied the monthly full moon. Fracking had brought crime like they'd never seen before on the Reservation. It was like the Wild West all over again: murderous bar fights, prostitutes galore, and two-dozen men for every woman. Dragged into the darkest corners of crime and corruption, the Blackfeet got the worst of it. Kimi held her breath, deciding whether to make a break for it or surrender. Before she could take off, Auntie Madge appeared in the hallway, arms akimbo, sheriff's hat perched atop her nest of dyed black hair. She was giving Kimi the evil eye.

"Where have you been Miss RedFox?" Auntie Madge asked knowingly.

Kimi flushed and answered, "Out jogging."

"Did you happen to jog out to the oilrigs behind the school?"

"Why would I…"

"Before you dig yourself in any deeper, I've seen the

surveillance tape with your beautiful face, big as day, knocking on the door of Danny's trailer." Auntie Madge put her arm around Kimi and led her into her room. "How the hell did you get involved with that outfit? Eco-terrorists, that's what they're calling them. Earth Liberation, my eye."

Kimi hung her head. "I'm sorry Auntie Madge." She'd known "Auntie" Madge all her life. When her mom died in the accident eleven years ago, Madge Blackthorn watched out for her and her sisters. From that moment on, she'd been like a second mother to the orphaned girls who were being raised by their maternal grandmother. While her grandmother imparted tribal legends and herbal remedies, Auntie Madge spoiled her with ice cream, candy, and afternoon cartoons. All the kids called her "Auntie" because she handed out lollypops from her squad car. She used to drive around with a bag of Tootsie-pops, probably still does.

"Is Danny Hall gonna be okay?" Kimi asked.

"You should've thought of that before you and your friends tried to blow him to kingdom come." Auntie Madge shook her head. "What was going through your mind, girl? It's a good thing your mother's not alive to see this, bless her soul."

My mother the saint. If she only knew. "That fracking is killing us, Auntie Madge. You know that. Our tap water catches fire and we're promised its safe to drink. Contaminated waste water pools in open ponds, and our air is filled with methane gas." Kimi ran her fingers through her long dense hair. She realized that she hadn't washed it in days. She unwound the tie from around her wrist and twisted her hair into a ponytail.

"That may be so, but you don't need to go blowin' folks up." Auntie Madge patted her shoulder. "Come with me. I tried to get ahold of the surveillance tape before the Chairman saw it, but I was too late. Now, he wants to talk to you."

Kimi cringed. "He's as corrupt as the rest."

"He means well. But he'd sell his own grandmother if she'd fetch enough." Auntie Madge chuckled, seized Kimi by the elbow, and led her outside to a squad car.

"Is this really necessary, Auntie? Can't you give me a warning or something?"

"Would you rather I take you over to the CCV compound? Maybe those Church Complete and Victorious nutcakes could knock some sense into you. Anyway, you know it ain't up to me now that the Chairman's involved." Auntie Madge used her fingernail to gently sweep the sticky bangs across Kimi's forehead and out of her eyes. She always managed to have freshly manicured nails, blunt cut with just a strip of white at the tips, and her beehive hairdo formed a pregnant helmet of hair under her sheriff's hat. Kimi suspected it was really a wig.

Auntie Madge was old school. She'd fight to the death for the women and girls on the Reservation, but she hated "that blessed women's lib." Kimi smirked and reached for the door to the back seat of the patrol car.

"Nah, why don't you sit up front, honey, so we can talk." Auntie Madge opened the front passenger door for her. "And wipe that silly grin off your face. This's no game."

Kimi and Auntie Madge had just arrived at the doublewide that served as the Tribal Police Station when

Tribal Chairman Dakota Rowtag swaggered through the door. With his shiny ponytail and freshly pressed Western clothes, he was an Indian version of the Marlboro man. In the political chaos over big oil companies leasing Blackfeet land, Dakota Rowtag had been elected Chairman of the Tribal Council with his promises of prosperity and wealth.

"Kimi RedFox," he said, "when did you become such a beautiful woman? I remember when you was just a scrawny thing riding that pink banana seat bike all over town." He embraced her in a bear hug. Kimi flinched and pulled away. She'd heard rumors about the old goat.

"Now Kimi, what have you gotten yourself involved in? Those tree-huggers aren't interested in what's best for the Reservation. The oil boom's brought prosperity where there was only poverty and despair. Why, your own family gets an allotment check every month from oil money, just like everyone else. Don't you remember what it was like before we discovered oil? Don't you remember the hunger? Sovereignty is impossible when you're hungry. Kimi, sit down. I want to tell you something." Chairman Dakota Rowtag pulled over a chair for her and then one for himself.

"Madge, darlin', go get us some coffee." He winked at the middle-aged woman and then turned back to Kimi.

"The oil is bringing sovereignty. Fracking is sovereignty by the barrel. It's the only way we can become independent from handouts from the Great White Father in Washington. We need this oil. It's good for you and your family. It's good for us all. Do you understand, Kimi?" When she didn't respond, Chairman Rowtag continued. "Sovereignty by the barrel. You want sovereignty, right? You don't want us always to be beholden to others. No price is too high to pay for the privilege of owning yourself."

When Chairman Rowtag patted Kimi's hand, she jerked it back and balled it into a fist like she might sock him. "The fracking has also brought toxic air and water, drugs, crime, and corruption," Kimi replied. "There's no sovereignty for meth or crack addicts. There's no sovereignty for our young girls sold into prostitution. You want to talk about sovereignty? What about my sisters? Where is their sovereignty? I'd rather have my sisters back than the blood money you send every month to placate us."

"Now Kimi, you have to listen to reason...."

"What's your reason for buying a ninety-five foot yacht when our brothers and sisters are going hungry? That monstrous whale looks ridiculous just sitting in the dirt..."

"Kimi you're treading on dangerous ground," Chairman Rowtag interrupted. "You're the one who has broken the law. You're the one facing a prison sentence. Why would you want to steal our livelihood? That oil is a blessing. It's our way out of addiction and poverty. We'll put that money to good use. Fracking means opportunity for our young people. Not just jobs, but education. We can build a new high school. We can expand the community college. We can give our young people a chance to succeed." Chairman Rowtag sighed and examined Kimi. She just stared back and waited for him to finish.

"What are we going to do with you, Kimi RedFox?" he asked. "Couldn't you at least have bombed Richard Knight's rigs instead of mine?"

"Sorry it took so long. I had to make a fresh pot. Here's

your coffee," Auntie Madge slid a chipped ceramic mug in front of the Chairman. She smiled as he lifted the cup to read what was written on it: "Feel Safe at Night, Sleep with a Police Woman." Hands on hips, she asked, "So what's the verdict? Has our princess decided whether she's going into the lockup or ratting out her blessed friends in ELF?"

Princess my foot. Kimi rolled her eyes.

When Auntie Madge sat down behind the desk, her coffee slopped over the rim of her cup. "Liver-worst and cheese!" she exclaimed as she popped back up, grabbed a paper-towel from the counter, and then used it to sop up the spots of brown liquid. She sat back down and took a sip. "Ah, that's better. Nothing like a fresh cup of coffee to lift your spirits."

"Right," said Chairman Rowtag. "Here's the deal, Kimi. Either you tell us the names of the ELF leaders or you stay in jail. It's as simple as that. You have 24 hours to decide. Auntie Madge, give her your best room while she's making up her mind." Chairman Rowtag chuckled. "Sovereignty by the barrel, baby. Don't you forget it!" He picked up his coffee and sauntered out the door.

"Hey, that's my cup," Auntie Madge called after him. "Suzy Little Eagle made it for me."

"You're the real criminal," Kimi called after him—once she was sure he was out the door. "And, I don't just mean stealing coffee cups."

CHAPTER ELEVEN

KIMI REDFOX SAT in the stinky jail cell waiting for Auntie Madge to return with lunch. She still didn't know if Danny Hall was going to make it. *What if he died?* Until now, she'd been so sure the Blackfeet had to get the oil companies off the Reservation any way possible and peaceful protests didn't work. Maybe violence wasn't the answer either. It would be one thing if it were a fair fight, if there were a chance good would triumph over evil. Somehow evil always had more weapons at its disposal. Evil would stop at nothing. Good didn't stand a chance. She remembered her grandmother saying, "There's no good or evil, just powerful medicine. Some have it, some don't." Maybe her grandmother was right—there was no good or evil. But power didn't come from medicine. It came from money. And, yeah, some had it, some didn't.

Kimi picked the dirt from under her chipped fingernails. Maybe she'd ask Auntie Madge if she could take a shower, to kill time if nothing else. The only other person in the jail was Abraham Old Person. He was passed out in the cell across the hall, snoring and smelling of piss and booze. Kimi scowled when Abraham Old Person vomited down the side of his bunk. She hated that so many of the older generation had succumbed to alcohol and detested that so many of her generation were surrendering to drugs. Given their lives on the Reservation, she understood why….but at the same time, she didn't understand how her generation could live with the rollercoaster of drug addiction. She'd rather stick to a steady diet of despair than get high. Kimi shook her head and sighed. A century of negotiations with the *Napekwin* had given nothing to the Blackfeet except bad medicine, drugs, and alcohol. White men and their poisonous gifts. She stood up and paced around the barren cell. She wished she could burn a sage smudge-bundle to counteract the stench emanating from Abraham Old Person.

She heard the front door shut and Auntie Madge called out, "I'm back with lunch!" The stout police chief appeared in front of the cell holding a paper bag from Nation's Burger Station along with a cardboard drinks tray. "Fry bread tacos and root-beer floats. Food of the gods," Auntie said as she dangled the greasy bag. "What in hell's name is that smell? Jesuschrist ala mode, Abraham, you stink!" She disappeared.

In a flash she was back with the keys and unlocked the door to Kimi's cell. "Let's eat in the office so we don't ruin our appetites." Auntie Madge opened the cell and gestured her out of the lockup. "It's nicer out there."

Without a word, she followed Auntie down the hall to the dingy office. At least they'd almost escaped the foul smells of Abraham Old Person.

"Here ya go honey." Auntie Madge handed her a Styrofoam container and a wad of napkins.

Her eyes widened when she opened the container and saw puffy fry bread smothered in beef and bean chili, topped with lettuce, tomato, cheese, and a dollop of sour cream. Kimi hadn't had a Nation's Burger Indian taco in years. As a special treat, her mom used to take them to Nation's for ice cream sundaes. Nation's could do anything imaginable with soft-serve ice cream. They had twenty kinds of milk shakes. If only her sisters had stuck with Nation's soft-serve instead of moving onto crack-cocaine.

Except for the occasional groan of pleasure, she and Auntie munched in silence. After wiping her mouth with a napkin, Auntie Madge stuffed the Styrofoam container back in the paper bag. Kimi savored the light, puffy, fry bread. Her cheeks full of taco, she asked, "Do you know the origin of Indian tacos, Auntie Madge?"

"I suppose you're going to tell me. And, don't talk with your mouth full. You look like a blessed chipmunk. Here, wipe your mouth." Auntie Madge handed her some napkins.

Kimi wiped the grease off her chin. "Fry bread. That's how it started. The butcher Kit Carson burned Navajo lands and forced thousands to walk three-hundred miles all the way to Fort Sumner. He didn't care that hundreds died on the way and hundreds more died of disease and starvation later in the camps. The government provided very little food. And the food they provided was rancid. So, the Navajo mixed the only supplies they had—flour, salt, lard, and soda—together and deep fried it. That is the sorrowful birth of Indian Fry bread."

"Well, I guess Fry bread's our silver lining," Auntie Madge said with a wink.

"Pretty meager reward if you ask me."

"I seen you lickin' your fingers." Auntie Madge changed the subject. "Are you ready to tell me what's going on, Princess?"

Kimi cringed. She hated bring called "Princess." "What do you mean? I already told you. Fracking is killing us. We have to stop them using whatever means necessary."

"Whatever means necessary. Ha! You sound like one of those blessed eco-terrorists. You know you could have killed Danny Hall?" Auntie Madge pursed her lips.

"I'm so sorry, Auntie. I didn't mean to hurt Danny. Is he going to be okay?" A lone tear sprouted from Kimi's eye, hung for a second on her lashes, and then traced a path through the dirt on her cheek.

"I outta' let you stew in your own juice. Luckily, he's going to make it. But his arm's burnt up pretty bad." Auntie Madge said with a soft sigh. "Dakota…The Chairman, wants you kept here until you tell us who's responsible for blowing up that rig and sabotaging his equipment. So, you'll have to start naming names, Princess, or you'll be rooming with Stinky Old Person tonight." She got up, fetched the coffee pot, and poured some sludge into a grimy coffee cup. "Want some?" she asked.

Kimi wrinkled her nose, "No, thanks."

"Well, what about it? Ready to tattle on your friends?" She grinned.

"They aren't my friends. I don't really know them." Kimi brushed the greasy hair from her face and troubled the soiled fringe on her collar. "All I know is the main guy's name is Leon Running Wolf, and he's on summer break from Yale or some other fancy college back east. He's an environmental activist and the brains behind the protests and ecotage."

"Ecotage." Auntie Madge rolled her eyes. "Give me a break. You can't stop trouble from vistin', but did you need to offer it a chair? Come on, Princess, fess up, who were the others with you last night? What are their names?" she asked, taking a pad and pen from her desk. "They have some fancy explosives for college kids. Where'd they get 'em?"

"I told you, I don't know. Really, I never met them before. They picked me up and we went to the oilrig out behind the Elementary School. They didn't ask my name and I didn't ask theirs," Kimi said.

Already on her second cup of coffee, Auntie Madge pulled a flyer out of her desk drawer. "Have you seen this? Those blasted college kids are handing them out on the street corners. Most folks are using those blessed flyers to plug holes in their walls." When Madge reached across the desk and handed her the flyer, she stared down at it. "*Fracking is chemical warfare, poisoning our water, the earth, and you.*" The words were printed over a picture of Indian kids wearing gas masks standing in front of a florescent green river.

"How'd they convert you?" Auntie Madge asked.

"You make it sound like it's a religion. They didn't convert me, Auntie. I went to a protest in East Glacier a few weeks ago where that guy Leon was giving a speech. I talked to him afterwards, and he asked if I wanted to get more involved. That's all."

Auntie Madge shook her head. "Why would you do something like that Kimi RedFox? You know better than getting mixed up with strangers who come around the Reservation just to make trouble. Fancy school in the East my eye!"

"Leon spoke the truth, Auntie. Big oil is raping our land, drugging and prostituting our girls, and assaulting our way of life. As usual, the *Napekwin* gets rich off of the spoils of our bodies and what little land we have left. Dakota Rowtag takes his cut, puts food in his own belly, and leaves the rest of us hanging out to dry like bison after a Buffalo Jump." Kimi's face reddened.

"What do you know about Buffalo Jumps?" Auntie Madge shook her head again and kept on shaking it. "Buffalo Jump my eye." She swigged her coffee and made a sour face.

"I read about them in school. Hunters chased herds of buffalo off cliffs."

"Dakota Rowtag is about as fierce a hunter as Winnie the Pooh." Auntie Madge scoffed. "You know the Chairman means well. He's looking out for all of us. We all get allotment checks." She took the flyer away from Kimi, crumpled it up, and tossed it into the trash can.

"You know what I mean, Auntie," Kimi pleaded. "Look what happened to Nadie and Hurit. As police chief, you know better than anyone that drugs and crime are side-effects of the oil boom."

"Yeah, I know what you mean," Auntie Madge replied with a sigh. She slowly sipped her stale coffee. "Speaking of your sisters, I may have a lead." She peeked up over her cup with pensive eyes.

"Really?" Kimi's voice rose an octave.

"Don't get too excited, Princess. It's not much," Auntie Madge put her coffee cup down on the desk. "James Black Hawk thought he saw Nadie in a bar in Sidney last weekend when he was over there doing some plumbing in one of the man-camps. He saw a pretty girl and said she stood out in that crowd of grease monkeys like a diamond in a goat's ass." Auntie Madge chuckled. "With her face and figure, Nadie would stand out anywhere. But they'd feast on her in a place like that."

Kimi narrowed her eyebrows and frowned.

"Sorry, Kimi. I shouldn't have said that. I've made you upset. Poor Princess. I know it's hard on you with your sisters missing and god knows what else. First your poor mother, then your brother, and now your sisters." Auntie Madge reached across her desk and grasped Kimi's hand. "We'll get 'em back, honey, don't worry."

"I'll find my sisters and I'll kill that filthy *Imitáá* that kidnapped them if it's the last thing I do," Kimi said and freed her hand. "And don't call him my brother. Call him by his name, Apisi."

"Okay honey, Coyote then." Auntie Madge pulled at her uniform and straightened her badge. "Yeah, I'd like to kill the filthy dog that took your sisters, but that won't end it. Another greedy heartless bastard will step in to take his place."

"Auntie, isn't it bad enough that my sisters are gone?

Do I have to stay in this reeking jail? Can't you just give me a warning this time?" Kimi smiled sweetly.

"This time! Darlin', you blew up an oilrig and nearly killed a man," Auntie Madge said.

"I didn't actually blow up the oilrig. I just checked to make sure Danny was asleep. I didn't mean to hurt him. Really, I'll never do it again. That was my first and last time with ELF." Kimi pleaded, "Just let me go and I promise I won't get in any more trouble."

"No more blowing stuff up, no more sabotage? You'll keep your nose clean from now on?"

"Yes, Auntie. I promise."

"Cheese-and-rice, you do know how to work me, Princess. What will I tell the Chairman?" Auntie Madge asked, speaking more to herself than to Kimi. "Guess I'll have to tell him you broke outta jail. Maybe you should sock me in the eye or something."

"I can't do that, Auntie." Kimi's eyes widened.

"I hope not! I was only joking. Don't worry about Dakota. I'll take care of that old dog." Auntie Madge winked. "Okay, you're free to go on one condition: you help us catch those blessed ELF nutcakes."

"How can I do that?" Kimi asked.

"Spy on 'em, that's how. Keep going to their blasted rallies, only let me know their plans before they plant another blessed bomb and kill somebody."

"Okay. Thanks, Auntie. You're the best." Kimi smiled and bounced up from her chair.

"I want to know your whereabouts at all times, young

lady. And, mind you don't get into any trouble or I'll make you bunk with Stinky Old Person."

On the way out the door, Kimi turned back and asked, "What bar?"

"Say what?" Auntie Madge replied.

"What bar in Sidney?"

"Oh no, you don't, Princess. You stay away from Sidney." Auntie Madge got up and marched to the door. "Promise me you won't go looking for your sisters in Sidney. It's too darn dangerous for girls over there. Promise me, or I'll lock you up again for your own good!"

"Okay, Auntie."

"Okay, what?"

"Okay, I promise that I won't go to Sidney." Kimi crossed her fingers behind her back.

CHAPTER TWELVE

KIMI REDFOX DROVE all the way across the state and by the time she pulled into Sidney in her mom's beater Ford pickup, it was nearly 9:00 P.M. Outside of town, the endless darkness was illuminated only by tongues of fire licking at the stars, flames from fracking burn-off. On the seven-hour drive from across the state, Kimi sped by fields of corn, soy and wheat, drooping in spite of constant irrigation. She'd passed out of the mountains and into the plains. She knew she was getting close to Sidney when crops gave way to fields of sand silos, water tanks, and shale rigs. Fracking equipment dominated the once peaceful prairie. Instead of the snaking wagon trains of the old West, now a snarled jam of trucks made it difficult to drive through town. The shiny King Ranch in front of her had a bumper sticker that read 'Keep Calm, and Frac On'.

Kimi googled "bars in Sidney MT," and got seven results, all near the main drag, Highway 200. Sitting in the traffic jam, she read the Internet reviews to help plan her strategy. "South 40 Casino and Lounge" with seventeen reviews about food, especially the prime rib and salad bar, went to the bottom of her list. Others, like "Ranch Bar," "great place for a good time," "Lucky Lexi's," "lives up to its name," and "Whispers Tavern," "DIVE, fights…skanky," moved to the top of the list. Since it was only a block away, she decided to start with "lives up to its name."

From the City Council website, she learned before the oil boom Sidney had been a sleepy little town on the North Dakota border known for growing and processing sugar beets. Sidney boasted one former Montana governor and one former Miss Montana, but she was eventually disqualified when the judges discovered she was secretly married. Now, the garbage rate had doubled, along with the crime rate, and rents had tripled. In one day, the Volunteer Fire Department had responded to three fires before noon. Then there was that schoolteacher found dead in a ditch. That did it. She couldn't read anymore.

She slid out of her truck and scanned the main street. The whole town of Sidney was a DIVE, fights and skanky. Browning might be a pit, but at least it was on the edge of heaven. Lucky Lexi's Casino, also known as Montana Lexi's, was a beige shack on the edge of nowhere. Kimi steeled herself when she saw the red neon sign in the window: 'SLUTS'. As she got closer, she saw it actually said 'SLOTS'. The parking lot was brimming with motorcycles, and parked right next to Lucky Lexi's banged-up metal front door was a shiny crimson Harley with a bumper sticker, "Well Behaved Women Rarely Make History." Hand on doorknob, Kimi stood under a faded pink awning that sported a picture of a buxom cowgirl riding a slot machine. Suddenly, the force of the door opening slammed her against the side of the building. A burly man with a gristly gray beard and a purple paisley bandana covering his greasy gray ponytail chucked a smaller man out the door. The little dog cursed as he landed on the asphalt.

"Excuse me, Miss," the burly man said. "Come on in." He held the door open and stepped backward to allow Kimi to enter. Inside, the place was hopping with bikers dressed in black leather chaps and jackets, sporting all varieties of bandanas on their heads, oil workers still covered in grease stopping for a beer on their way home, roustabouts dressed-up in tight jeans and fancy cowboy shirts, and every low-life kind of man in between. Every slot machine had a cigarette smoking, beer swilling baddie hanging off it. A couple of chubby women dressed in black leathers to match their men laughed in a corner booth. A few rough faced women with floppy boobs and saggy bellies danced on the bar wearing nothing but G-strings and cowboy boots. One exceptionally well-endowed younger woman was racking up twenty-dollar bills under the elastic of her sparkling G-string. Unlike the others, she looked like a professional. Kimi had heard prostitutes were flying in from Vegas for the weekend and stuffing their carry-ons with thousands of dollars in oil money to take back. Could she blame a pretty girl for trying to make a buck off these sex starved dogs? Kimi's stomach flipped and she wanted to puke thinking about her sisters and the brutal pimps prostituting them.

No sooner had she made her way up to the bar, than a nest of men swarmed her. "Hey Pocahontas, nice rack," one said, staring at her breasts. She zapped him with the evil eye, folded her arms over her chest, and squeezed into a stool at the crowded bar. The hairs on the back of her neck stood on end, and she instinctively pulled her shoulders up around her ears. An older woman in a cowboy hat was tending bar. She conjectured that was Lucky Lexi, the proprietor. Kimi shouted over the ruckus, and pulled out her cell phone to show the bartender a picture of her sisters. The lanky lady shook her head "no" and abruptly departed to attend to a commotion at the other end of the bar.

Kimi stood up to see what was going on. A black boot connected with a young buck's jaw and sent him flying onto the end of the bar. One of the go-go dancers shrieked, jumped off the bar, and was cowering behind it. The black boot belonged to a willowy young woman, a tornado of legs threatening everything in its path. Her jet-black hair soared as she whirled around, and the neon lights flashed off her sage-green eyes. Kimi was leaning on the bar to get a better vantage point when she felt burly arms screw around her waist. Struggling, she twisted around to face her attacker. When she did, the drunken pig kissed her hard on the mouth.

When Kimi tried to shove him away, he only laughed and yanked her closer. She clawed at his cheek, and he yelped, then lifted her up and slammed her onto the bar. He tugged at her blouse so hard, the buttons flew off. She kicked and screamed, but no one paid any attention. The drunk tore her shirt clean off and pinned her arms to the bar. She squirmed and tried to wriggle away, but her tormenter was too strong. Tears were now streaming down her face as the bastard "kissed" her neck. She bit his ear as hard as she could. He slapped her and then mounted her, a knee on either side of her hips. Glasses sailed off the bar and crashed onto the floor. Beer splashed on her face. She squeezed her eyes shut tight and turned her head from side to side to stop him from kissing her mouth. The image of her father breathing hard and grunting relentlessly came into her head. Her shoulders shook with silent sobs.

The black boot whizzed past her face and slammed into the side of the bull's head. The wallop sent the monster flying off the bar and onto the floor behind it. The bartender yelled, "Hey, you can't be back here." Kimi caught a whiff of jasmine as a pair of long figured hands locked under her armpits and hauled her off the bar. When her savior's strong arms set her on her feet, she was face to face with the most striking woman she'd ever seen.

"Let's get you out of here," the beauty said in an unrecognizable accent. One arm around her bare waist and the other outstretched to shield her from the vicious pack of men, the Amazon whisked her through the crowd to the front door.

Once they were outside, shaking, Kimi gulped the night air. Her guardian angel wrapped a leather motorcycle jacket around Kimi's shoulders.

"Are you okay? Do you need a lift anywhere?" she asked.

"Thank you," Kimi answered in a weak voice. "I'm okay. My truck is right here." She pointed to the beat up Ford.

"Should I take you to the hospital? Or would you like to get a coffee or something?" the woman asked.

"No, thank you." Kimi gazed down at the asphalt.

"How about dinner?"

"No, thank you." When Kimi glanced up, the woman's steely green eyes melted into lush pastures that went on forever. Startled, Kimi quickly glanced away again.

"Are you sure? My treat." The beauty reached out, grasped the jacket, and guided Kimi's arms into the sleeves. Then, she held the front corners together and zipped it up. The motorcycle jacket was surprisingly heavy. Enveloped in the scent of jasmine, enfolded in the worn leather outside and the silk lining inside, for the first time in her life, Kimi felt safe. She inhaled deeply.

"What's your name?" she asked the beauty.

Her steely sage eyes compounded the contrast between her jet-black mane and luminescent alabaster skin, while angular bangs accented her high-boned face. Kimi gazed up at her guardian angel, enchanted by the tiny gap between her front teeth.

"Lolita. Lolita Durchenko."

CHAPTER THIRTEEN

JESSICA JAMES HADN'T seen her roommate since she'd snuck out before dawn after that disastrous dinner with David Knight. When she asked, the manager told her Kimi had been fired for missing her last two shifts. Turned out, she'd given them a bogus address and phone number, and they hadn't bothered to check, so now no one knew how to reach her. David was gone too. They'd both just disappeared.

She was sure she'd recognized David's voice at the mill, but she couldn't believe the mild-mannered, surfer boy with his curly locks and sparkling eyes was really a ruthless businessman. Her instincts about men couldn't be so wrong, could they? Her whole life, her passions had meant swimming upstream through a torrent of men—from horsemanship and rodeos when she was a kid, to studying philosophy in the big leagues as a graduate student. But she was determined to kick the shit out of the idea that she was just an ornament in a man's world. Even if riding in the rodeo meant chewing plenty of gravel, she'd never be content as just a buckle bunny groupie, padding her bra and cheering from the sidelines.

She stocked up on Snickers bars and Coke from the garage vending machine, then climbed aboard the Ruby Red bus. Distracted by the disappearance of David and Kimi, she had a hard time making small talk with the passengers. She couldn't wait for her shift to end so she could get back on the scent of the missing persons. Driving faster than usual put her ahead of schedule but didn't make her shift end any earlier. She chewed her fingernails, snacked on candy bars, and drank too many Cokes biding her time until she could go looking for her mysterious missing roommate and the shady cute businessman.

Driving back and forth on the curvy mountain roads, Jessica tried to force herself to pay attention, but around every corner, something reminded her of Mike. If only he hadn't subbed for Little Bear or Bear Cub or whatever his name was. What was Mike talking about, a woman and baby at the Snow Slip Inn? Why was he going to the hospital to check records? What records?

In her fog, she'd almost forgotten to stop at Rising Sun Motor Inn, maybe because Rising Sun was the dumpiest hotel in the park. The others were majestic lodges built by the Great Northern Railroad in the nineteenth century to bring wealthy tourists to Montana as part of the "See America First" campaign. But Rising Sun was an ugly little motor inn with yellowed shower curtains, dog pee stained carpets, and moldy linoleum, where stunning views were the only compensation for crappy accommodations.

After the last passenger exited the bus, Jessica put the

Ruby Bus in high gear and headed out of the park. She had no choice but to take the Ruby of the Rockies into Browning to find her missing roommate and get the dirt on double-dealing David.

The drive from Glacier to Browning was dismal. In the rearview mirror, stunning panoramic vistas of jagged peaks and alpine forests contrasted with the flat barren plains up ahead. It was as if she'd dropped off the edge of one world and into another, it's evil twin. There was nothing gradual about the descent onto the Reservation. The mountains were still there in the distant background, but only as a vague memory, shadows flickering on the horizon, forever just out of reach.

Her first stop in the stolen Ruby Bus was the man-camp on the edge of Browning. She hadn't been to a man-camp before and was surprised by the haphazard snaking strings of shabby trailers and crappy campers as far as the eye could see. In contrast, dozens of brand new silos and water tanks lined up in neat rows just beyond the camp. Decks of steely hydraulic arms pumped up and down, while armies of monstrous torches burned into the clouds. Legions of tanker trucks, platoons of train cars, and convulsions of pipes of all shapes and sizes comingled on giant scabs of earth dug into hay fields. The Montana plains had sprouted new crops. In a state where cattle outnumbered people, vast fields of green hay turning to straw bails were a common sight. Now, instead of grain towers marking the long distances between one-horse towns, gas towers blistering around boomtowns signaled a new era. The townsfolk thought they'd won the lottery—that was, until their tap water started catching fire.

Jessica parked the vintage bus at the entrance to the man-camp and hoofed it towards the office. She'd walked only a few feet when a swarm of roughnecks buzzed around her. When she asked if they'd seen David Knight, a guy with teeth so crooked he could eat corn on the cob through a picket fence yelled, "Hey honey, what do you want with the brass, when you can have my ass?"

Another punched the air, singing, "Why take the boss when you can have Hoss?" The men's laughing and jeering made Jessica's skin crawl. When she repeated her question, a smooth faced boy, who didn't look old enough to drink, said, "Miss, why don't you try the Warbonnet. I'd be pleased to take you there."

"Thank you, but I've got my own rig," Jessica replied and pointed to the bus. The men hooted and hollered when they saw the Ruby Bus.

"Yes, Miss," the boy continued with flushed cheeks, "But what I mean is you might want an escort to go into a place like that. I'd be honored to take you."

"Thank you. But I'll be okay."

"It's really no place for a nice girl like you," the boy said and followed her to the Ruby Bus. "Hey, isn't that one of the tour buses from Glacier Park?"

"That's right," she said as she slammed the door. The old bus belched a plume of black smoke as she revved the massive engine and squealed off towards town. She turned off the highway into another world, one doused in a toxic cocktail of Indian Reservation and Hydraulic Fracking.

The Warbonnet Saloon was a rough place. Even the wooden façade was rough, paint peeling off a giant Indian Chief's face and feather headdress—half of the Chief's mouth was gone and his grotesque eyes were flaking off. Jessica stepped over a patch of half-dried vomit on the dirt path to get to the front door. Although it was only eleven in the morning, the place was hopping. All eyes turned as she crossed the threshold. One of the only women in sight, she was a magnet for the sex starved oil workers. She was used to being the only woman in a room full of men, but not this many and not this dirty— at least not on the outside. At Northwestern, they wore threadbare blazers and quoted Hegel, but deep down even with their Ph.D.s and O.E.D.'s there wasn't much difference between her lecherous professors making inappropriate remarks during office hours or cornering her in the deserted departmental library and these oil men whistling and hooting at her or grabbing her around the waist. The well educated had simply learned to do behind closed doors what these men did out in the open.

As she shoved her way to the bar, Jessica's cowboy boots stuck to the tacky floor of the fusty tavern. Broken, mismatched furniture slumped in the center of the room, a tired band of abused misfits, and a well-used jukebox slumbered in the back corner. Jessica recognized Danny Hall from television news, a tall young Indian with a single ponytail braid down his back. He was leaning on the jukebox with one arm, bandages covering the other. She blew at her bangs, set her teeth, and made a beeline to the corner before some creepy ogler could stop her. Danny Hall was staring into the jukebox deep in concentration and didn't hear her call his name. She tapped him on his good shoulder and he turned and narrowed his brows, glaring down at her. The jukebox came to life and he had to yell over Dolly Parton's "Stand by your man."

"Do I know you?"

"No, I saw your picture on TV after the rig explosion," she said. "I'm so sorry about what happened to you." She'd heard he'd been released from the hospital and that the police were looking for the people who sabotaged the oil-rig. "Have they caught the idiots who blew it up yet?"

"Only one. Kimi RedFox," he said.

"Kimi RedFox? Did you say Kimi RedFox?"

"Why, do you know her?"

"She's my roommate."

"Well, she was my best friend when we were kids and this is the thanks I get." Danny Hall pointed to his bandaged arm.

"Have you seen her? Where is she?" When Jessica grabbed his arm, he pulled away.

"I never want to see her again. I hope Auntie Madge keeps her in that poor excuse for a jail until she's gumming her food and peeing in diapers." He stomped off to the bar and left Jessica to fend for herself. As she turned to follow him back to the bar, a roughneck with a lewd grin shouted at her from a barstool, "Hey, Blondie, how 'bout givin' us a nice smile?"

"Hey Baldy, how 'bout you wipe that shit-eating grin off your face," she snapped back, and then regretted it as soon as she noticed a couple of greasy men coming towards her. *Just like horses, can't let them smell fear.* She continued walking without making eye-contact, trying not to stumble over her wobbly feet, cold sweat saturating her wooly socks.

"Grumpy, aren't we?" one ugly mug said. "Must be that time of the month."

"She's probably bleeding like a stuck pig," his pock marked buddy chimed in.

Jessica fled toward the bar, and voice trembling, asked for a shot of whiskey. A knot of men tightened around her, some of them shamelessly looking her up and down, nasty glints in their eyes.

A sweaty tattooed fella laughed, and said, "Hey, I like her. She's got grit."

"Yeah, and you're a masochist," one of his buddies said.

"What did you call me?" the sweaty guy asked.

"Careful with those big words," Jessica said, red faced. "You might hurt yourself." Emboldened by the encouragement, she slammed her empty shot glass onto the bar. The glass skiddled across the slick surface and smashed onto the floor next to her boot. She slid off the stool and kicked the broken glass further under the bar with the toe of her cowboy boot. Exhausted from fighting off sex starved oil workers, Jessica motioned to the bartender—one of the two other women in the bar. One buxom "little gal," as the men called her, had a protuberance of men around her and was collecting hundred dollar bills in exchange for lap dances in the storeroom off the bar. The bartender, a "big boned gal" wearing a plaid flannel shirt, answered to "Butch." Until she heard the high pitched voice, Jessica thought she was a dude. A double take revealed telltale bulges on her chest and purple highlighting in her crew cut.

When she asked Butch about David Knight, the beady-eyed woman responded, "Oh yeah. He's a sweetheart. Comes in here nearly every day. But I ain't seen him lately." Butch wiped some milky liquid off the counter. Jessica hoped it was a spilled drink.

"Sweetheart, my arse," Jessica said. "If you only knew."

"What's that honey?" Butch looked up from her wet rag.

"Nothing." Jessica turned to face the throng gathered between the bar and the door and fought her way back outside.

CHAPTER FOURTEEN

EMBOLDENED BY HER guardian angel's heavy motorcycle jacket, Kimi RedFox skipped "a good time" at Ranch Bar and drove straight to Whispers Tavern: "DIVE, fights, skanky." Just before midnight, the bars were bulging with grease stained men eager to spend their hard earned oil money. Kimi veered into the parking lot behind Whispers just in time to see a tumble of drunken dogs roll out the back door, fists flying. She waited in her pickup until some *kitoki*, prairie chicken, was lying unconscious on the pavement and the others were stumbling back into the bar. Stomach in knots, she opened the back door and slipped into the dive. Inside, the dark dank joint pulsated with masculinity, a liquored-up rodeo of cowboys, roustabouts, and painted ladies. Trying to remain invisible, Kimi glided along the back wall and pressed herself into a corner so no one could surprise her from behind. With her curves and long silky hair, she had about as much hope of blending in with a crowd of sex starved men as a magpie at a Buffalo Jump.

Once Kimi's eyes had adjusted to the dark, she saw

several scantily clad Indian girls sitting at the bar, faces heavily made-up. Their thick eye shadow, rouge, mascara and lip-stick might as well have been a death mask. She watched as two rough men commandeered the girls, handing them off one by one to waiting Johns. A prepubescent girl about her youngest sister's age slouched over the counter, moaning, strung-out on drugs or in pain. Another girl's concave stomach and pointy ribs jutting out from under her halter-top contrasted with her painted face and made her a ghastly, emaciated doll. The men treated the girls worse than animals. They prodded and poked, pinched and grabbed, smacked and bashed, forcing them to do all variety of unsavory sex work, some in plain sight in the bar. Kimi hated to imagine what happened in private in the backrooms. She gritted her teeth, pounding the wall behind her with her fists, she resisted the urge to charge headlong into one of the sleaze bag pimps.

She scanned the room for her little sisters but didn't see them. A filthy *Imitáá* with tattooed biceps the size of melons grabbed one of the semi-conscious girls and dragged her to the back room, while a skinny creep with missing teeth collected cash from a smiling young buck before he followed the muscleman to the back room. Kimi slithered along the wall to the corner for a better view of the back. She slipped into the dingy women's bathroom and peeked through a crack in the door. The store room had been converted into a makeshift whorehouse. Cases of beer and liquor loomed over a grubby queen-sized mattress lying on the floor with a boom-box and cracked lava lamp plugged in next to it. The lamp's obscene bloodshot glow lit up the stains on the mattress, lewd evidence of the girl's nightly abuse. These two sleaze bags were selling delusional girls so vulgar oilmen could rape them in a filthy storage room. Maybe it was good the girls were strung out on drugs. Disgusted, she watched the two creeps selling dazed girls for the rest of the night. Still no sign of her sisters.

When the bar closed at two, Kimi zipped outside to her pickup and ducked down in the cab. Peeking up over the truck's door, she saw the two filthy *Imitáá* roundup the spent girls and throw them in a horse trailer. When the truck and trailer pulled out of the parking lot, she followed at a discrete distance. The rig stopped in front of an old barn a few miles out of town, so she killed the lights and motor and coasted into a pullout alongside the road. Across the highway from the barn, she craned her neck to see what was happening with the trailer.

The two pimps hauled the girls out of the back of the horse trailer and dragged them to an old airstream parked next to the dilapidated barn. Whenever the girls cried or tried to resist, the bastards slapped them. Kimi cranked the window down and listened into the night. She heard one of the girls sobbing and then a high pitched scream. A brute yelled, "You bitches shut up or I'll give you something to cry about. Your shit's inside, don't worry. You'll have your medicine soon enough my little whores."

Kimi could smell cigarette smoke mixed with an unrecognizable acrid odor. If she concentrated hard enough, maybe she could sense whether Hurit or Nadie were in the trailer. She closed her eyes and inhaled deeply. Below the pungent smoke, she could smell sagebrush. And, she heard bird song, a Yellow Warblers in its spring migration. She relaxed into the night sounds, conjuring strength to find her sisters. In the far distance, she caught the lonely sound of a wolf howling, followed by the all too human wailing of a pack of coyotes. The music of the night coalesced into an eerie chorus with haunting solos by the warbler and the wolf that transported her back to her childhood when she and her sisters would sit cross-legged on the shag carpet listening to her grandmother's stories about the triumph of good medicine over evil.

Kimi bolted from her truck and dashed across the highway, past the trailer, through a small field, and into the abandoned barn. Panting, she bent over, hands on knees. She caught her breath and listened for any sounds emanating from the trailer. She heard soft giggling and the pop music playing in the background. She got her second wind and sprinted to the airstream window, standing on her tiptoes to peek inside. Through the small opening between the grubby oval window's faded curtains, she saw a slice of life inside: brown legs, black hair, almond eyes, and a small pipe passing around in a flash of chipped pink fingernail polish. She pulled herself up and pressed her nose against the glass to get a better look. Two familiar amber eyes stared back at her through the curtains. The girl looking back at her through the window screamed and snapped the curtains shut.

Startled, Kimi fell backwards onto the ground and landed on her wrist. She heard it crack and yelped. A booming voice descended on her, "What the fuck is going on in there?" She saw a large shadow round the corner from the barn where the truck was parked and recognized it immediately as the silhouette of the ruthless monster who'd kidnapped her sisters. She was sure it was Nadie's face that had appeared in the window and knocked her on her butt.

"What have we here?" the brute said with a chuckle and scooped her off the ground. Kimi kicked and writhed and then bit at his face. Laughing, he jerked his head back out of her reach. He carried her into the trailer and dropped her on the floor. Pain shot up her arm from her broken wrist.

"Whores are coming to us now," he said. "What's wrong, little bird? Broke your wing? Someone take care of her. I'll be back with breakfast around noon. Get some sleep. Tomorrow's a busy day, my little chicks." He slammed the trailer door shut and locked it from the outside. They were trapped, seven girls in a tin can. The other girls were in no shape to help themselves, let alone help her. They were all high and messed up. Kimi scraped herself off the floor and flew one-winged to her sister who was sitting on the edge of a thin grimy mattress in the corner swaying trance-like back and forth, holding her knees.

"Nadie, sweetie, it's me," she said softly, using her good hand to stroke her sister's stringy hair. Her little sister looked up with sorrowful eyes, lips trembling, as tears rolled down her cheeks. Kimi put her good arm around her sister and pulled her closer. Nadie wept until she fell asleep against her older sister's shoulder. Once her sister was asleep, Kimi slowly pulled her arm away and laid her back on the soiled mattress. Kimi's wrist was killing her and she had no idea what to do next, so she searched the trailer for something to use as a weapon or a tool to pry one of the windows open.

The airstream trailer was confining and claustrophobic. Yellowed linoleum curled up from the corners. Stuffing bulged from filthy upholstered seat cushions on tiny gouged wooden benches. The teeny table had one broken leg and was littered with crumbled Mountain Dew and Coors cans, some had been made into makeshift pipes. Between the empty aluminum cans there were a couple of teaspoons with black marks on them, a stubby pencil, and several wads of aluminum foil. Piled on the floor underneath were uncapped yellowed syringes and a few lengths of fat rubber-bands, beige tapeworms lying in wait. After trying one handed to force a window open using a spoon, and then banging on the door until her fist hurt, exhausted, frustrated, and in terrible pain, Kimi collapsed onto the grimy mattress between her sister and another passed out girl.

CHAPTER FIFTEEN

JESSICA JAMES TURNED on Google map on her phone and looked up directions to the tribal lockup on the Reservation in Browning. She was running out of time. She'd better get the bus back to East Glacier before dark. Soon, everyone would come looking for her. As it was, they'd probably figured out by now that the bus had gone AWOL.

On the outside, downtown Browning with its dilapidated shacks and rusted trailers seemed the opposite of downtown Whitefish with its cute brick buildings, fluttering awnings, and antique streetlights. Her friends used to say, "Blink and you'll miss Browning and be glad you did… unless you need an outhouse." The oil boom hadn't done much to spruce up the two-horse town, and feral packs of dogs still roamed the streets, harbingers of the poverty at the root of the robust fracking industry. If anything, oilrigs and man-camps had ruined the beauty of the surrounding area. Now, noisy pickups and belching oil tankers fouled the once desolate dirt roads.

Just off the main drag, Jessica spotted the police station.

In case her boss was already looking for her, she parked the Ruby Bus a few blocks away and hiked to the pokey. If it hadn't said, "Tribal Jail" outside, she wouldn't have guessed it was a lockup. The police station was a twin to the derelict doublewide mobile home right next to it; both had rusty metal siding and cracked windows. Inside, the air-conditioning was blasting even though it wasn't hot outside. Jessica wrinkled her nose in response to a foul stench circulating through the ventilation system.

A solidly built, middle-aged Indian woman sitting behind a desk greeted Jessica. "Can I help you, Honey?" Her well-coiffed black curls donned a tiny silver halo at the roots.

"I'd like to visit Kimi RedFox," Jessica said.

"Kimi. Are you a friend?" the policewoman asked. She got up from behind her desk, tugged on her tight uniform, and came around to face Jessica. "I'm Madge Blackthorn, Chief of Police, but young folks around here call me Auntie," she said extending her hand. "Would you like a cup of coffee or a piece of toffee?"

"No thanks. I just wanted to talk with Kimi for a few minutes, if that's okay."

"Fine with me, but Kimi's not here." Madge Blackthorn stood arms akimbo and smiled.

"Oh, my mistake. I heard she was in jail." Confused, Jessica turned to go.

"She *was* here. Last night. But we didn't have enough evidence to keep her," Madge said. She cocked her head to one side then scrutinized Jessica.

"So, she wasn't involved in that explosion? I knew…."

Madge interrupted. "I didn't say that."

"Oh. Do you know where I can find her?" Jessica asked.

"She's working over at East Glacier Lodge as a maid. Why, I don't know." Madge sat back down behind her desk and sipped coffee from a grimy chipped ceramic mug.

"I know. I'm her roommate there. But she missed her shift today and got fired." Jessica worried she was ratting Kimi out by telling this policewoman she'd missed work. On the other hand, maybe she'd been kidnapped like her little sisters and this policewoman could help.

Madge jumped up from her chair. "Oh shit!"

"What's wrong?" Jessica asked, fearing the worst.

"I knew I shouldn't have told her about Nadie." Madge fetched her hat and gun belt and then marched toward the door.

"Told her what? Where are you going?" Jessica took long strides to keep up. For a short woman, Madge sure could move fast.

"Guy thought he saw Nadie in a bar over in Sidney. Knowing my princess, she's over there right now trying to rescue her sister, getting herself into six kinds of trouble. Dang girl. She promised."

"Princess? Kimi? She may look like a princess, but she sure doesn't act like one," Jessica said, catching up and holding the rickety door open for the policewoman.

"You can say that again. She was the sweetest little thing when she was a toddler. An angel." Madge shook her head. "Now, she's a daredevil. But believe you me, she's more bark than bite. I've got to find her before she gets herself into a deadly fix."

"Your jurisdiction goes all the way to Sidney?" Jessica

didn't know about tribal law, but Sidney was at least seven hours away.

"No, it doesn't. To hell with jurisdiction! Come on, I've got to lock up here. Out ya go." She shooed Jessica out the door.

"I'm going with you."

"Like hell you are," Madge said, brushing past her.

Jessica darted around the squad car, hopped in the passenger seat, and slammed the door.

"Oh no you don't, Blondie. Get out of my car," Madge ordered.

"What are you gonna do, arrest me?" Jessica asked.

"Don't give me any ideas."

"You're going to find Kimi and so am I." Jessica buckled her seatbelt, crossed her arms over her chest, and stared straight ahead.

"You're not by any chance driving that mammoth Ruby Red parked over yonder, are you?" Madge asked.

Jessica's cheeks the color of the bus. "Why do you ask?"

"Because it's got four flat tires. Looks like someone played a prank on you, Blondie." Madge laughed.

"That's not funny. I'll lose my friggin' job!" Jessica shouted.

"You shoulda thought of that before you drove it over here, shouldn't you now, Hon." Madge glanced over at her. "Well, if you won't get out of my squad car, I guess I'll have to take you with me. We're going into the wolves' den. Are you ready, Blondie?"

"My name's Jessica, Jessica James." She reached into a bag of candy sitting on the console and pulled out a handful of individually wrapped bonbons. "Lunch."

"Glad to meet you Jessica James. But if you get a belly-ache from all that candy, I'm not pulling over."

"You're more like a bossy mommy than a lady cop," Jessica whispered to the side window.

"I heard that, Blondie."

CHAPTER SIXTEEN

KIMI REDFOX WOKE up when one of the girls rolled over onto her wrist. Her cry bounced off the tin walls and brought her back to the nasty fact that she was imprisoned with six other girls in a tiny stuffy trailer. She was desperate for air, but all of the windows had been sealed shut. She made her way to the miniature bathroom. The toilet was rimmed with dark brown stains and dried vomit crusted the floor around it. The bathroom reeked of female bodily excretions. Peeing as fast as she could, she held her nose with her good hand. When she flushed the plugged toilet, it moaned but didn't discharge its contents, so she leapt out of the water closet—literally a closet—and slammed the accordion door shut behind her. The dingy airstream's bowed walls created the sensation of being in a cramped cave. Kimi was on the verge of screaming and clawing her way out when she noticed Nadie awake, sitting on the edge of the unhappy mattress, with her head in her hands. Haggard and gaunt, she looked ill.

"Are you okay? Where's Hurit?" Kimi asked, squeezing in between the other girls, next to her sister.

"I don't know," Nadie answered. "I'm sorry." She sobbed. Kimi cradled her with one arm.

"Don't cry, Sweetie. We'll find her. We're going to get out of here. Then we'll find Hurit. You'll see. Please stop crying," Kimi was whispering into her sister's ear.

A woman shouted outside the trailer, "I told you to get those sluts off my property! And, you owe me lease money from last month. Post the pony and get out!"

The brawny kidnapper's voice yelled back, "You'll get your money. Don't worry. And these are respectable girls. We aren't causing you any trouble."

"We'll see about that. I don't want no whoring prostitutes on my land!" the woman screamed. "I should send all of yous over to CCV. Those crazy kooks would straighten you up!"

A rattling at the door, then a gust of fresh air and sunlight preceded the burly *Imitáá* appearing in the doorway, his gold front-tooth winking in the glare. He slid a box of Dunkin Donuts across the floor. "Breakfast girls. Eat up. I'm bringing someone to see you in an hour, so get cleaned up." He shut the door and once again Kimi was trapped in the dim aluminum cylinder. The donut box lay in the middle of the floor like a mangy dog. No one moved to touch it.

A rumbling noise outside was getting closer. Soon the trailer was shaking and skidding. It rocked back and forth, being pushed along the ground. Cramped between her sister and the side of the trailer, Kimi braced herself against the side window, peered outside, and saw the airstream slide sideways, heave a few times, and then settle

into place in the middle of the wide road. When the rumbling stopped, Kimi could still hear the woman shouting,
"I'll get you off my property myself, you sluts. I don't want
to see you round here no more." Kimi glanced out the back
window and saw an old woman in a ratty faded housedress
and rubber boots backing away in the John Deer tractor
she'd used to ram the trailer off her property and into the
middle of the highway.

Her stomach growled, and Kimi realized she hadn't
eaten since her tacos in jail the day before. To keep up
her strength, she reluctantly poked at the donut box and
opened it with one finger. Inside an assortment of gooey
pastries greeted her. She picked the least offensive plain cake
donut and handed it to Nadie, then passed the box around
to the other girls. The ones on heroin grabbed donuts and
stuffed their faces. The ones on meth shook their heads and
covered their mouths. Kimi had to coax those to eat. After
eating, two of the girls immediately vomited their donuts
onto the already disgusting mattress.

When Kimi asked them questions, they stared through
her with blank faces. Finally she got them talking and
learned that Butterfly, the youngest was twelve and had
been captive for months. Whenever she spoke, her milky
tongue poked through the hole where her missing teeth
had been. The ones she had left were brown from meth.
An older girl known as Fawn had sores on her arms where
she'd picked at her skin until it bled. She gasped, grabbing
her calves, complaining of cramps. The color drained from
Kimi's face when she noticed the track-marks on Nadie's
inner arms. Those filthy *Imitáá* supplied the girls with

uppers like meth and coke during the day and then dosed them with heroin at night. That's why they were all in a stupor when she joined them last night. Three of the girls were sisters from Fort Peck Reservation and the other one was from Belknap. Kimi and Nadie were from the furthest away. Except for Kimi, they were all in their early teens. And from what she could tell, they were all addicted to meth and crack cocaine, and some of them heroin too.

The sound of the lock rattling on the trailer door filled Kimi with terror. The burly kidnapper burst through the door.

"What the fuck happened? How'd this trailer get into the road?" he asked. "Answer me!"

"An old woman pushed us with her tractor," Kimi shouted when he raised a fist to punch one of the girls.

"That old hag. Hang on while I pull you off the highway then," he said and slammed the door. He hooked up his pickup truck and pulled the trailer to the side of the road. When he reappeared, he said in a chipper voice, "Time for your medicine, girls." Then he turned to someone behind him, "See, we have a new one."

A strapping young buck with a big blonde beard and a baseball cap glanced around the doorframe. His lively blue eyes widened when he saw the girls. "This place stinks, Mack." He wrinkled his crooked nose and grimaced. "What kind of operation is this?" Waving the tail of his flannel shirt back and forth, he let out a, "Peeewww."

"Don't worry. All of our girls are clean. But this new one might even be a virgin. We just got her last night." The brawny pig pointed straight at Kimi. She kicked at him when he grabbed her and pulled her from the trailer.

"You can have her now over in that barn, if you want. Cash in advance."

"No!" Kimi screamed, kicking his shins.

"Look Mack, I just want to meet a pretty girl. This whole scene is kinda freaky."

"Do you want her or not?" Big Mack held her at arms length.

"What's your name?" the prospective john asked Kimi. When she didn't respond, he turned to the big pimp and asked, "What's her name, Mack?"

Kimi struggled to loosen Big Mack's grip on her arm. Her wrist was throbbing and his abuse was aggravating the pain.

"What's wrong with her hand? It's all swollen and bruised." The newcomer lifted Kimi's wrist, and she instinctively yelped in pain and then retracted her arm.

"She needs to see a doctor," the newcomer said. "It looks broken."

"Oh, come on, for Christ's sake, do you want her or not?" Big Mack asked.

"What's your name? I'll take you to a doctor." The young buck looked at Kimi with kind eyes.

"Kimi RedFox," she said to the gravel beneath her feet.

"What happened to your arm?" he asked, glancing at Big Mack.

"I fell on it," Kimi told the truth.

"I'm taking her to a doctor."

"She's my property. She don't need no doctor," Big Mack said. "Do you want her or not?"

"How much to have her for the whole day?"

"You want her for the whole day?" Big Mack wrinkled his face and counted under his breath. "Two grand. But you have to have her back by 9 tonight. Cash in advance."

The young buck reached in his back pocket and pulled out a fat wallet bursting with receipts, credit cards, and cash.

"My sister needs a doctor too," Kimi said. "Please, Mister, take her, too. I won't go unless she does. I'll do whatever you want if you take her, too."

"What's wrong with her?" the buck asked.

"She's pregnant," Kimi said. She'd tried to deny the little basketball poking out from Nadie's shirt, but it was obvious.

"That pregnant bitch is your sister?" Big Mack asked.

The young buck shook his head and sighed. "What have I gotten myself into? How much for both girls?"

"For the day? Two grand each, so four grand," Big Mack said.

"Can't I get a discount for two? Anyway, one is knocked up." The buck adjusted his baseball cap to cover his bald head.

"Okay, two grand for both. Cash on the barrel. But I want them both back at Whispers Tavern tonight by 9, or I come lookin' for you and it won't be pretty for any of y'all," Big Mack said.

The man counted out two thousand dollars in hundreds and handed the wad to Big Mack. "There. Now give me the girls."

"Hold onto this one, while I fetch the other bitch." Big Mack handed Kimi to the bearded man, then unlocked the trailer door, stomped in, and reappeared carrying Nadie in his arms. She was only semi-conscious. He tossed her into the cramped backseat of a messy white Toyota Tundra, and the young buck led Kimi to the passenger's seat.

As the bearded man pulled out onto the highway, Big Mack shouted after them, "You'd better bring 'em back to the club tonight, or there'll be hell to pay. Remember, I have your little sis and she'll get hurt real good if you aren't back tonight."

CHAPTER SEVENTEEN

EVEN THOUGH JESSICA James had seen it hundreds of times, the view of the Rockies from the cop car startled her. She soaked in the vista and almost forgot she was with a bossy tribal policewoman searching for a surfer dude oil mogul and a beautiful taciturn Native girl. She imagined herself instead living amongst the grizzlies and wolves, grazing on wild huckleberries and pine nuts. She wondered what it would be like to be a bobcat, or a fox, or even a rabbit, sniffing her way through the world with her hyper-vigilant sense of smell. She considered her sense of smell her superpower. She was sure she was part wild forest animal because she could smell stuff no normal human should: cutthroat trout swimming upstream, morning dew vaporizing, wild tiger lilies in bloom, horses sweating in summer, and, of course, the pungent smell of fear. Then she realized they were going the wrong way.

"Hey, where you going?" Jessica James asked. "That's not the way to Sidney!"

"I'm taking you back to East Glacier, Blondie,"

Madge said, looking over her shoulder to see if she could change lanes.

"But the Ruby Bus... I'll lose my job... How am I going to explain?" Jessica's face fell and she was on the verge of tears. "Sheriff, please, I was just concerned about Kimi. I don't have a car. I didn't know where she was. I was desperate, so I drove the Ruby Bus. My boss'll kill me if he finds out I drove the bus to the Reservation."

"Guess you should've thought of that before you left the safety of your National Park and ventured onto our treacherous Blackfeet territory." Madge raised her eyebrows and smirked. "Anyway, I doubt old Stanley would kill you. Fire you, maybe, but not kill you."

"I didn't mean... Please, officer take me with you to find Kimi. She's a pain in the butt, but I've got to find her." In spite of her efforts to control her emotions, silent tears rolled down her cheeks.

Madge swerved off the highway and onto the gravel shoulder. "Don't cry, Blondie," she said. "We'll figure it out." She handed Jessica a lollypop and smiled. Once Jessica's sobs turned to whimpers, Madge flipped on her siren, did a U-turn in the middle of the highway, and sped off in the opposite direction leaving behind a layer of skin off her tires on the blacktop.

Jessica clung onto the dashboard. "Are you sure you're a police person?" The whiplash U-turn had knocked the crying right out of her.

"Police people, my eye. Sounds too much like pod-people," Madge said with a wink. She reached into the candy bag and pulled out a handful. "Dessert."

"Pod-people?" Jessica perked up. "I love *Invasion of the Body Snatchers!*"

"What?"

"Pod-people, that's from *Invasion of the Body Snatchers*. Didn't you see it? The remake's even better. These aliens come to earth, inhabit people's bodies, and turn them into emotionless shells of their former selves. Whenever the pod-people see a person who's still human, they let out a piercing scream."

"Aliens my eye. Don't tell me you believe in all that UFO hog wash? Little green men from Mars? You might as well join those goofballs over at the Church Complete and Victorious." Madge scoffed. "What would you do if you saw a UFO land over there on Sweet Grass Hill?" She pointed out the window.

Jessica pondered. "I'd hide behind a tree and watch."

"Blondie, there ain't no place to hide on Sweet Grass Hill. Look out the window. Those plains go on forever." Madge laughed. "I'd run like hell and I bet you would too." Her countenance turned grim. "Honey, the only body snatchers around here are those dirty dogs that took Kimi's little sisters, and that ain't science fiction but all too real."

The mountains had long ago disappeared into the rearview mirror, and after riding in silence for two hours, somewhere in the desolate plains around Chinook, Madge asked, "How well do you know Kimi RedFox?"

"I just met her a couple days ago. She's an angry little bird."

"Honey, you'd be angry too if you had a deadbeat dad, your mom and baby brother were killed in a stupid accident, and you had to raise your younger sisters. She was only thirteen when Coyote was born. When he and her mom died a month later, poor little princess had to grow up fast."

"Where's her dad now?"

"That pale faced trucker only stopped by the Reservation every other weekend. He wasn't around much during Kimi's childhood, but when he was, it was bad news. She's better off without that rattlesnake."

"Why? What'd he do?"

"Not my place to say. That's for Kimi, in her own time." Madge tightened her lips.

Jessica imagined the worst.

"After Koko died that good for nothin' snake just up and disappeared. We ain't seen him since." Madge's countenance darkened and the kindly policewoman transformed into mamma bear protecting her cubs. "Good riddance," she growled. "Poor little princess. Her anger is really the armor to protect herself from a world of hurt. Inside, she's just a scared kid missing her mama."

Three hours later when the squad car pulled into Sidney, the town was hopping. It was 9:30 on a Friday night and every tavern in town was spilling oil workers out into the streets. Jessica had never seen anything like it. A redneck hoedown, rowdy fellas hollered and drank whiskey straight out of the bottle. The sidewalks around the entrance to Whispers Tavern glistened in the streetlights, a pond of broken glass. The one-horse town was overflowing with stallions of all shapes and sizes, lit up on booze and nicotine, shiny eyes dancing devils, as they staggered from bar to bar.

Madge parked the squad car behind the tavern. "Don't want to attract more attention. Are you ready, Blondie? This could get ugly fast. Stick close."

"Ready Sheriff," Jessica said. She inhaled sharply and stepped out of the car. A six-pack of oil workers shooting a revolver at a tree in the corner of the back parking lot turned to stare as she got out of the squad car. Most of the vehicles in the lot were motorcycles, and Jessica counted twenty-eight when she spotted a familiar crimson Harley Superlow with turquoise fringe saddlebags. She came up behind the bike to confirm. Sure enough, Illinois plates.

"I'll be dipped in shit. Lolita's here!"

"Who?" Madge asked.

"My best friend, Lolita Durchenko, and the most badass woman you'll ever meet. Russian mafia trained her to fight. You'll see. She looks like a supermodel, but she fights like a Kung Fu master. Think Megan Fox meets Bruce Lee."

"Fox meets what?" Madge asked.

"Never mind. You can't miss her. Five-eleven, long black hair, chameleon eyes, and skintight black leathers. Never bothers with phones, just shows up." Excited to find Lolita, she swung open the door to what had to be the nastiest saloon she'd ever seen. The stench alone stopped her in her tracks, bouquet of fetid men's locker room with overtones of and rancid beer and subtle hints of stale vomit. She stood in the malodorous doorway until her eyes adjusted to the darkness and scanned the bar. It was so crowded she couldn't even make out individual figures in the molten mass of flesh.

"In or out, Miss," a bouncer the size of the Rock shouted at her. "Don't just stand in the doorway. In or out."

Jessica held the door open for Madge, and then they squeezed into the throng. The saloon pulsated with sweaty bodies. It reminded Jessica of her favorite dives in Chicago, dark and dingy with lots character. Of course, the locals were a lot harsher in the middle of the Bakken oil field than back in her Polish neighborhood in North Chicago. The most dangerous creature in the Polish Falcons, her favorite local hangout, was Jellyroll Chlebek, the chubby seventy year old bartender who proposed to her every other week. Here, instead of sweet old Polish pastries, the bar was filled with tough young beefcakes looking for trouble.

Jessica squeezed through a nub of roustabouts and made her way to the bar, scanning the room for Lolita, who was nowhere in sight. Once she got her Jack-'n'-Coke, she lifted it above her head and elbowed her way back through the throng back to Madge, trying not to spill her drink.

"Watch yourself, Blondie," Madge yelled in her ear. "These men are hungry coyotes and you're a tasty rabbit."

"Did you just call me a tasty rabbit?"

"Look at all those leering lecherous Ying-Yangs." Madge grabbed her elbow and led her through the crowd toward the back of the bar. "You shoulda seen their eyeballs glued to your ass as you walked to that bar."

"Hey ladies, can I buy you a drink?" A young bull in greasy overalls came out of nowhere.

"Can't you see she's a cop," his friend said. "Don't mess with cops. Anyway, she's probably at least forty years old, bro."

"I love a lady in a uniform," the loudmouth said as he turned back to his friend. Even drunken cowboys knew better than to mess with the Tribal police. Madge pulled her highway patrol style Stetson down over her ears and marched onward as the sea of men parted in her wake.

When they reached the back of the saloon, Jessica spied a group of young Indian girls huddled in a corner booth a few feet away and pointed them out to Madge. The two of them swam against the current to reach the eddy of girls floating on the edge of this angry ocean of men. Once there, crushed up against the edge of the table, Jessica grabbed the cool Formica for support. She was bobbing back and forth with every wave of bodies that crashed her from behind. Madge slid in next to the girls and put her arm around a petite teen with braids tucked behind her ears. The girl looked up at her in surprise, "Auntie Madge!"

"What's going on here, Nuna?" Madge asked.

"You know her?" Jessica asked.

The little girl started to cry. "Auntie Madge, they're making us do terrible things with these horrible men."

"Who's making you, darlin'?" Madge asked.

"The men who took us from home," Nuna replied, sniffling into Madge's uniform.

Jessica reached into her pocket, pulled out a wad of Kleenex, and handed it to the little girl.

"This is a friend of Kimi's," Madge said, tilting her head toward Jessica. "Have you seen any of the RedFox girls?"

"Nadie was here until this morning. When I woke up, she was gone," Nuna said.

"Gone? Where'd she go?" Madge asked.

"I don't know, Auntie, I was asleep."

Madge gently rolled up Nuna's sleeve to check for track marks on her inner elbow. "Oh dear, what have they done to you, my poor little Sweet Pea?"

"I'm so ashamed, Auntie," Nuna hung her head and blew her nose into the Kleenex.

"It's not your fault." Jessica pounded her fist on the table. "Those fucking human trafficking bastards should be castrated with rusty scissors." The girls stared at her with empty eyes, pod-people possessed by alien forces. She wanted to scream and kick the shit out of whoever did this to these poor little things. "These are just little girls!" she shouted. "It's sickening."

"First things first," Madge said. "Let's get you girls out of here. Girls come with me." The policewoman took charge, pulling the girls out of the booth one by one. She'd rounded them up and was escorting them through the wolf pack when a burly man appeared out of nowhere and shouted, "What the fuck are you doing? Those are my girls!" The tattooed brute seized Nuna with one hand and punched Madge square in the jaw with the other. Madge hit the concrete floor with a thud and lay there prone.

Jessica tried to kick the thug in the balls, but he grabbed her foot and she fell backward on top of Madge. Jessica clawed at his feet trying to pull him down, but the bull kicked her in the face with the sole of his boot and she tumbled back to the floor. When her hands flew to her mouth from the pain, she felt warm liquid trickling down her neck. She checked her hand and sure enough it was covered in blood. She didn't know if he'd split her lip or knocked out some teeth. Her head was spinning and everything went black.

PART TWO

CHAPTER EIGHTEEN

"RUN, GIRLS…" JESSICA James sputtered as she came to on the sticky bar floor. But the poor strung-out girls didn't move. They were cowering behind their burly pimp, some of them quietly crying. Jessica rolled toward the tribal policewoman and started shaking her. "Wake up, Madge. For god's sake, please wake up!"

Big Mack snagged Jessica by the arm and hauled her to her feet. She glared into his bulging eyes and spit blood into his ugly face. "Why you little whore… I outta." He jerked his arm back to sock her in the face when a black boot flew into the side of his head. When the creep dropped her arm, Jessica stumbled backwards, tripping over Madge, who was still unconscious on the gummy floor. The burly man swayed to one side and then turned to face his attacker. When he did, the boot slammed into his chin, and Jessica heard the unmistakable cracking sound of bone breaking. The wounded brute staggered backwards clutching his face. As the black boot flew up to kick him, he lurched forward, catching Lolita's foot in midair with both hands. The rest of Lolita came into view as he dragged the karate kicking avenger across the floor.

By now, the wolves in the bar had made room for the fight and were howling and hooting from the sidelines. Some of them were placing bets: "Hundred bucks on Adolf Titler," one guy shouted, and they all laughed. "I'll take fifty on the Poker Tsarina," said another, and they started chanting "Tsarina, Tsarnia." With her one free leg, Lolita vaulted off the floor, flipped herself up, and head-butted the burly pimp smack in the groin. When he dropped her leg to grab his crotch, Lolita sprung to her feet and landed another kick on his chin that sent the monster hurling back into the side of the bar.

Out of nowhere, a wiry thug with a pig-sticker lunged at Lolita from behind. When Jessica reached down, unsnapped Madge's peacemaker from its holster, flipped off the safety and fired the 9mm Glock straight at him, the hunting knife clattered to the floor and the wiry pimp followed. *Holy Shit!* She'd just shot someone.

"Good to see you too," Lolita said, extending her hand toward her friend. "And nice shooting Jessica James. Let's get out of here."

Shaking, Jessica grasped her friend's hand and Lolita pulled her to her feet.

"Watch out behind you!" Jessica yelled. The gorilla was coming at them again from the bar. Lolita swung around but wasn't quick enough and the brute clipped her around the waist. She clasped one hand around the other for leverage and jabbed her elbow into his thick neck, then she spun around and thrust her knee into his saggy nuts. Cursing, he crouched over but continued coming at the karate black-belt, when Jessica shouted, "Stop or I'll shoot!"

Still on the floor, Madge sat up holding her head. "What's going on?" she asked, slurring her words.

Someone in the crowd said, "Little lady's got a gun and ain't afraid to use it. She's gotcha by the balls, Big Mack." The guys laughed. No one cared that the wiry weasel was still lying bleeding on the floor. Jessica hoped she hadn't killed him.

"If you roustabouts want any more pussy, you'd better help me stop these crazy bitches," Big Mack said.

"I'll shoot," Jessica warned, scanning the bar with the pistol.

"Blondie, maybe you'd better give me my gun back before you kill someone," Madge said, brushing off her hat and smashing it back onto her off-kilter hairpiece.

"I think I already did." Jessica pointed the gun at the wiry guy lying on the floor in a pool of blood next to the bar.

"I'd better call for backup."

"Let's get the hell out of here," Lolita said. "There is no backup in this lawless country."

The bulls were getting restless. No longer laughing and cheering, now snarling and spitting, they swayed back and forth, some of them holding broken bottles, ready to charge the women.

"Anyone move and I'll shoot," Jessica shouted, her voice trembling. "Madge, get the girls outside while I cover you."

"Come on, now, Blondie, be reasonable," Madge said. "Give me the gun."

"Do it!" Jessica shouted at the top of her lungs.

Startled, Madge followed orders and herded the girls out of the tavern.

"I mean it, I'll shoot" Jessica said brandishing the handgun again.

"You boys don't want to mess with my friend, Jessica James." Lolita laughed and tossed her ebony hair over her thin shoulder. "She's one tough cookie. She's the Cowgirl Philosopher!" she said beaming.

Some of the guys chuckled, but backed off. "Any friend of yours Tsarina, is a friend of ours," one of them said. "Yeah, we know better than get on the bad side of the Poker Tsarina, 'specially if we want to keep playing," said another.

Jessica gave her friend a concerned look. "You know these guys?"

Lolita strode to the door and flung it open. "Time to go," she barked.

Jessica staggered out of Whispers Tavern backwards, pointing the gun back into the bar. As she stumbled across the threshold, Lolita gently took the gun away from her. Once outside, shivering, Jessica slumped to the ground. Lolita flipped the safety on the handgun and jammed it down the front of her black leather pants. "Come on." She put a hand under each of Jessica's armpits and lifted her to her feet. "Let's see if the girls and your cop friend are okay. What's up with her anyway? That hair?"

When they reached the squad car, the girls were crammed in the backseat. Madge rolled down her window. "Now, can I please have my sidearm back?"

Lolita handed her the gun and introduced herself, then glanced in the backseat at the zombie girls.

"I'm going to get these girls to the clinic and then take them back home," Madge said. The girls were munching and passing the bag of candies. "Are you coming, Blondie?"

"Thanks, I'll hop a ride with Lolita." Jessica turned to her friend. "Can you take me back to East Glacier? That's where you're headed, right?"

"Eventually," Lolita said with a sly smile.

"What do you mean, eventually?" Jessica asked, knitting her brows.

As always, heads turned as Lolita shook out her glossy black hair before stuffing it into her helmet. Every stupid man that saw her was smitten, but the Russian beauty never fell for any of them. She always said, "Men are for business, not pleasure." Jessica wondered where her lithe friend did find pleasure, that is, besides karate chopping assholes.

"After the big poker game." Lolita kissed her friend's cheek. "I'll stake you if you want to take these redneck *Súchka* for a ride. The bitches won't know what hit 'em." As she threw her long leather clad leg over the bike, someone whistled from the backdoor of the bar, but she ignored him. "Hop on. I want to show you something."

CHAPTER NINETEEN

BILL "CANNON" SILVERTON adjusted his new paisley tie as he waited in the lounge at Whitefish's only fancy restaurant and ordered a glass of wine to calm his nerves. Then he thought better of it.

"Can I get a Coke?" Bill asked the bartender. "No, make that a coffee." Coke was childish, wine too relaxed, but coffee, that would make the right impression. Coffee drinkers were taken seriously. Or maybe he should order a martini like the movers and shakers on Mad Men with their three martini lunches.

He'd been dumfounded when Mr. Knight's assistant had called asking for a lunch date. Richard Knight was the big-shot owner of Knight Industries and its dozen subsidiaries across the globe. He was one of the richest men in the country, if not the entire world, and lately he was investing in Montana.

"Excuse me, you must be William Silverton," said a well-groomed gentleman with a single malt voice. "Yes, handsome, wholesome, and probably very photogenic, that's all good."

"Yes, Sir, chez moi," Bill said. *Come on Billyboy, get a grip.*

Heads turned in the restaurant as the hostess buzzed around Richard Knight. "Mr. Knight, can I take your coat? Would you like a cocktail? The usual? And your usual table?" With his tailored wool navy suit, starched white shirt, and red tie, he stood out, a patriotic peacock amongst the casually dressed tourists and Montana elite.

Richard Knight nodded to the enthusiastic hostess, and then extended his hand to Bill. "Pleased to meet you Mr. Silverton. I hope you like Café Kandahar. Did you know Kandahar is what Persians called Alexander the Great when he founded the city and gave it his name? I've always admired Alexander the Great." Richard Knight put his hand on Bill's shoulder and led him to a corner table. Something about this guy was strangely familiar, his touch triggered a vague sense of déjà-vu. When Knight waved to the waiter, he dashed over, leaving a table of local society ladies gaping at their Caesar salads. "What can I get for you Mr. Knight?" the waiter tilted his head and aimed his plastered-on smile toward the big cheese.

"We'll have the Chef's Tasting Menu with the wine pairings," Knight replied.

"Always a good choice, Mr. Knight." No sooner had the waiter scurried off then he was back with the first course.

"Sashimi grade tuna and Dungeness Crab Salad, nestled on a bed of local microgreens," he said as he put a small plate in front of each of them. "Accompanied by a Heidei Schröck, Furmint. Enjoy."

Bill heard the words but had no idea what the hell they meant. The waiter poured two glasses of white wine, and waited for Knight to taste it. When Bill followed his lead, his lips puckered involuntarily and his taste buds bristled at the sweet and sour combination.

"The original Furmint wine was made in Hungary and grown in soil high in iron, rust actually. Amazing that something so sweet is born from corrosion, isn't it?" Richard Knight swirled the wine in his goblet, put the glass to his nose, and inhaled. "Ripe yellow plums and greengages," he sighed. "With a hint of cinnamon."

Bill swirled his glass, took a big whiff, but all he smelled was sour fruit. "Do you own distilleries too?" he asked.

Knight laughed. "You mean wineries? No, for me, wine is just a hobby. Some men fish, I drink wine."

In Montana, if men drank it wasn't a hobby but a sport, especially in bars around the oil fields. Roughnecks, roustabouts, and even ginsels were serious about their drinking. So much so a guy could get killed over a bottle of whiskey. *There but for the grace of God.* Bill's wrestling scholarship to Montana State in Bozeman had given him the college degree that saved him from those dirty backbreaking jobs.

They'd hardly finished their salads when the waiter whisked their plates and glasses away and appeared with another set."

Knight began swirling, so Bill did the same. Swirl, sniff, swirl, sniff, sip, sip. He was getting the hang of it.

"What do you smell, Mr. Silverton?" Knight asked.

Bill swallowed hard. "You mean the wine?" he asked.

"Well, I don't mean your aftershave, which, by the way is perhaps too man of the people even for a junior representative from Flathead Valley. Maybe I can at least help you upgrade from Walgreens to Macy's. Well? What do you smell?" Knight demanded. "First thing that pops into your head!"

Bill took a long drag of the golden wine. "Lemon Meringue Pie?"

Knight laughed. "Well done. This Viognier has a strong lemon finish. I think we're going to make a great team, Mr. Silverton. I hope your instincts are as good when it comes to politics."

"Team?" Bill asked. He wiped his sweating palms on the legs of his trousers.

"Mr. Silverton, I don't beat around the bush. I invited you to lunch to talk about your future in politics. I think you have promise, a lot of promise. If you play your cards right, you could work in Washington someday and serve on important committees in the House or Senate. You, Mr. Silverton, are the future of Montana. America's finest." He waved his knife in the air for emphasis.

Bill's face was beaming, but his stomach was doing flips. He may be from the boonies in Montana, but he'd been around enough to know that when some rich businessman waved a steak knife, talking promise and futures, he wanted something in return.

"You'd like a future in politics, isn't that right, Mr. Silverton?"

"Yes, Sir. Of course I would. I care about this land and its people. But I'm just a City Councilman. Why come to me?" Bill asked.

"William Silverton, you won't always be just a city councilman. I see you in Washington helping to shape this country." Knight dabbed the corners of his mouth with his napkin, and then nodded when the waiter brought the next course.

"Pork Belly Confit, Maple, Rosemary, Honey, Winter Squash, and Frisee, paired with a Domaine de Font-Sane, Gigondas," the waiter said and did an about-face.

"Speaking of pork belly," Bill said. "What do you want in exchange for your support?"

"My, my, William—can I call you William? You are direct, but let's not get ahead of ourselves." Knight chuckled. "Take this wine, for example." He lifted his glass and examined the maroon liquid. "It's purposeful and direct. But it's got a raw nose, and it's painfully dry. Yes, it's a manly Gigondas with its feet on the ground, but it lacks real passion. Compare this to the Viognier. Your lemon pie is big and bold, but it's also complex and generous with freshness and length on the finish." Knight put his glass down on the table and stared across the table.

"William, you don't have to sock someone in the kisser to prove your strength."

The waiter arrived with another course. "Washington Rack of Lamb…"

"I'm with you there, Sir," Bill interrupted, eyeing the rare lamb. "I believe in violence only as a last resort."

The waiter set out two new wine glasses and poured yet another burgundy liquid into each. Knight took a sip. "Yes, well, this Cabernet Franc is an act of violence. Take my advice and pass on this pairing."

Bill couldn't shake the funny feeling he'd met Richard Knight before.

"This lamb's delicious," Bill said.

"Yes, sheep are made to be eaten," Knight said with a wink.

Bill narrowed his eyebrows. "You still haven't told me why you invited me to lunch." He was beginning to worry he was the sacrificial lamb.

The waiter interrupted with another course.

"There's more," Bill blurted out. "Man, how many courses are there?"

The waiter gave him a dirty look. "This is the penultimate course, Sir. Save room for dessert!" He exclaimed and pranced off.

More swirling and sniffing, swirling and sipping. "This is what I'm talking about," Knight said smiling. "Quilceda Creek Cabernet Sauvignon. Bold and muscular with nerves of steel. Its sheer power is matched only by its grace, and dare I say, subtlety. Yes, it's powerful and subtle at the same time like you, William. I suspect you'll ripen into something dominating. That's why I'd like to make a donation to your campaign."

"That's very generous of you, Sir, but, but, why?" Bill stuttered.

"Call me Richard for heaven's sake. I have confidence in you. And I know that you understand that Montana needs strong economic growth. It needs to reopen public lands to private industry and keep our neighbors employed and happy, isn't that right?"

"Ah," Bill said. "You're interested in timber on government lands, is that it? You know I have absolutely no power to influence the use of state or federal lands." *Tit for tat, rich bastard thinks he can buy everything.*

"Let's just enjoy our lunch," Knight said. "Remember the importance of subtlety. It's a lesson that applies to *almost* everything in life."

The waiter whisked their plates away and scraped the tablecloth clean with a gold table-crumber. Right behind him, the underwaiter delivered mounds of dark chocolate, surrounded by eddies of crimson and topped with fresh raspberries. Bill thought he'd burst if he ate another bite. But after the first taste of molten chocolate heaven, it was easy to clean his plate. "I'm stuffed," he said and sat back with a sigh, using his napkin to scrub at the red wine mustache he suspected had formed over his upper lip.

"That cougar on the wall is stuffed, William. You, on the other hand, are about to become a live contender for the State House." Knight reached inside his designer suit jacket pocket and retrieved an envelope with "William Silverton" typed in black letters on front. The way he slid it across the tablecloth made Bill think of *The Godfather*. He remembered Michael Corleone saying, "keep your friends close, but your enemies closer." He thought of the corrupt Senator demanding the mafia pony-up, "I'm going to take a nap. When I wake up, if the money's on the table, I'll know I have a partner."

Bill reluctantly picked up the envelope and turned it over in his trembling hands.

"Well, open it!" Knight said. "It won't bite." He smiled and raised his bushy eyebrows.

Bill seized his steak knife and sawed open the envelope. He reached inside and removed a cashier's check for $100,000.

"Oh my god! I can't take this." The cashier's check was a rabid bat threatening to bite him and Bill flopped it into the middle of the table.

"Why not? It's well below the limit on campaign donations." Knight said. "William, my boy, you'd better practice accepting money with grace, and dare I say, subtlety." Knight unclipped the Montblanc pen from his breast pocket and wrote on the back of a business card. "And here's the number for my tailor," he said. "Call him."

Bill looked down at his paisley tie, now spotted with molten chocolate, and glanced back at Knight. *Something sweet growing out of corrosive soil, my ass.* "I'm going to regret this," he said under his breath as he pocketed the check.

Chapter Twenty

"SO, WHY IS a nice girl like you in a dump like this?" Lolita asked. "I thought you were working at some fancy lodge in a National Park."

"I am. I was. I've probably been fired by now." Jessica James blew her tangled bangs out of her eyes. "Why didn't you call to tell me you were in Montana?"

"Montana's a big place and I'm still a long ways from your neck of the woods. Anyway, I'm not done here and I wasn't sure when I'd make it over to Glacier. How'd I know you'd come looking for me?" Lolita winked.

"I'm looking for my roommate. Her sisters were kidnapped by some friggin' human traffickers. They're prostituting out young girls from the Blackfeet Reservation to service those bastard oil workers. Now, she's disappeared. We've got to find her."

Lolita unlocked the back compartment on her bike, and removed a bowl shaped helmet. "Here, put this on." She shook out her shimmering mane, wrapped it into a bun on the top of her head, and slapped her own helmet on top. "Describe these missing girls. I've been hanging around every shady bar in this town for the last week gathering marks for my game. Maybe I've seen them."

Jessica balanced the small helmet on top of her head and then snapped its strap under her chin. She always felt silly wearing the stupid thing. "My roommate, Kimi RedFox, is a snarky Indian girl, woman really. She must be about my age, maybe younger. She's adorable until you get to know her. She's got a chip on her shoulder the size of Montana. Her little sisters have been missing for the last month."

"I've seen a lot of Native girls being prostituted around here. It's fucked up." Lolita threw her long leg over the bike. "Hop on," she said over her shoulder. "Last night, I knocked out a jacked-up fucker who grabbed my ass. And, a couple of nights ago, I dragged a horny bastard off of another terrified Native girl.... I wonder what happened to her. I swear I'm going to find out."

"Maybe we can look for her and my roommate at the same time." Jessica climbed on the bike behind her friend and clamped her arms around Lolita's waist. She couldn't put her finger on it, but something was different about her friend. "Where's your motorcycle jacket?"

"I gave it to that sweet girl. She needed it a lot more than I did." Lolita revved the engine.

Even in the pitch dark with her crappy sense of direction, Jessica could tell they were headed the wrong way back to East Glacier. She yelled at her friend to turn around, but Lolita ignored her. She gestured wildly, pointing in the other direction, until the bike hit a bump, and she was forced to clutch Lolita around the waist again with both arms. Winding along the Yellowstone River on a dirt road, the bike was throwing up so much dust that Jessica had to pull her sweat-shirt up over her mouth. The drought had made the countryside even dustier than usual, and she wished Lolita had given her goofy goggles to go with the silly helmet. She trusted her friend knew what she was doing. She'd obviously driven this road before, at least Jessica hoped to hell she had.

After twenty minutes on the windy road, they pulled off into an imposing Blue Spruce tree lined driveway. In the distance, floodlights popped on the moment they pulled in off the county road and illuminated a magnificent log house. The front yard—if you could call it that—was a magnificent manicured park with underbrush cut down and trees trimmed up. It reminded her of a friggin' Christmas tree farm, perfect triangular evergreen trees standing erect on a blanket of pine needles.

Lolita slowed down and coasted her bike into a four-car garage off to the side of the mammoth house. The cavernous garage was empty except for a case of Prosecco sparkling wine, a case of George Dickel barrel select whiskey, and four green felt-covered card tables. The concrete garage floor was so clean it shone.

"What the hell's going on?" Jessica hopped off the bike, careful not to burn her ankle on the exhaust pipe.

"You didn't think I'd be holed up in some rattrap in Sidney or Williston, did you? You know me better than that."

"But whose mansion is this?" Jessica asked. "What are you up to? Why so much booze?" She pointed across the cave. "You aren't really hosting a poker game here, are you? Can't you come out to visit without organizing cursed card games?"

"Why yes, that's exactly what I'm doing. You don't think I'd let all that oil money floating around here go to waste? This place is ripe for the picking and I'm just the girl to pluck this low-hanging fruit." Taking off her helmet, Lolita laughed and shook her silky hair. "This place belongs to an Exxon oil baron out here for the fracking. We're going to clean up out here." She rubbed her elegant hands together.

"You're insane. These roughnecks and roustabouts aren't like the gentlemen back in Chicago. They kill folks over a friendly game of poker out here," Jessica warned.

"Gentlemen, my ass! You mean the mob boss, a gun totting art dealer, and that rapist quarterback. I haven't met a man I can't handle. They're all the same. They only respect you after you give them a butterfly kick to both sides of the head. Follow that with a good Kin Geri, and either they'll never mess with you again or fall hopelessly in love." Lolita sighed and unlocked the door, then flipped on the lights and gestured her friend inside.

"Kin Geri?"

"Kick to the nuts."

"Holy shit!" Jessica exclaimed as she walked into the living room. "This place is amazing."

Huge expanses of window glass stretched between floor to ceiling logs—not little prefab jobs, but giant, hand hewn Lodgepole pine. In the center of the great-room, overstuffed leather chairs and sofas surrounded a two-sided stone fireplace. The honey stained, tongue and groove vaulted ceiling peaked fifty-feet overhead, and when Lolita opened the living room windows, the sounds of running water trickled in.

"There's even a stream running through the property." Her friend gestured Vanna White style out the window.

"How'd you get this place?" Jessica asked, forgetting she was talking to the "Poker Tsarina." She'd set up the most famous games in Chicago for elite athletes, movie stars, high stakes billionaires and other illustrious (and notorious) rich men, and raked in a lot of chips in doing so.

"You've got to know how to work the system. I'm planning a big poker game for this weekend. And there's fly-fishing on the Yellowstone River thrown in for some daylight fun. Low hanging fruit," Lolita repeated with a sly smile.

"What? You don't know how to fly fish!"

"I don't know how to play poker either, but that's never stopped me." Lolita flipped a switch and the gas fireplace came to life in blazing glory. "But I do know how to throw a party. And, I know men."

That was an understatement. Lolita was paying her tuition at posh Northwestern University hosting lavish poker games in the city. With professional athletes, famous actors, futures traders, and yes, even mobsters, playing in her high stakes games, no matter what, she always came out a winner because she knew how to make men feel important, and it paid off in thousands of dollars in tips. It helped that she looked like Russian royalty. In a sense, she *was* Russian royalty—that is if you counted being the exiled granddaughter of the richest and most revered mafia boss in Moscow.

"You can help me run the game. That is, unless you want to play," Lolita said. "You might want to hedge your bets, so to speak, in case you've really lost your job. You know you'd clean up." She smiled and winked.

"I might have saved my job if we'd gone straight back to East Glacier, but now forget it. I'll probably never be able to show my face around there again." Jessica collapsed into one of the oversized chairs, threw her legs over one huge arm, and leaned her head against the other. She sighed and stared at the ceiling. "If I'd known I was going to host a fancy party, I'd have brought some clothes. Hell, I'd have brought my toothbrush."

"As usual, my parties are all inclusive. You'll look like Drew Barrymore when I get through with you, my Montana friend." Lolita sauntered to the wet bar and poured herself a vodka. "Would you like some wine or a cocktail?"

"I'd like to sleep for about twelve hours. Can you just put some whiskey in a to-go cup and send me to bed?"

"Sure thing, Sweetie." Lolita poured two fingers of sipping whiskey into a crystal glass, handed it to Jessica, and led her down the hallway to a suite at the very end of the house.

"Your room." She gestured into the huge room. The bathroom was the size of the room Jessica shared back at the bunkhouse. Sliding glass doors opened onto a patio; and when she opened them, she heard the soothing sounds of the stream again. The night air was brisk and just perfect for sleeping. Lolita blew her a kiss as she shut the bedroom door. "Get your beauty sleep. You'll need it! I have a surprise for you tomorrow."

CHAPTER TWENTY-ONE

BILL SILVERTON PACED back and forth in front of Glacier Bank on the main drag in downtown Whitefish. Richard Knight's mammoth check was burning a hole in his jacket pocket. He knew if he cashed it, he'd be beholden to the damned billionaire Texan businessman. And, if he didn't, he'd stay a little fish in a little pond for the rest of his life. This might be his only chance at the big time. He hadn't even cashed the check and he already felt like a thief.

He wondered what Jesse would think of Mr. Richard "High Falutin" Knight of billion-dollar Knight Industries backing his candidacy. Why should he care what she thought? All through high school, she never gave him a second look. If she had...if she had, who knows? He remembered how he used to tease her because her trumpet playing was so atrocious. Before he even entered the band room he'd recognized her horrific squealing. Playing the sax had been the only thing in life that ever came easy to him. Back then, he'd planned to be a professional musician, but in college Annie had convinced him to study agricultural economics.

Bill scrolled through his contacts until he found Jesse's freshly entered number on his cell phone. He tapped the green button, then immediately regretted it and tapped the red one. Instead, he speed dialed Annie.

"Oh my god, Honey!" Annie exclaimed. "That's great!" He stopped pacing and stared dumfounded into the bank window. When one of the bank managers gawked at him through the tinted glass, Bill stepped away from the window and leaned against the bank's brick façade.

"You really think so?"

"Of course, Sweetie. This is the big break we've been waiting for. With Richard Knight's support, who knows how far we can go!" Annie hadn't sounded this excited since they'd put the down payment on their house. Given her reaction, he had no choice but to deposit the check. No sooner had he tucked the deposit slip into his wallet than his cell phone rang...a number he didn't recognize.

"Richard Knight here," a familiar voice responded to Bill's "Hello." He was searching his memory to place it. "You probably heard that I bought the old Specht Mill. Naturally, I want to get it up and running again as soon as possible to get our local boys back to work, but I've run into a snag with the local constabulary. They're insisting the mill is a crime scene. Those accidents were tragic, yes, but not criminal. The only thing criminal about those deaths is that old man Specht didn't keep his ancient equipment updated. But I assure you I intend to fix everything. I'm going to outfit the mill with a new debarker and gang-edger, and I'm going to replace that old fire hazard of a kiln. I plan to make the mill safe and profitable again, but I need your help."

Bill got chills remembering the gruesome scene after Mike James was chewed up and spit out by the debarker. He didn't know what to say. Knight was already asking special favors when the ink was barely dry on his fat check.

"William, I'm sure you agree it's in the best interests of Whitefish and all of Western Montana to get that mill up and running again and put those boys back to work."

"Ah, okay. But you have to understand that law enforcement needs to do their job. If there's been a crime committed out there, that's pretty serious business, and we don't want to interfere with justice."

"Of course, we all want justice. That's why I'm backing your campaign, William. You are a man of integrity and stand for justice. You're also a man of loyalty who can get things done. I'm counting on you." The line went dead.

In spite of himself, Bill was pulled towards Alpine Vista, a magnet drawn to its opposite pole. He had to see Jesse again. As he reached the turnoff to the trailer park, he thought better of it, stomped on the accelerator, and broke the speed limit getting back to town. Hoping to sober up, he gunned it all the way to Whitefish police headquarters where they always had a fresh pot of coffee, and where Annie's brother—detective Dial Davies—could talk him down. It wasn't just the wine that had gone to his head.

When he arrived at the police station, Bill found his brother-in-law at his desk and on the phone. Dial held up one finger and then pointed to a chair. Bill sat down in the spotless, cerulean upholstered chair and admired the ultra-neat surroundings while waiting for Dial to get off the phone. Dial was calmly telling the person on the other end of the line, "That's okay. Just do it over again, and do it right this time." Dial was unflappable; that's how he got his nickname, "Dial Down." When he got off the phone, Dial strolled to a table in the corner of his office and popped a shiny purple bullet into the silver capsule container at the top of his Nespresso machine.

"Regular or decaf?" he asked.

"Full octane, dude." Bill waited for his brother-in-law to finish fiddling with his fancy espresso machine.

"What can I do for you Councilman Silverton?" Dial asked. "It's been a while." He handed Bill a demitasse on a small saucer.

"Too long." Bill made a show of crossing his legs and sipping his coffee with his little finger extended. "Hey, what's the latest on the investigation out at Specht Mill and Mike James' death?"

"You came to see me about the mill?" Dial narrowed his eyebrows. "Is it a matter of City Council business?"

"What happens at our local businesses is always a matter of City Council business." Bill looked up at the detective over the edge of his cup and waited. "Anyway, Mike James was a friend of mine."

His brother-in-law just stared at him for a few long seconds. "Well, this is strictly confidential, but someone was out there nosing around. They cut through the barrier tape. We found a piece of a bloody shirt near the fence, but it doesn't match the blood of the victims. We've called in a team from Helena to check out the equipment to confirm they really were accidents. Someone snooping around an inoperative mill is curious. Makes me curious anyway." Dial swigged the rest of his espresso. "Want another?"

"How many of these deadly bullets do you drink a day?"

"I don't know, four or five, maybe six." Dial smiled. "How else could I keep up with crime in Whitefish?"

Bill stared at his cup and then glanced up at his brother-in-law again. "So, except for the recent trespassing, sounds like you don't think there was any foul play."

"I didn't say that," Dial said. "As you know, the detectives from Helena took over as soon as there was a question of homicide. They don't keep us in the loop. We're just the lowly local boys. But we're investigating the trespassing. There were a few sets of tire tracks, a bloody shirt—looks like a girl's...."

Bill interrupted, "A girl?" He thought of Jesse James stranded out by the mill. A shiver ran down his spine as he remembered her silhouette in the surreal light of dawn, so different from the old days when she used to tuck her ponytail into a baseball cap to pass for a boy...a very sexy boy.

"I should say 'a female'." Dial made air-quotes. "Probably just some high school kids looking for a place to make-out, get high, or something."

"You know, I picked up an old friend of mine out there. Her car had broken down near the mill. Remember Jessica James from Whitefish High School? Her cousin, Mike, was killed in the latest mill accident." Bill tightened his lips.

"Jessica's back in town? I thought she'd gone off to some Ivy League school back East to become a doctor or something," Dial said. "Talk about beauty and brains."

"Yeah. She's back for the summer. She's getting a Ph.D. in psychology back in Chicago," Bill said. "Mike told her something weird was going on out there the day before he died."

"Really." Dial took out a pen and pad. "Now, that's interesting. How can I get a hold of our old friend Jessica?"

"She's working in East Glacier. Her mom still lives out there in the same crappy trailer park. Alpine Vista." Bill retrieved his phone. "I'll text you her cell number." A knock on the door startled him, and he had to re-type his text. The door opened and a uniformed officer poked her head in.

"We've picked up James Dalton. He's waiting for you in the conference room."

"Okay, thanks Sergeant Hodges."

"Jim Dalton? You picked him up?" Bill asked. "Why?"

"His little brother Tom has skipped town. He was working out at the mill the day Mike James died in the debarking machine. Those Helena detectives couldn't find him, so they asked us to help. I'm going to find out if Jim knows where his brother is hiding and why." Dial got up from his desk. "I have to go, but I'll keep you posted on the mill investigation."

After he left police headquarters, Bill drove straight to Alpine Vista. A pang of guilt stabbed at his heart as he knocked on the door to the rundown doublewide and noticed its rotten wooden siding and cracked peeling paint. He hadn't been over to help Mrs. James in years, not since Jesse left for college. When Mrs. James answered the door, he was surprised at how much she'd aged in the last few years. Still, shining through her leathery face were Jesse's same sapphire eyes. Her tight jeans, flannel shirt unbuttoned to reveal the lace of her black bra underneath, and bare feet with bright pink toenails reminded him of the flirtatious girls in high school. When she hugged him, he realized just how tiny she was. She invited him inside, and he sat across from her at a small, rickety table in what passed for her dining room. She refilled a tall glass with vodka and tonic, added a few ice cubes, and then asked if he wanted one. He took a glass of water instead. He smelled alcohol on her breath, and her glassy eyes suggested she'd been drinking since breakfast. It reminded him of Jesse's sixteenth birthday party when her mom had gotten drunk and was inconsolable, balling her head off about The Accident, as if she were the only one in pain. Jesse, the birthday girl, left her own party unnoticed, and he'd found her later in the barn sobbing, clinging to her horse.

"Is she in some kind of trouble?" Mrs. James asked.

"No, Mam, I just need to talk to her, that's all," Bill lied.

Mrs. James ran out through the broken screen door after him and gave him a big drunken hug before he climbed back into his pickup. He tried to call Jesse again, but her phone went right to voicemail. He just had to find her, even if it meant driving on damned Highway US 2 over to East Glacier. He hadn't driven over Marias pass or past Snow Slip Inn since The Accident eleven years ago. But if anything happened to Jesse, he couldn't live with himself. He hoped it wasn't too late.

CHAPTER TWENTY-TWO

J ESSICA JAMES WAS awakened by the smell of strong coffee brewing, tempered by the sweet aroma of distant skunk. She'd always loved the smell of skunks, not the freshly killed ones lying alongside the highway, but the lingering spicy odor left after they were long gone. The trace of skunk made her feel at home. She identified with that defensive smell of fear, long dissipated, and subsequent relief when the fearsome threat retreated into the forest.

Lying in the king sized bed under a down comforter, the freezing early morning air drifting in through the screen door, she didn't want to get up. She stretched and yawned. When she rolled over to go back to sleep, it hit her. She was with Lolita in some posh log mansion on the outskirts of friggin' Sidney Montana, about to host a poker game for a bunch of lousy oilmen. The realization jerked her out of bed, and she padded barefoot into the bathroom. In the natural stone steam shower adjoining her room, she enjoyed the luxurious rush of hot water spraying from all directions.

Lolita was waiting for her in the kitchen with

homemade yogurt smoothies and freshly ground coffee. "There you are sleepy head. I wondered if you'd ever get up. It's already almost noon, and we have a lot to do today." Lolita handed her a glass of purple smoothie and a cup of steaming java. "Have you heard of huckleberries?" she asked.

"Ha! One summer when I was about eight, my cousin Mike recruited me to haul gallons of huckleberries down to the highway in a wagon he'd jerry-rigged to the back of my bicycle. He'd bribed me to pick with stale Halloween candies he'd saved up from the year before. We'd pick all morning and in the afternoon we'd join old Hippies with hair below their belt-buckles parked alongside the road. With our propped-up cardboard sign, we'd sell the precious berries for a whopping thirty-five dollars a gallon. After two days, I was so bored I insisted on getting my share of the loot. And my gosh if I hadn't earned just enough to buy a pink Cricket 22-caliber rifle and a pink saddled white horse for my Barbie doll." Jessica had lost her appetite and put her smoothie on the counter. "I miss Mike." She sighed and shut her eyes tight.

"Time is the best doctor for a broken heart. Come on. This will distract you. We have work to do." All business, Lolita handed her a list of chores. "This is what we need to do for the poker party this evening," she said. "The guys are coming out for some evening fly fishing just before dusk, then dinner, followed by cards."

"Tonight! I've got to find Kimi and get back to East Glacier," Jessica moaned.

"You can do better than minimum wage, my card sharp

friend. I guarantee tonight will be very lucrative. Do you know how much money these guys have to burn?"

"What about my roommate?"

"I promise, as soon as we take down these marks, we'll find her. And, I'll kick the shit out of the assholes that took her. Now, let's get to work."

"What if she's in trouble?"

"I can't back out on my guys now, and believe me, you're going to need my help to take down the fucking pimps around here. We'll take care of business tonight and begin our search tomorrow at dawn. Don't worry, if she's here, we'll find her."

Just before dusk, fancy pickups and SUVs began pulling into the driveway. Lolita provided flies, rods, and waders, everything the players needed for some evening fishing. She even distributed felt-bottomed wading boots in each of their shoe sizes. Jessica should know better than to underestimate her resourceful friend. Chicago's "Poker Tsarina" had become a fly fishing outfitter with the best of them.

When the twenty odd players came in from fishing at dark, Lolita's staff of pretty girls offered them cocktails as they sat in the mudroom removing wet boots and waders. Jessica had no idea where her friend had found such attractive professional waitresses in the backwoods of Montana. And, who were these guys? These weren't the horny oil workers in the bars or the man-camps. Like all of Lolita's "marks," they were beyond loaded and sported brand new high tech clothes. One guy was wearing a sports jacket made of fine cashmere and when she complimented him, the dandy said it was made from "baby Persian goats' hair." *Dickhead.*

The catered dinner was spectacular: shrimp cocktail appetizer, followed by sea bass en paupiette, with rustic new potatoes on a bed of creamed spinach, then chocolate lava cake á-la-mode with homemade huckleberry ice cream for dessert. Half way through dinner, there was a knock on the door. Lolita answered it, and then escorted none other than David Knight into the dining room. She introduced him to the other players, including the head of Shell oil in the Bakken, the owner of Plum Creek lumber mills and the richest dude in Montana, and Pat Frazer, a retired professional footballer who'd come back to his roots.

Jessica couldn't believe her eyes. "David, where have you been?" she asked between her teeth. "Can I talk to you in private?" She snatched his arm and dragged him to the fireplace where she sat him down on the leather sofa. Even the warmth of the fire couldn't thaw her frozen heart against this blackguard. "You said you didn't buy Specht Lumber Mill. But you did. You were over there weren't you? I heard you, you bastard."

"Slow down, cowgirl" David said calmly, looking down, and smiling at her the Ropers she'd painted red with model paint. "My big bro' ordered me back to Dallas to go over the purchase of said lumber mill. I didn't know when asked that he'd already purchased it. I've never seen it, and frankly I don't know why he bought the thing. It's been losing money and has a record of accidents...."

Jessica interrupted him, "My cousin Mike was killed in one of those so-called accidents. And you had something to do with it!"

"What?" David looked dumfounded.

"Why are you in Sidney? What are you doing here?" Jessica asked, raising her voice.

"I'm undercover, looking for Kimi's sisters." David's hazel eyes twinkled.

"Undercover as what? A rich dickhead?"

"Well that wouldn't be much of a disguise now would it?" When David winked at her again, she wanted to sock him in the eye and wipe the stupid grin off his handsome face.

CHAPTER TWENTY-THREE

BILL SILVERTON CRINGED as he veered onto Highway 2, and clicked on the country radio station to calm his nerves. He was wailing along with Blake Shelton's "I Don't Wanna Be Lonely Tonight" when he reached Essex. Almost to Marias pass, the Snow Slip Inn loomed ahead, and Bill stopped singing. His palms were sweating as he turned off the radio. The log Inn looked exactly the same as it had when he'd carried his injured teammates to safety there eleven years ago. He held his breath as he drove past, trying to look straight ahead up the highway, but the Snow Slip Inn tugged at his gaze, a melancholy magnet pulling him backwards.

As he drove past the curve where The Accident had happened, a sinking sensation overpowered his gut, a gravestone descending into his bowels. The repulsive smell of burning flesh assaulted his memory. He saw her face again, the Indian woman thrown from the truck, bleeding on the road, pleading with him to save her baby. The pool of blood in the snow, a crimson halo encircling her head, the cacophony of screams echoing through the dark canyons, the strange mixture of adrenaline and numbness as he carried his teammates all the way to the Snow Slip Inn, the sharp, shooting pain attacking his hip when he finally sat down. It had been so unreal. He'd been numb and dazed when he'd dragged his bloody friends from the school bus. But as soon as everyone was out of danger, he crumpled to the floor because his hip was broken.

He'd almost lost it on the ambulance ride to North Valley Hospital with Jesse's dying dad. Her father had regained consciousness just long enough to beg Bill to take care of Jesse and her mom. He'd made Bill promise to look after them. That's why Bill had gone to Alpine Vista every weekend to help out. At first, he'd thought little Jesse was a goofball—she was such a klutz. As he got to know her though, he fell in love with Jesse's determination and high spirits. It didn't hurt that even with dirt on her face, blisters on her hands, and wearing a backwards baseball cap on her head, she was the prettiest girl he'd ever seen. The Accident had taken her father away forever, and all Bill had ever given her in return was yard work...and the alleged forgotten kiss. No way he'd forgotten kissing Jessica James.

Driving by the scene of The Accident, Bill shuddered as he tried to suppress another memory, a secret burned into his heart in the explosion. But he'd promised his best friend he'd keep it until his dying day. "Cannon, swear to God you won't tell anyone, ever." Later, people called him a hero. He hadn't been a hero, just a traumatized teenage boy in shock. The Accident hadn't killed him, but it had killed his dreams. Now, Annie was the keeper of his dreams. She dreamt big for both of them.

By the time he reached East Glacier Lodge, he was shaking so bad, he had to get a shot of whiskey at the bar to take the edge off. The staff told him Jesse had disappeared with one of the tour buses and hadn't been back to work since. They'd found the Ruby Bus with all four tires flattened across from the police station in Browning. But no one had seen Jesse. The pink-faced girl behind the front desk leaned over and whispered, "She's in big trouble."

Bigger than you know. Bill lumbered out of the lodge, climbed back in his truck, and drove to Browning. He hadn't been there since the wrestling meet on that terrible day during his junior year, but nothing had changed. The town was still a rundown dump, populated by dilapidated trailers covered with pointy rusted tin hats to keep the snow from caving them in, and weathered wooden shacks. The Blackfeet Museum and Bureau of Indian Affairs were the nicest buildings in town. Stray dogs chasing each other through downtown reminded him of a joke Tommy Dalton told about "Two-Dogs-Humping."

When Bill got to the Tribal Police Headquarters, the door to the office was locked, but through the grimy glass he saw a guy sitting inside with his cowboy boots up on a desk. Bill knocked on the door.

"Can I help you?" the big man asked, opening the door just a crack. Bill was stocky and muscular but at six foot three and two-hundred and fifty pounds of beef, this guy towered over him.

"My name is Bill Silverton and I'm looking for a friend of mine, Jessica James. She's about 5' 7" inches tall, 120 pounds, very pretty, big blue eyes, and long wavy blonde hair. Have you seen her?"

"Can't say as I have. Did you say your name is Silverton?" The guy leaned against the door. "Silverton, I've heard that name somewhere. Do I know you?"

"I'm a city councilman over in Whitefish. And, you are?"

"Oh sorry. I'm Dakota Rowtag, Blackfeet Tribal Chairman." He held the door open with his big booted foot and scratched his head. "Councilman Silverton. Yes, *Napekwin* mentioned you to me."

"*Napekwin?*" Bill asked.

Dakota Rowtag's big belly shook with laughter. Grabbing his huge silver belt buckle with both hands, he tugged at his pants. "That's what I call Richard Knight and other powerful white men. It's a tribal joke."

"Richard Knight mentioned me to you?" Bill asked with concern.

Rowtag gestured for him to come into the office and offered him a seat on a metal folding chair across from his desk. As he sat down, Bill smelled a strange odor, freshly brewed coffee with an undercurrent of something rank and rotten. "Could I maybe get a cup of that coffee?" he asked.

"Of course you can." Rowtag sauntered over to the pot, poured a cup, and handed it over. "Mr. Knight tells me you're helping him get the mill up and running again so he can supply lumber to my new construction company. I'm going to build housing for the oil workers over here. It's a booming business, a godsend, really." When he extended a chipped mug full of steaming coffee, Bill noticed a diamond studded watch with turquoise inlay on his wrist, and then his matching bolo-tie and earrings, all solid silver with precious stones. The turquoise jewelry stood out against the black wool shirt stretched across his potbelly. Rigid creases down the front of jeans suggested they'd just come back from the drycleaners. With his ragged, pock marked, brown face and twin braids trimmed with blood red leather fringe, he could have been on a souvenir postcard: Dakota Rowtag, leader of the brave Blackfeet tribe.

"Mr. Knight told you that?"

"Yes, he says you're on our team, a real team player. He says he's backing you for office."

Bill flushed. "So, you're doing business with Knight Industries?"

"Sure am. Knight Industries owns most of the shale oil leases on Blackfeet land. And, he's going to mill the lumber for my housing development." Rowtag troubled the silver tip of one of the leather cords on his tie.

"Sounds like Knight Industries has cornered the market." Bill felt queasy. "Fracking, lumber, housing contracts…."

"All perfectly legal," Rowtag interrupted. "All perfectly legal."

"Of course, I wasn't suggesting otherwise." *Yeah right, how do you spell corruption?*

"Fracking, lumber….That's not why you're here, is it, Mr. Silverton? You were asking about a friend, and I'm sorry to say, I haven't seen her." Rowtag stood up, towering over him and gestured toward the door.

After making two loops around the main drag, Bill stopped at Nation's Burger Station. A colorful turquoise and red chicken coop attached to a small kitchen, Nation's drive-up window was busy all day. Like everywhere else in Browning, stray dogs roamed at will, crossing back and forth across the road and sniffing around trashcans. Bill parked on the street and walked over to the tiny shack to order Nation's famous Indian tacos and a Rez Chili Cheese Burger. Food helped him think. Right now he didn't have any darned idea where to go next. No one had seen the missing blonde girl or the missing red bus. He sat out front at a picnic table and gobbled his taco and burger, both on heavenly fry bread, a cross between scrumptious scone and delicious cake donut, but much tastier than either. *Man, they were good.* Nothing like some greasy Indian fry bread to calm the nerves.

He couldn't help overhearing a group of natives sitting at a picnic table behind him. Stuffing their faces with burgers and tacos, they were gossiping about the Tribal Chairman. One of the Indians complained about an oilrig in Rowtag's own backyard where the Chairman had them release wastewater right onto the ground, and dump used radioactive frack-socks in a ditch nearby instead of disposing of them properly. "Shady *Napekwin* come to the Chairman's house at all hours hauling away oil in tankers or bringing fine looking *Aapaiai*, white ermine for the Rowtag to bang."

Bill's eyes widened and he stopped chewing mid-bite to listen. He'd read about corruption on the Reservation. If the Tribal Chairman wasn't on the up and up, then Richard Knight and Knight Industries were also implicated; and if Knight was in on some corrupt oil deal, then Bill had essentially accepted his first bribe when he cashed that darned check. Blood money. He shuddered. To keep his integrity intact, not to mention his political career, he had to return that filthy check. He went across the street to his truck to retrieve his phone, but when he turned it on and saw Annie and the girls on his screen, he was gripped by guilt. Just as he was putting the cell phone back in his jacket pocket, it buzzed.

"Dial, long time no see," he said, eyeing the caller ID.

"Look, Bill, there's been a development in the Specht Mill case. The federal inspectors found evidence of tampering with the machinery. Tommy Dalton is the prime suspect. We still haven't found him. I'm determined to get my hands on him before those federal boys do. They think we're a bunch of incompetent hicks out here and I aim to prove them wrong...."

"Wow, Tommy's suspected of murder," Bill interrupted. He shoved his plastic tray across the table and slurped the dregs of his coke through his straw. "I always knew he was dangerous."

"I'm telling you all of this because we still haven't found our mutual friend, Jessica James."

"You think Jesse's involved?" Bill's heart skipped a beat, and he dropped his paper cup, splashing the last drops of coke down his flannel shirt.

"No, not in the accidents. But you were right. We think it was her bloodstained shirt we found out at the mill. If she was snooping around the mill, she may be in danger. Whoever is responsible for this is very dangerous. Have you seen her? She's not answering her phone."

"I know, dude. I've been trying to call her too," Bill said. "No one has seen her. I'm in Browning now asking around."

"Browning? I thought she worked in East Glacier. Why would she be in Browning?"

"That's what I'm trying to find out." Bill pinched the phone between his chin and shoulder, unlatched the bear proof trashcan, slid the crumbled taco wrappers into it, and then returned the tray to the drive-in window.

"Let me know as soon as you find her." The line went dead.

If Tommy Dalton knew Jesse had been snooping around the mill, she was in real danger. Bill leaned his forehead against the steering wheel. "Where the hell are you, Jesse?" he asked the dashboard. When he glanced up over the dash, he saw a lean snowshoe rabbit chewing on some lettuce off of a discarded hamburger wrapper behind the drive-in, its mangy coat transitioning from winter white to summer gray. Amidst gravel, asphalt, and the overflowing dumpster, the scrawny hare concentrated on its lunch. For some reason, he thought of Jesse James in the big city, far from her friends and family.

Glancing up from the wayward rabbit, Bill saw a familiar figure walk into Nation's Burger. He ducked down in his seat, waited a few seconds, and then peeked up over the dash. It was Tom Dalton all right. He considered a citizen's arrest, but thought better of it. Lying between the seats and the floor of his truck, he retrieved his phone, searched recent calls, and pressed call back.

"Dial, I just saw Tom Dalton."

"Where?"

"Over here in Browning at Nation's Burger Station."

"Don't approach him. But don't let him out of your

sight. He may be dangerous. We don't have jurisdiction on the Reservation. But I'll get there as soon as I can. Follow him. Don't lose him. It'll take me at least two hours to get there at top sped."

"What? I should follow him?" Bill asked.

"Be discrete." Dial hung up.

"But, I've got to get back..." Bill mumbled into the dead phone. He tried Jesse's number again for the dozenth time. Still no answer. *Where the hell could she be?* He put one hand on each side of his head and squeezed until his temples hurt, discretely watching Tom Dalton order then sit outside at a picnic table, as big as life, eating Indian Tacos.

CHAPTER TWENTY-FOUR

THE POKER GAME was in full tilt, and even though Jessica James was chip leader, sitting across from that smug scoundrel David Knight, she'd lost her appetite for cards. If David had really been looking for her roommate, he wouldn't be yucking it up, drinking George Dickel and betting wads of cash in a high stakes poker game while Kimi might be kidnapped, hurt, or worse. Seeing the self-satisfied jerk so cheerful when her roommate was still missing and possibly in grave danger made her livid. The last thing he said as he scooped up his winnings was, "I promise. I'm going back to Whispers Tavern after this next hand. I'll find her." But he was still playing when she cashed in her chips and slipped off to bed two hands later. The other players grumbled, expecting her to give them a chance to win back some of their losses, and Lolita gave her a sour look. Her friend had been counting on her to help out hosting the game, or at least help her fleece these rich oil dudes.

Alone in her bedroom, the scent of freshly cut pine on the cool evening breeze wafting through the screen door was a calming tonic. She'd just finished reading Willa Cather's *O' Pioneers*. Cather's tough, stoic Swedish immigrants resembled her friends and family in Montana, where the land's harsh demands had taught them to fetter passions. But the Rocky Mountains couldn't be more different from the flattened plains of Nebraska, where the landscapes, inside and out, were the color of baked earth, everything chalky and dry. Still, she identified with Cather's heroine, Alexandra, so independent, and determined to succeed when everyone doubted her. She marveled at Alexandra's ability to detach herself from her own feelings and those of others around her. Jessica wished she wasn't so affected by everything and everyone, a raw nerve exposed in an open wound. If only she could be more like Alexandra and evacuate all her emotions (and stay away from men) then she might be able to concentrate on getting her cursed Ph.D.

She downloaded the last in Willa Cather's Great Plains trilogy, *My Antonia* and scrolled through the pages: more immigrants homesteading in Nebraska, more hard soil and harder characters, more farming and premature death, more beaten-down women swimming upstream in a man's world. Jessica sighed, put her kindle on the nightstand, and stared at the ceiling. Stewing about David and worrying about Kimi, she couldn't sleep. She suspected the smart-mouthed surfer dude was involved in some shady business; and she was terrified to even think of what might have happened to her roommate.

She padded down the hallway to Lolita's bathroom and rifled through her toiletries until she found the right prescription bottle, twisted the lid open, shook a little purple football into her palm, and popped it into her mouth. She palmed another Xanax for good measure, in case her insomnia got worse. Back in the bedroom, she settled into the luxurious sheets under the down duvet on her king-size bed and waited for the pill to kick in.

Before long, she was drifting off to her happy place, a heavenly waterfall along Sprague Creek near her very favorite lodge in the park, tiny Sperry Chalet, high up on rugged Gunsight Mountain, accessible by foot or horseback. Forged from local rock, Sperry Chalet survived when the other railroad lodges were destroyed by fire, avalanche, or time. Wavering between consciousness and sleep, she was back on her first horse pack trip to Sperry when she was five and her dad had taken her up there, just the two of them. Sitting high on her child-sized saddle, she'd ridden Mayhem all by herself, and at the summit, they'd eaten baloney and sliced cranberry jelly sandwiches she'd made before they left home. She'd loved those trips with her dad. Forged in the mountains of Montana, he'd been made from local rock too, but that couldn't save him.

She awoke to a hand stroking her hair. "Lolita?" she asked, still half asleep. A rough hand clamped over her mouth, and she kicked at the bedcovers. When a man jumped on top of her, Jessica bit his hand, tried to scream, but only managed to squeak. She jerked up and clawed at his face, but the bastard punched her hard on the jaw and she fell back, hit her head against the wrought-iron headboard, and then went limp. By the time she realized what was happening, her kidnapper had scooped her up and thrown her over his shoulder. He was carrying her outside across the lawn toward the road. She grabbed at his torso to keep from bouncing up and down, and yelled, "Help! Let me go! Stop!"

"Quit your damn strugglin' and this'll be easier for both of us." She recognized Tommy Dalton's high-pitched voice. He just cackled when she pounded her fists on his back. She'd had enough of these Dalton arse-holes. She knew they were all friggin' crazy, but this was going too far, way too far. When she realized she wasn't wearing her pajama bottoms, and Tommy's arm was pressing against her bare butt cheeks, she hollered, "Tommy Dalton, put me down! What the hell do you think you're doing?"

"Behave, girl, or I'll sock you again. You ain't gettin' away from me this time, my pretty." He spit a revolting stream of tobacco juice onto the grass.

"What do you want, Tommy? Just tell me." Jessica pleaded.

"I told you before, it's Tom. Just Tom, okay."

"Okay, Tom. Please put me down." Jessica tried to push against his back to right herself, but it was no use. The wiry redneck was stronger than he looked. He clumsily removed a key from the front pocket of his jeans with one hand and then opened the back hatch to his van. He threw her in with a thud, then climbed on top of her, pining her to the dirty carpet with his knees. She screamed, "No! Stop." When he reached over her head, his armpit was directly above her face, and she was overwhelmed by the rank smell of sawdust and rotten cheese. With both hands, she shoved at his chest as hard as she could. Her push had no effect except to make her hands more accessible for Tommy who produced a ball of twine and grabbed her wrists with one hand, then wrapped the twine around them with the other. She tried to kick, but he was sitting on her legs. When she opened her mouth to scream, Tommy stuffed a dirty rag inside it. Grit scratched her tongue, and she could taste stale motor grease. As Tommy set to work binding her feet, she continued kicking at his arms.

"Nice muff," he said, laughing as he tightened the twine around her ankles. "Trussed up like a Thanksgiving turkey. Hey, what if insteada turkey, the Injuns gave the Pilgrims bobcat? Then on Thanksgiving we'd all be eating pussy." Hooting, he slammed the van door shut. Jessica's eyes filled with tears. She couldn't breathe through her mouth and felt like she was suffocating. She closed her eyes, and sucking in deep breaths through her nostrils, she rehearsed her yoga mantra in her head. The van stunk of Tommy's acrid body odor, stale chewing tobacco, and greasy fast food.

Bare thighs pressed against cold steel, lying face down, Jessica was freezing in the back of the van. With every bump in the road, her head bounced against the unforgiving metal frame of the spare tire. Her restraints and the erratic movement of the vehicle made it impossible for her to right herself. Every time she tried to sit up, she fell over again. The carpet's stiff tuft pressed into her cheek, making it itch. The best she could do was wedge her bound wrists up under her head as a boney buffer. Twisting her neck, she managed to peer out the back window. The night was black as homemade sin.

Jessica had no idea of the time. They'd been driving for what must have been hours when Tommy pulled the van off the highway, got out, and locked the doors. Finally, in the stillness, with all her effort, she slid into a child's pose, and then sat up on her knees. Propping herself up against the side panel, she saw Tommy had stopped at a rest stop. She glanced around for help. Not a soul in sight. She pounded on the window with her tethered fists anyway, but no one came. She tugged at the gag with her fingertips and managed to loosen it enough so it slipped below her chin, and she gasped and gulped the brisk night air.

When Tommy came back to the van, she didn't know if she should speak or not. She didn't want him to gag her again, so she waited until he'd started the engine, and then she decided to risk it. She was shivering, and her toes and hands were numb from cold and lack of circulation.

"Tommy…. er, Tom. I don't know why you're doing this, but I promise not to scream, or run away, or anything if you could please untie me and give me a blanket or coat or something. Please? I promise I won't give you any trouble. I'm freezing back here, and my wrists are bleeding. Please," she begged.

Tommy stared back at her from the rearview mirror, grinning like a weasel in a hen house. He removed the round tin from his back pocket, screwed open the lid, pinched a big wad of tobacco, stuffed it into his mouth, and smiled back at her with an ominous bulge in his lower lip.

She tried another tact. "Remember when we used to hold hands in the bleachers, Tom? We were pretty close back then, weren't we? For old time's sake, please, untie me and I'll keep you company while you drive," she said with as much honey in her voice as she could muster. Her grandmother always said, "You catch more flies with honey than vinegar."

"How 'bout a BJ? You don't need untied for that." He turned his head and flashed his yellow teeth at her. "Why is car insurance higher for men? Coz women don't get BJs while driving." His laughter sent shivers up her spine, and she silently weighed her options.

"Oh, alright," he said, pulling off the highway. "But if you so much as peep, I'll knock you inta next week." Tommy hopped out of the van, and whizzed around to open the back hatch. He pulled her out, helped her baby step to the passenger seat, opened the door, and shoved her into the passenger seat. He leaned over her lap, and she flinched as he dragged a grease stained camouflage hunting parka over her lap from the backseat, then, he slammed the door and jogged back around to the driver's side, stopping to spit before he hopped back in.

"Thanks." Her voice reverberated in her head, the squeaking of a timid mouse. "Tom, tell me why you're doing this. Why are you kidnapping me? What do you want from me? Just tell me. Please. "

"Promise you won't be mad?"

Jessica rolled her eyes. *Is he insane?* "No, Tom, I won't be mad. Just tell me," she said through clenched teeth.

"My boss don't want you nosin' in our business."

"What are you talking about? What boss? Your boss at the mill?"

"You knows too much so I'm takin' carea you."

"What do you mean? What do I know? Take care of me how?" Jessica's voice rose an octave.

"You jus wish I'd take carea your sweet thing." Tommy's laughter sliced at her eardrums.

"Is that what you want, Tommy….. Tom? Just like old times?"

"Old times. That's a laugh. You never put out then neither, Lil' Miss Tight Ass." Tommy chuckled. "What do ya say to a virgin when she sneezes? Guzintight." His laughter was making her sick to her stomach.

"Say Tommy, what's the last thing a redneck says before he dies?" She glared at her captor. "Hey, y'all. Watch this!"

"You callin' me a redneck, Miss College Girlee? You think yous so damned smart. But who's your daddy now, Miss Flat Chest?" Tommy cackled. He spit his nasty juice into a Coke can in the cup holder.

Jessica instinctively drew the parka over her chest, and stared out the side window to avoid looking at Tommy. The sight of him brought back bad memories. She wondered what had happened to the cute teenager who had asked her to the seventh grade prom. As a man, he was uglier than a burnt boot. Nothing about him was the same, except maybe the nasty glint in his eyes and the way he flapped his foul mouth. The wind was howling, and the sun was coming up behind them as they crossed over Marias Pass. The gilded mountains flashed a searing bright light and she squinted. Usually, she enjoyed this drive through blades of rock slicing upward through rolling mounds of earth, evergreen trees giving way to stark rock. Now, she dreaded whatever awaited her on the other side.

CHAPTER TWENTY-FIVE

BILL SILVERTON FOLLOWED the beat up Dodge van at what he hoped was a discrete distance. He wanted to confront the punk, but Dial had told him to follow Tom Dalton, not to engage him. He switched off the country music blaring from his wife's favorite radio station and inserted a CD into the player, Cannonball Adderley's "Something Else." Annie wouldn't let him listen to jazz when she was in the rig. She said it sounded like "cats screeching." But jazz sax was the language of his soul, and he'd had to stuff his entire emotional life into those moments alone in his pick-up with Cannonball Adderley, Charlie Parker, and John Coltrane.

Hypnotized by the monotony of the plains, Bill settled into the despairing grooves of his favorite mournful jazz. No matter how many times he heard it, he was still mesmerized by Cannonball's soulful alto solo on his favorite tune, "Autumn Leaves," with its trills, elliptical leaps, and rhythmic novelties. Bill's eyes filled with tears as the horn wailed in despondent woe, the perfect backdrop to the high lonesome of the central plains.

With the mountains long gone, asphalt stretched in a straight line all the way to the sparse horizon eternally receding into the distance until the road met the sky. His truck and Tom's van were the only two vehicles on the highway, so he fell back even further. He'd been following Dalton's van for over a hundred miles now and there was no sign of Dial or his damned men. If Tom Dalton was heading for Canada, he sure was taking the long way around.

By the time the beat-up van stopped alongside the Yellowstone River outside of Sidney, Bill was exhausted. *Where the hell were the police?* He couldn't do their job for them. In the distance, across from the riverbank and through perfectly spaced evergreen trees, he saw lights glowing in a sprawling house set back from the road. There were several vehicles parked in the long tree lined driveway. For the next hour, he watched for Tom's next move, but there was no sign of life in the van. Maybe Tom had pulled over to sleep. Staring into the darkness, waiting, Bill tried to stay awake. He rolled down his window to let in the cool night air. He must have dozed off because the roar of a large vehicle driving by woke him up. Cold, hungry, bladder bursting, Bill rubbed his eyes and looked for Tom's van, but it was gone.

Bill glanced down at his phone, just after three in the morning. He called Dial, but got no answer. Not knowing what else to do, he got out of his truck, took a quick piss alongside the road, and hiked up the driveway to the big house, hoping by some miracle the path would lead him to Jesse. He breathed deeply and knocked on the door, then heard music coming from inside, the kind of stupid smooth jazz he associated with elevators—whoever was inside knew nothing about real jazz. When no one answered, he hovered his finger over the doorbell for a few seconds and then pressed it hard. An extraordinarily beautiful young woman answered the door, and he stumbled backwards.

She regarded him with steely eyes, "Can I help you?"

"Sorry to bother you, Miss. My name is William Silverton. I'm on the City Council in Whitefish." *Why the hell did he always need to say that?* "I'm working with authorities there to locate a man who came this way in a Dodge van. Have you seen him? Mid-twenties, longish brown hair, wearing a checkered flannel shirt, dirty jeans, and work boots?"

"Did you say Councilman Silverton? Come in and have a seat, Mr. Silverton. Can I offer you a drink?" the pretty young woman asked, as she slung her ebony hair over one shoulder and gestured for him to enter the house. "My name's Lolita. Lolita Durchenko." She extended her pale hand, her long fingers tipped with scary looking red nails.

"Councilman Silverton from Whitefish. Are you by chance related to Cannon Silverton?"

Confused, Bill narrowed his eyes. "Do I know you? That's my nick-name from high school."

"No, but you know my good friend Jessica James, also from Whitefish," Lolita said. "It's a small world, especially out here where there are so few people."

Bill's eye's widened. "You know Jesse? Actually, that's why I'm here. Do you know where she is? She may be in danger."

"She's asleep in the back room. Safe and sound, I assure you, Mr. Silverton."

"Can I talk to her?"

"Go ahead. But she won't be happy you're waking her up before sunrise. That girl likes to sleep! I think she's part lazy cat." The skinny Russian gal pointed to a long hallway off the living room. "Don't blame me if she throws something at you."

Bill followed the hallway to the very end and rapped lightly on the door to the bedroom. When there was no answer, he knocked louder. His stomach plummeted. Now he knew why Tom Dalton drove all day to get here, somehow he'd known where to find Jesse. Bill pounded on the door and then tried to open it. It was locked. He felt a pang of relief. At least she'd had a good sense to lock herself in.

"What's going on? She's a sound sleeper, but your racket would wake the dead." The Russian gal was on his heels.

Mind racing, he imagined Jesse lying dead on the other side of the bedroom door. Instinctively, he kicked at the door.

"Hey, what do you think you're doing?" The Russian gal stepped between him and the door. "Let's not wreck the place, Councilman." She pulled a tool from her inside her wide patent-leather belt and worked the lock on the door. Within a few seconds the door popped open.

Bill was stunned. Who was this crazy woman with the trick belt? He followed her into the room. Even in the faint twilight of morning, he could tell the bed was empty. Its flat silhouette seized his heart and squeezed. The curtains on the sliding door blew in the breeze, slapping back and forth through the gaping openness. Bill dashed to the sliding door and gazed out into the expansive grounds behind the house. Darkness choked him. When the Russian gal flipped on the bedroom light, the dead certainty revealed an empty room, bed sheets strewn across the floor. Bill flailed out into the twilight calling her name, "Jessseeeee, Jessseeeeee." In his haste, he tripped over the threshold to the slider and stumbled into the yard. Panting, he scanned the grounds, but it was no use. She was gone. Tom Dalton had got away, most likely with Jesse in tow. Numb on the outside, sharp toothed regret chewed at his guts, and he held onto the door jam for support.

"Maybe she went for a midnight stroll. Or, perhaps she sneaked off with that handsome David," Lolita Durchenko said.

"Who? I don't think so." Bill said, stunned. "I'm afraid she's been kidnapped and I aim to get her back."

"Kidnapped? Why would someone want to kidnap Jessica?"

"No time to explain. I've got to get back to Whitefish and find her." Bill called Dial Davies and gave him the bad news. "Get some men out to the Dalton place. Now!" he barked into his phone.

"What's going on?" Lolita Durchenko grabbed his arm. "I'm going with you."

"It's not safe, especially for a...."

She interrupted him. "I'm a black belt in karate and could knock you across this yard. I can take care of myself. And, I'm not about to abandon my best friend."

"Have it your way." In a daze of guilt and remorse, Bill

stumbled back through the hallway, a pinball bouncing from wall to wall. He leaned against a high backed chair in the living room to steady himself, then made a beeline for the front door, and slammed it on the way out. The Russian flung the door open and yelled after him, "I'll follow you on my bike." He ignored her and strode towards his pickup. Tom could be halfway across the state by now. He could have disposed of Jesse any place between Sidney and Cut Bank.

CHAPTER TWENTY-SIX

THE SPEED LIMIT was eighty miles an hour along most of the Hi-Line section of Highway 2. Bill Silverton's truck was shaking at ninety miles an hour, but he kept his foot on the pedal all the way to Shelby. Hours of speeding across the plains had made him delirious. His right Achilles tendon hurt from jamming his foot to the floor, and his hands ached from gripping the steering wheel. His neck was killing him from staring hard at the centerline, not to mention the stress. He should have insisted Jesse go to the police back when he'd found her out by Specht Mill. If anything happened to her, it would be his fault. Guilt seized his throat, almost choking him.

Clutching the wheel with one hand, eyes still on the road, he reached across the seat for his cell phone. He glanced back up at the road, and then punched up Dial's number again. No answer. For hours he tugged on the seatbelt where it pressed into his doughy gut. Finally, the mountains came into view on the horizon. A blazing orange halo hovered in the sky above the distant mountain range. He was close to the Blackfeet Reservation. When he glanced in his rearview mirror, he saw the crazy Russian gal right behind him on her Harley. He'd been driving for five hours nonstop and she'd been on his tail the whole way.

Heading onwards towards Whitefish, he came up over the Continental Divide at Marias Pass. The sun was blinding as it reflected off of the obelisk, marking the highest point, and the wind howled down from the peaks. Bill's bladder was about to burst, so he swerved off the highway to a roadside outhouse. He would have just pissed out on the side of the road if that darned Russian gal hadn't been following him. Behind the wind worn, parka and aviator hat clad statue of the engineer who charted the railroad pass, were two outhouses, men's and women's, both with stinky toilets, basically long shafts plunging into human refuse decomposing ten feet below, harsh lye added by park rangers monthly devoured the foul sewer but not its stomach turning stench. Bill remembered a story he'd heard about a Flathead Indian on the lamb from the law and hiding out amongst the Blackfeet. The engineer bribed the Indian to lead him to the only natural pass through the mountains, and then took all the credit. There were no statues of the Indian. After pissing out buckets, Bill bounded out of the out house, waved to the Russian chick, jumped back into his truck, revved his engine, and took off.

Up ahead, the Snow Slip Inn came into view, and his stomach sank. Before The Accident, he'd thought Snow Slip, a charming refuge in the middle of nowhere, a cute log house with red trim and Christmas lights all year round. Now, it was a haunted shack relentlessly pursing him. His skull was throbbing, and he needed caffeine. Determined to face his demons, he swerved off the highway and into the gravel parking space in front of the Snow Slip. Rocks flew as he skidded to a stop. The Harley squealed in right behind him.

As Bill stumbled through the wobbly front door, he was transported back to the chaos of the restaurant during The Accident. To this day, he couldn't believe he'd carried his teammates a quarter mile down the highway to the Inn with a broken hip. All eleven years crashed down on him with an avalanche of memories. The tiny bar and grill hadn't changed, a deceptively innocent, inviting gold hewn log cabin nestled in the mountains. Inside, tiny inlaid splotches of red in the scuffed gray and white linoleum became tokens of blood not easily washed from his memory. The walls were adorned with the same vintage sled, antique skis, and old fashioned ads for beer and whiskey. Even the old black cat sleeping next to the pot bellied woodstove was the same. Time stood still for Snow Slip. Only Bill was different. Since The Accident, he'd wrapped his fragile heart in cotton lest it be broken again. He was haunted by nightmares of all the ways his own daughters could be taken from him: accidents, pedophiles, diseases, poisons... The list was endless. On the outside, he'd kept his easy manner and quick smile, but on the inside his guts were still scorched and scarred from that horrible night.

As if it were yesterday, he recalled the image of Arnold Specht covered in blood, disappearing into the frosty night. When Bill joined the junior high school wrestling team, Arnold taught him how to use the snap from a double wrist tie-up to throw his opponent off balance. He flushed thinking of all the times Arnold had pinned him down, staring hard into Bill's eyes, both of them breathing fast, two warm bodies heaving together as one. The last time he'd seen Arnold was on the gristly night of The Accident, the night Arnold had sworn him to secrecy, then flung his silver watch across a snow berm and down the cliff below. In shock, he hadn't asked what Arnold was doing, but he'd kept his secret to this day. Where had Arnold gone, shards of glass embedded in his face, crawling up the snow bank behind the blazing bus?

Bill tried to banish the haunting images of Arnold Specht from his mind, but his hands were trembling as he paid for two coffees to-go. In the time it took for the same grumpy waitress to get his coffees, he'd relived the nightmare of that dreadful night. Luckily, she hadn't recognized him.

"Why are we stopping at this dump?" the Russian gal asked, as he passed her on his way out the door of the Snow Slip Inn.

"Exorcising Ghosts." He handed her a coffee.

"Be careful. Casting out demons you might exorcise what's best in yourself," she said as she grabbed the Styrofoam cup.

Without looking back, he got in his pickup, and headed down the highway at top speed towards Hungry Horse and the Dalton's lair, still over an hour away. That hour could mean the difference between life and death for sweet Jesse.

CHAPTER TWENTY-SEVEN

JESSICA JAMES HAD no idea why Tommy might be taking her back to the Dalton place in Hungry Horse. When she leaned her head against the window of his van and closed her eyes, the cool glass was soothing against her hot cheek.

"Don't worry none, go ahead and sleep. Don't worry none. My lips are sealed. I won't make another peep whiles you get some shut eye," Tommy said, spitting into a Coke can.

Jessica's eyes flew open. "Don't worry none, my lips are sealed...." Now she recognized that voice she'd overheard at the mill. Smoky voice had accused him of killing people. Her stomach churned like she'd eaten dirt as she realized Tommy might be responsible for the accidents at the mill. Tommy was a jackass, but she couldn't believe he would kill someone.

"Tomm...er, Tom. You were there the day my cousin Mike died, right? Did you see anything unusual?" she asked.

Tommy turned towards her, his face paled. "I didn't want to hurt Mike. I don't want to hurt you neither. I'm sorry Jesse. I really am, but Mr. Knight...."

Her face burning, she interrupted Tommy. "Did you say Mr. Knight? He told you to do this to me? David Knight?" she asked, tears in her eyes, without warning she had a desperate need to pee. She squirmed so much in her seat that the parka fell off her lap and onto the floor around her feet. She bent over to rake it back up over her nakedness.

"I only mean to kill them dirty Injuns who was takin our jobs. I never mean to kill good folk like you and Mike. She's the one what wanted him dead coz he knowed her from before."

"What? Who wanted him dead?"

"You and Mike. We growed up together. I ain't mean to kill Mike, only them Injuns."

"You killed Indians?"

"I thought I was riggin' the debarker to take out Little Bear and his long greasy braids and shit. It weren't supposed to be Mike in there. I swear. I didn't know he was in there. I thought it were that Injun. When she asked me to do it, I ain't knowed it was Mike she wanted. I swear. And I feel mighty bad. I really do. You knows I's still sweet on you, Jesse. You think you could care 'bout someone like me?" Tommy gawped at her with pleading eyes.

She shuddered so hard her head hit the window. "Why, Tommy? Why'd you do it?" A tear rolled down her cheek, and she wiped her runny nose on the twine holding her wrists together.

"That Johnny greasy bear fucker got my promotion. Injuns ruined my life. Me and my brothers grew up without a daddy coz your damned daddy give them dirty Injuns a ride. Them Injuns killed my daddy and yours too."

"What are you talking about?" She shook her head.

"Them dirty Injuns what your dad picked up off the side of the road. That dirty squaw with the little papoosa. You know, *them* Injuns." He spit into his Coke can, then stared at her. "If he woulda minded his own business and not drove them stinkin Injuns across the pass…"

Jessica knew her dad had picked up hitchhikers the day of the accident, but she didn't know they were Indians. Too busy mourning her dad, at ten years old, she'd never paid attention to his passengers.

"It's not my dad's fault and it's not their fault," she mumbled. "It was an accident. It's not anybody's fault." She was trembling, trying not to sob. Suddenly, she realized where he was taking her. Through her tears, she saw Specht Mill in the distance. Trembling, she thought of the debarking machine, and her captor's intentions became clear.

CHAPTER TWENTY-EIGHT

JESSICA JAMES PLEADED with Tommy to let her go. She promised not to say a word to a single soul. In tears, she relented and even offered sexual favors. When that didn't work, she tried another strategy.

"Tommy Dalton, what would your father think if he saw you now?" she asked, wiping her teary eyes on the sleeve of her pajama top. "Shame on you! Your dad was an honest man. He did an honest day's work and provided for his family. He raised you and your brothers after your mother died. He wanted more for you than…..than…. than." She couldn't say it, *murder*. Tommy hung his head and glanced over at her out of the corner of his eye. He'd stopped in front of the gate to Specht Mill.

"You don't have to do this, you know. The accidents at the mill weren't your fault." She lied. "Everyone knows they were accidents. But this…this…." She took a deep breath. "Killing me here can't pass for an accident. Think about it, Tommy. You'll go to prison. Or, more likely, you'll get the death penalty. Do you fancy the electric chair? Or, maybe they'd hang you." Her speech was having an effect on Tommy. He leaned his head against the steering wheel and gazed over at her with droopy sad eyes.

"Why do you have to be so pretty?"

Jessica was surprised by his question. She'd thought he was contemplating his neck in a noose.

"Let's go, punkin'," he said, unlocking the van. "Don't worry bout me. I ain't gonna wear no Montana collar." He ejected a stream of brown liquid onto the ground after he opened the driver's side door.

"You'll lose your job, everything you've worked for. Remember you told me you were going to make something of yourself, that you wouldn't always be a mill worker? Now you'll go to prison for life. Think about what you're doing, Tom."

"I used to be a lumberjack, but when I couldn't cut it, they give me the axe!" Tommy started crowing again. Just then his cell phone rang. He stared at the screen and slid his finger across it. "Brother Frank? What's up? I'm kinda busy. Whaat? Hold tight. Don't tell 'em nothin'. Is Jim there? Well, where is he?"

Jessica watched Tommy's face go white and his jaw drop. She wondered what his older brother Frank was telling him. Whatever it was, Tommy was worried.

"Tell 'em I's gone to Canada. They ain't got no warrant. They ain't got nothin' on me. I ain't done nothin'. They can't arrest me for doin' nothin'. I ain't comin' home. Just coz your older, you ain't the boss of me, Frank." Tommy slammed his palm against the steering wheel.

"Never mind where I am. Get them dirty cops off our property. No, I swear Frank, I ain't done nothin'." Tommy tapped his phone off and swore under his breath. Red faced, he sat staring out the front window of the van. After several seconds, he made a phone call. "Jim, the cops is out at our place. Frank called. He's hoppin' mad. I'm at the mill. I got her. Where're you?" Tommy slumped in his seat. "Ain't that too close to town? No, don't go home. Call you later."

"What's wrong Tommy?"

"None of your wax. And, for the last time, Tom. If you calls me Tommy again, I'll backhand you!"

Tommy got out of the rig, and came around to the passenger door, spit, and then opened it. "Get out," he yelled.

She stared straight ahead out the front window of the van toward the river, and didn't budge.

"I said, GET OUT!"

Moisture sprayed her cheek and she flinched. When he yanked her arm, she clawed at the dashboard and sunk her gnawed fingernails into it. He wrenched her off the dash. The hunting parka had fallen to the floor and Jessica's bare legs were exposed. Tommy wrapped his arms around her legs, then hauled her out of the van feet first. She screamed as her head hit the doorframe. He dragged her across the gravel to the gate. With one hand holding the twine around her feet, he tried to unlock the gate with the other. He dropped her completely when he couldn't get the key into the lock. Using both hands, he finally got the lock open and pushed the mammoth gate out of the way. While he was busy with the gate, Jessica had managed to roll herself off the driveway and into the ditch. Wrists and ankles still bound, she tucked herself into a fetal position, braced her legs, and shoved off the embankment with her feet. Her bare bottom scraped against sharp rocks and thorny brush on the way down. She rolled a good eight feet before she bounced off a boulder and came to a painful stop.

"What the hell are you doin'?" Tommy slid down the embankment after her. "You stupid cow. Are ya tryin' to kill yourself?"

He put one hand under each of her armpits and pulled her back up to the gate. "You's heavier than ya look, sweetheart. I can't keep carryin' ya."

Jessica spit out a wad of dirty grass. "Then untie my feet so I can walk."

"Run away, more like. Do ya think I'm an idiot?"

She couldn't resist saying, "I don't think you're an idiot, I *know* you're an idiot!" Tommy shoved her through the gate. She was shuffling as fast as she could to keep up with him and keep herself from tipping over. Blood was running down her left leg from a cut on her behind. She had gravel embedded in her thigh, dirt under her eyelid, bruises forming on both legs and arms, her hair was covered with grimy muck, and she had grass stains on both knees. She hurt all over.

When Tommy tugged on her wrist wraps, she fell forward, and he caught her. "Just like ole times, huh, Jess?" He smiled his lopsided smile and she felt nauseous. He put one hand on each side of her waist and toddled her into a warehouse across from the main office where she'd overheard his conversation with that bastard Knight. He heaved her onto a wooden bench and tied her to a metal pole directly behind her. Lacerating twine around her wrists and her ankles, a thick itchy rope around her waist, the splintery bench rough against her sensitive raw skin, she was vulnerable, exposed, hurting, and more than anything, exhausted. She wished Tommy would get it over with and put her out of her misery, but he'd disappeared.

Monstrous machines with giant saw blades and steel claws big enough to hoist an elephant loomed in front of her. Row after row of steel beams, interlocking wheels, sharp blades, conveyor belts, and control panels with giant red and green buttons, filled the huge room. The floor was speckled with sawdust and black grease spots.

Even now the heady perfume of fresh pine combined with earthy grease reminded her of her dad. He'd worked at this very mill from the time he was a boy until he died. She'd heard herself telling Tommy that the accident wasn't anybody's fault. Not the hitchhikers, not his dad's, and not hers. Maybe she'd been wrong and her dad was right. Maybe generosity was the only thing in life worth dying for.

She wondered what happened to Tommy. Maybe he'd left her there to rot. She pulled against the rope around her waist, but it sprang back and slammed her back into the pole with a painful thwack. Even if Lolita realized she was gone, how would she know where to look for her? Jessica hung her head and closed her eyes, remembering once when she was a kid, she'd beg her dad to take her with him to the mill. One Saturday, the mill had a family day picnic and invited everyone to a tour. Jessica had been in awe of the giant machines picking up handfuls of logs like they were toothpicks. When she'd informed her dad she planned to work there someday, he'd scolded her. "Never use your body when you can use your brain. Not to make money anyway. Unless it's riding a horse."

The florescent lights buzzed and flickered as the metal monster came to life, claws closing, teeth buzzing, red eyes shining. The noise from the grisly machinery was deafening, and Jessica snapped upright when it came on. The imposing automated equipment rolled logs along wheeled belts, dropped them into a steel trough; the logs rode back and forth until a thin red laser beam encircled the wood and finally straightened into a line that signaled the saw head to buzz rectangular boards, back and forth, back and forth, until the log was no more. She imagined her boney body riding back and forth with the laser pointing to the best spots to slice her into something marketable. If only she had her jeans on, the whole thing would be more bearable. As if pants would protect her from the lurid teeth of that enormous saw blade.

Tommy appeared out of nowhere and was standing right in front of her. He grabbed her head in both hands, bent down, and when he kissed her hard on the mouth, she was assaulted by the smell of stale Copenhagen. She squeezed her lips together as tight as she could, and he yanked her head backwards by her ponytail. She saw his tobacco stained teeth but she could only imagine his high-pitched laughter over the earthquake rumbling of the machinery. Wearing bright yellow earplugs, Tommy pulled a box-cutter from his back pocket and cut the rope at her waist, then he waved the knife in the air and said something she couldn't hear. He put both hands through the twine wrapped around her wrists and heaved her to her feet. Her feet were numb and a prickling sensation was crawling up her legs as he dragged her toward the ravenous machine.

CHAPTER TWENTY-NINE

AFTER THREE DAYS of degradation and despair, Kimi RedFox felt like she'd lived an entire lifetime at Whispers Tavern. Every day was the same. Big Mack would throw them some meager food in the morning, fix the girls up with dope, haul them to town and pimp them out at the bar until the wee hours, and then stuff them back into the crowded trailer. Most of the girls were sick or strung out or both. Maybe that stuff transported them to a better place, at least temporarily. She buried her nose in the collar of her guardian angel's leather jacket and inhaled the lingering scent of Jasmine, remembering the barely visible turquoise capillaries dancing at the delicate corners of Lolita's keen eyes.

As usual, around four in the afternoon, Big Mack bought the girls burgers and fries and installed them in a corner booth at Whispers. About an half-hour later, when men poured in after their shifts, Big Mack lined the girls against the bar, offered each one to the highest bidder, then collected cash in advance and sent the girls and their johns to the store room or out to the trailer to have sex. If the men wanted something kinky, Big Mack charged extra. These oil workers had cash falling out of their pockets. Flashing wads of hundred dollar bills, they'd buy two or three girls at a time. The girls were drowning in beer, shots, and cocktails bought for them each night. Inevitably, one or two of the girls would spew out their burgers before the night was over. But the oilmen didn't care if a girl smelled like puke or had dried vomit on her shirt. All they cared about was getting laid. These filthy white dogs might hate Indians, but they loved to rape them.

Luckily, the thick elastic bandage on her wrist and the scowl on her face meant Kimi RedFox wasn't the first pick of the filthy snakes in Whispers Tavern. Unluckily, the young buck didn't take her to the hospital to get her broken bone set like he said he would. Instead, he took her back to his trailer in the man-camp, wrapped her arm, then tried to kiss her. At least the bearded bastard stopped when she resisted. But he promptly drove her and Nadie back to Whispers and dropped them off. Now Big Mack was threatening to kill both her sisters if she didn't cooperate. He had Nadie and the other girls on a tight schedule of crack cocaine, just enough to keep them craving more. So far at least Kimi had managed to avoid the ravages of that bad medicine.

The roughneck's day shift had ended, and they were lined up at the back of the bar. Kimi was waiting for her sister to get back from her latest trip to the trailer. Nadie and the younger girls had been sent out there with a pack of wild dogs who wanted a private party with some "virgin whores" in the trailer parked behind the tavern, across the back parking lot, next to an empty field. Sometimes, not wanting to wait their turn, men would take girls into the vacant lot and use them there on the ground. When she heard a scream coming from the trailer, Kimi ran outside through the back door, but Big Mack caught her on her way out, and pinned her up against the building. His bicep was as big as her head, and he held her there with one hand around her throat. Trying to catch her breath, she swallowed hard and turned her face towards the sky.

Hundreds of stars pierced the dark fabric of the celestial ceiling. Seeing so many bright lights in the sky reminded Kimi of her grandmother's story about the Orphan Boys, abandoned on earth by their people, befriended by a pack of wolves, and eventually sent to play together in the sky to escape their loneliness and sorrow. Each night the wolves would howl at the stars to remind the boys of the cruel people who'd abandoned them.

"Let her go!" a murky voice called out from the darkness. "Put her down."

With the giant palm around her throat, Kimi couldn't move her head enough to see who was yelling, but the voice sounded familiar.

"Yeah, who's going to make me?" Big Mack answered. "Not you, pretty boy."

"How much do you want for her?"

"She's not worth it," Big Mack said. "She's as dry as a bone and as tough as shoe leather. I've got something tender and juicy inside though."

"No, I want her. I'll double your usual rate. How much do you want?"

When Big Mack let go of her throat and grabbed her by the arm, his grip made Kimi's wrist throb. She shook her head to get the hair out of her eyes and mouth, and saw that the john was actually Mr. Naïve himself, David Knight.

"Oh shit. Not you," she said.

"You two know each other?" Big Mack asked.

"No," David said. "I've never met this girl. She's delirious. What do you want for her?" Behind the gorilla's back, David was mouthing something she couldn't understand.

"No!" Kimi played along. "Please, Mister, leave me alone."

"Okay. Five hundred cash," Big Mack said. "You'll have to wait your turn for the trailer, unless you want her here in the parking lot. I like to keep an eye on my girls."

David took out his wallet and counted out five crisp hundreds. "I'll wait."

"What about my sister?"

"What about her?" Big Mack said.

"Is your sister as pretty as you are?" David grinned and winked.

"She's even prettier than you!" Big Mack said. "Especially in the dark."

"All cats are leopards after dark," Kimi quoted her grandmother without thinking.

"I'll take both girls." David counted out another five bills, and then gently took Kimi away from the brutal pimp. "Do you mind? I don't want you to bruise my merchandise."

"Whatever you say, Hotshot. Just because you're paying double, doesn't give you double time. You get the regular half-hour like everyone else."

The metal door banged open on the trailer and a string of boisterous men spooled out with some bedraggled girls following behind. When she saw her sister, Kimi broke away from David and ran to her.

"There, there, Sweetie." Kimi tucked a strand of hair behind her sister's ear. "I'll take care of you." She put her arm around her sister's expanding waist.

"Okay, Hotshot, they're all yours. Remember, thirty minutes, no more. I'll be waiting right here by the tavern door."

"Right you are, Sir." David saluted. "Come along girls. We've no time to waste."

Once inside the trailer, Kimi stood arms akimbo, staring at David. "What are you doing here? If you think we're going to have sex with you, you've got another think coming."

"No, no," he chuckled. "I'm here to rescue you!"

"Yeah, and how are you going to do that with those filthy dogs just outside this tin can?"

David flashed his expensive smile.

"Just because you're against evil, doesn't make you good." Kimi brushed the sticky hair out of her face and smiled in spite of herself.

David scanned the trailer, then pulled a chair into the middle of the tiny space, and retrieved a Swiss Army knife from his hip pocket.

"Turn the music up," he said, standing on the chair, using the little screwdriver tool on his knife to loosen the roof vent, and pry it fully open, then removing the center bar from its frame. "Girls, I'll hoist you up and you'll have to climb down the back side of the trailer before Big Mack sees you. Can you do that? Run across the empty lot, and to your left you'll see a 7-11 convenience store. Duck in there and then I'll come pick you up."

"This is your brilliant rescue plan?" Kimi asked, shaking her head. "We're supposed to jump off the roof of this rattletrap?"

"Ha! I brought a rope ladder. Clever, eh?"

Kimi put her hands on her hips. "Remember, Mr. Naïve, there's only a few inches difference between a halo and a noose."

"Look, this is the best I can do. Do you have a better idea?" David asked. "Will your sister be able to make it? She looks awful."

"That's nice of you to say. Yes, she'll make it. Come on Nadie. We're getting out of this shit hole." Kimi pulled her sister to her feet. "Hoist her up first," she said to David, then whispered into her sister's ear, "Sweetie, when you get up there, lay down on the roof and we'll go down the ladder together. Okay?" She kissed her sister's clammy forehead.

David lifted Nadie up by her waist and squeezed her through the small opening in the roof. Then he offered his hand to Kimi. She stepped up onto the chair next to him. "I'm too heavy," she said. "You can't lift me. You'll have to give me a leg up."

With her good hand on his shoulder and one foot in David's cupped hands, she clawed at the metal edge of the vent while he gave her a boost. She hooked her elbow, cast and all, over the lip of the opening. David held her thighs while she pushed herself onto the roof with her good hand. Then, she scooted her curvy body onto the roof of the airstream. Hanging her head back down through the opening, she snatched the rope ladder out of David's hands. "You have to fasten it securely to the trailer. Be sure it's on tight," he said.

When she popped out the vent onto the roof, her sister was curled up like a little worm nearby. Kimi used her elbows to pull herself along the roof. The metal was so cold on her bare arms, it burned. She tied the end of the ladder onto a metal bar at the corner of the airstream closest to the vacant lot. Then, she nodded for Nadie to climb down. Once her sister was half way down, she swiveled around, dangled her right leg over the side, and put her foot on the second rung. Carefully, she slid her right foot over to make room for her left. Then, she grasped the rope with both hands. The ladder swayed back and forth. Nadie was already running across the vacant lot. Kimi scurried down the ladder, and sprinted past her sister. As kids they used to race each to the end of the block and back. Now, they were running for their lives.

CHAPTER THIRTY

KIMI REDFOX TURNED around, but didn't see her sister. In a panic, she ran back towards Whisper's Tavern parking lot. Nadie had fallen and was lying in the weeds moaning. Kimi pulled her sister to her feet and struggled to get a good grasp on her limp body. "Shhhh. Be quiet." Taylor Swift's "We are never ever getting back together" was still blaring from the stereo in the trailer, and she hoped the moonless night had absorbed their movement.

She glanced back and saw Big Mack coming across the parking lot. "Come on, Nadie! We've got to get out of sight. Come on! You can do it!" Kimi whisper-yelled into her sister's ear, and then dragged her to the street, prodding her to move faster. By the time Kimi got her to the convenience store, Nadie was whimpering. She had a bloody cut on her face and a bruised knee. This wouldn't be the first time Kimi had to bandage scraps and scratches for her younger sister. From behind a row of chips, she peeked out the window of the cramped store. The deserted road taunted her.

"Can I help you?" asked the Asian man at the cash register. "Are you girls going to buy something?"

Startled, Kimi whipped around to face the man and bags of chips went flying. "We're waiting for someone," Kimi replied, picking up the chips.

The Asian man looked her up and down. "Well, wait outside. You can't loiter in here."

"But, it's...."

"Shoo. Out with you!" the man interrupted. "We don't want your kind in here."

"Please, Mister...."

"Get out now! Or, do I have to throw you out?" The Asian man came closer and Kimi flinched. She led her sister by the hand.

"Come on, Nadie. Let's go." Her voice shrunk.

She pulled her sister around to the side of the building and yanked on the door to the women's bathroom. It was locked. Someone had kicked-in the door to the men's bathroom and it swung open. She ducked into the foul smelling closet, hauling her little sister in after her, and held the door shut with her foot. A dim green glow from the sickly florescent light cast a sinister pall on a smiling crack in the tiny porcelain sink. The tiles behind the toilet and urinal were broken, revealing a cavernous hole in the wall. When she noticed Nadie shivering, she put her arms around her sister and pulled her close.

"There, there, Sweetie. It will be okay." She hoped she was right.

A car pulled up and screeched to a stop, but she didn't dare peek outside. She waited and listened, then sniffed the air, but all she could smell was rank urine and fetid vomit. A car door slammed and footfalls exploded on the asphalt. Next, the front door of the store squealed, followed by ominous bells jingling. She hugged Nadie tighter and matched her breathing to her sister's. As one being, she concentrated their life force on willing David Knight to find them. Closing her eyes, she gathered energy from the universe. Hoping her ancestors were right, she whispered incantations to the Sun and the Moon, and then let out a slow controlled breath through her nose. The bells jangled again, more footfalls, and a car door. If that was David Knight, he must have given up on them. He was leaving.

Kimi took a gamble and heaved open the twisted metal door. With her good hand locked around Nadie's wrist, she pulled her sister out of the bathroom and into the menacing glow of the streetlight. With its tinted glass, she couldn't see inside the black sedan. She hoped the driver was David Knight. Whoever it was, she lunged at the passenger door and pounded on the window. The dark glass withdrew to reveal Big Mack's vindictive grimace. "Get in," he yelled. "You girls belong to me and no HotShot Texan do-gooder is going to change that. Get in now, or Hurit is dead."

CHAPTER THIRTY-ONE

JESSICA JAMES SCREAMED at the top of her lungs, "You're insane! Stop! No! Please, Tommy," as her captor dragged her towards the fierce machine.

"I'll call ya flower after I's put ya through the mill." Tommy cackled as he hauled her across the floor. She doubled over and dug her bare feet into the sawdust to make it harder for him to drag her. He'd almost toppled her onto a conveyer belt when the lights died a slow death. She crouched on the floor, trembling. Tommy yelled, "What the hell!" just as the machinery whizzed to a gentle whorl and then fell silent. Tommy's groping hands were dangerously close to Jessica's head, but she didn't dare move or he'd find her for sure. She listened to the equipment winding down and hoped the person who'd stopped it was there to help her. She wanted to yell, but she was afraid the lunatic might throw her onto the dying conveyer belt and she'd travel through the lasers and saws, only now in excruciatingly slow motion.

Jessica heard a scuffle nearby. Tommy bumped into her in the dark and fell on top of her. With both fists, she propelled him off, and then scurried on all fours in the other direction. She came to a dead stop when she crashed head first into something very hard. The lights flipped on. She was crumbled up against a metal cabinet that housed the control console. Dazed, she glanced up and thought she saw Cannon Silverton pushing buttons.

"Untie her and I'll finish off this little fucker." She looked around in time to see Lolita's kick send Tommy flying onto the conveyer belt, then covered her eyes with the crook of her arm.

Cannon tugged on the twine around her wrists, but he was just making it tighter.

"Ouch! That hurts."

"Sorry," he said. "Got a penknife or some clippers or something?" he shouted at Lolita.

"You've got to be joking," Lolita shot back. She reached into her boot and pulled out a switchblade. "Here, will this do?" She tossed it. Cannon reached out as it sailed by and hit the floor. He picked it up, and turning it over in his palms, carried it back to where Jessica was lying.

"Wow, how do you work this thing?" Bill was admiring the ivory handled instrument.

"Jesus, can't you do anything?" Lolita stomped over, snatched the knife from his hands, and with a couple of deft slices, freed her friend. "Are you okay?" she asked Jessica.

"Holy crap, you're naked!" Cannon exclaimed.

"Give me a break and shut it," Lolita said. "Take this rope and go tie up that crazyass Sawyer. Then call the police. I'm taking Jessica home."

"Shouldn't you wait for the police?" Cannon stammered. "They'll want a statement, and..."

"You wait for the police. I'm taking her home," Lolita interrupted. "You know where to find us." She gently helped Jessica stand up. When she saw Jessica's scratched and bruised naked body, she said, "Jesus Christ, did that pervert...."

"No, he just tied me up, and he would have turned me into a few board feet of lumber if you hadn't shown up. I think he's lost his mind."

"Before you go, I need to tell you something, Jesse."

"Not now," Lolita barked. "I need to get her out of here."

"But there's something important eating away at me, and I'll regret it for the rest of my life, if I don't..... Jesse, I...I," he stammered.

Jessica put her hand on his arm. "I know. Cannon, you're like a brother. I'll always consider you part of my family."

Bill's face fell as he repeated her words, "Brother, family...."

"Let's get you home, Sweetie." Lolita steadied her friend and led her outside. "Oh dear. We can't have you riding on the back of my bike like that." She unlocked the travel trunk on her Harley Superlow and pulled out black leather bell-bottom chaps and a matching vest. "Put these on."

Jessica did as she was told. "I look like a gay cowboy pinup with my bare arse hanging out."

"Better than nothing. Anyway, won't be the first time. Let's go." Lolita swung her lanky leg over the shiny red fender and sat down. "Get on."

Heads turned from Main Street to High Street as they drove through the streets of Whitefish. One nail takes out another. And, soon Jessica forgot about her bare bottom. Instead, she dreaded showing Lolita the hole where her mother lived and where she'd grown up. Sure, the surrounding scenery was stunning, but the trailer park itself showed its age. Except for a couple new singlewides and a shiny retro Airstream, all of the mobile homes were flaking and sagging. Lolita's family was practically Russian royalty. The only "royalty" in Jessica's family was her mom, who'd been the Flathead County Rodeo queen. That's where her mom and dad met. He was riding bucking broncos and she was riding on the rodeo float.

As they drove through her hometown, Jessica imagined seeing it for the first time through her friend's eyes. Its cute wooden façades with second story balconies, and brick buildings with decorative awnings, made the historic district more like a movie set than a real town. At Christmastime, covered in snow and adorned with fresh evergreen streamers, adorable red bells, and antique streetlights, the place was enchanting. Just five miles away, any time of year, Alpine Vista Trailer Park was a royal dump.

When they pulled into the driveway, Jessica's mom was sitting on the porch, cat in lap, drink in hand, and cigarette in mouth. When she saw them, she stopped petting the cat and put her hand to her brow to shield her eyes from the sun. She just stared as Lolita and Jessica got off the motorcycle and staggered across the lawn to the porch. A glint of recognition finally crossed her face.

"Oh my god. Jesse, what happened to you?" she asked in alarm.

"I got bucked off a horse."

"You what?" Her mom raised one eyebrow. "Where? The Raunchy Rodeo? Come inside. You girls look like you could use a drink."

CHAPTER THIRTY-TWO

HEART STILL RACING from their failed escape, Kimi RedFox was only half listening to the rich white pup whining about how his plan to rescue her went wrong. She glared at him across the tiny airstream table and then glanced over at her sister. Curled up in a fetal position, shivering, Nadie was asleep nearby on the filthy mattress in the rear of the trailer. Kimi removed the black leather jacket she'd worn every minute since her guardian angel gave it to her, then climbed over a strung-out girl sleeping on the floor, and gently placed the coat over the top of her sister. Once again, thanks to David Knight's stupid plan, she and her sister were prisoners in the claustrophobic airstream, now lurching down the winding highway behind that dirty dog Mack's truck.

"We're going to need to get her to a treatment center or clinic or something. Poor little blossom's hooked on drugs," Kimi said. "Auntie Madge'll sort her out."

"Auntie Madge?" David asked from across the table, interrupting his own soliloquy on his "heroic" rescue attempt.

"Madge Blackthorn, tribal police chief and surrogate mother."

"Mother?"

"Never mind." Kimi crossed her arms over her chest and huffed. "We're lucky you didn't get us all killed." Secretly, she was glad he was there.

"How could such a sweet girl get mixed up with such bad people?" David asked. "A teenage drug addict. It's terrible."

"Are you really such an idiot? Have you lived your whole life in a protective bubble? Evil isn't always ugly. Sometimes it's beautiful. Sometimes it draws us close and whispers into our ears as a lover might." Out of the trailer window, she watched trees passing, shadowy creatures threatening her from the dark of night. She trembled and gazed over at her sleeping sister.

"I guess you're right. Evil is sometimes beautiful." David sighed. "Look at my big brother Richard. The clinking of coins is his siren song."

"And I suppose you're different?" Kimi smirked.

"Well, it's true I've had a comfortable life. And lots of opportunities, most of them I've wasted. At least that's what my brother says. He thinks I'm worthless, that I only want to play and have fun."

"Do you?" she asked.

"What?"

"Just want to have fun?" Kimi rolled her eyes.

"What's wrong with fun? You have something against enjoying life?" His tone of voice changed. "Maybe we'd better just focus on finding a way out of this tin can."

"What? You're going to jump out of a moving vehicle

at sixty miles an hour, Mr. Superhero? For you everything's a game, isn't it? Life is about more than amusing yourself, Mr. Knight."

"What's the point of living if you can't enjoy life?"

"Making the world a better place, for one thing. Helping others. Working for justice. Keeping your loved-ones safe. Things you wouldn't understand. Not everyone gets to have fun, Mr. Knight. For some of us, life is full of pain while others profit from our suffering."

"Look, I'm just trying to get through the day like everyone else, okay."

"When you don't know what you're living for, you don't care how you live from one day to the next. You're happy the day has passed and the night has come, you've had your fun, and in your sleep you bury the tedious question of what you lived for that day and what you're going to live for tomorrow."

David folded his arms across his chest and didn't respond.

"I don't suppose you read Russian literature, or any literature for that matter," she said.

They sat in silence, facing each other across the tiny foldup table, as three sweaty teenage girls, spent and strung out on drugs, slept fitfully on the nasty foldout bed.

"*Cat's Cradle*," David said out of the blue. "Does that count?"

"What in the hell are you talking about?" Kimi asked.

"Does *Cat's Cradle* count as literature? I read that. And in high school I read *To Kill a Mockingbird*. Well, it was assigned and I was supposed to read it."

"Good for you, Mr. High and Mighty. You can read.

There are plenty of people who can't read. If you can and you don't, you might as well be illiterate."

"I can read and I can add too. Actually, I'm pretty good at math. That was my major at the University of Texas. I admit, I mostly read sports magazines. I'm also a pretty good surfer. I'm not a total loser."

"Just a total snake." Kimi sneered. "Whatever you read, it's what you take away that matters. You have to know how to look."

"I mostly look at the pictures," he said with a chuckle.

"Figures."

The trailer jolted to a full stop. Doors slammed in unison. Kimi's pulse quickened when she heard Big Mack talking to someone outside, and she strained to hear what they were saying, but the voices receded. Crunching gravel signaled someone approaching, then the trailer door flew open, and Kimi was staring straight into Big Mack's grizzly sized chest as he brandished a tire iron. Sailing into the trailer, he pulled David to his feet, whacked him across the knees with the iron, and then dragged him out the door by his preppy collar.

"You sonofabitch!" Big Mack pushed the yuppie down into the dirt and raised the tire iron. "I'm going to smash your brains in. That's what you get for fuckin' with me."

All the girls were awake now watching through the greasy side window of the trailer. Kimi jumped up, rushed out the door, and mounted the gorilla's back. "Stop it!" she shouted. "You're killing him!"

Out of nowhere, a wiry weasel with a bandage on one ear and jagged homemade orange flames tattooed all the way up his sinewy forearms grabbed Kimi around the waist, and then yanked her off of Big Mack. He was dragging her back toward the trailer when the crack of a shotgun firing cut through the thick night air. The thin man dropped Kimi on the cold ground just outside the threshold to the trailer, and then stared out into the darkness. "Who's there?" he demanded.

Big Mack ignored the shot, seized his heavy metal bar in both hands and was about to bring it down on the defenseless rich boy, when a familiar voice shouted, "Put your blessed hands up, or I'll blow your bleeping head off."

"Auntie Madge!" Kimi exclaimed.

Madge stood feet hip distance apart, pointing the shotgun at the dirty dog, just ten feet away.

Mack stood up and raised the tire iron over his head again. "You're not going to shoot me, Grandma?" he asked with a sinister chuckle.

Auntie Madge pumped her shotgun. The sound of the barrel sliding and snapping into place stopped him in his tracks.

"Don't make me use this, Mister, because believe me, I will," Auntie Madge said.

The gorilla held the tire iron over his head and charged ahead. "I don't think so, Grandma."

Crawling on all fours, David heaved himself at the monster pimp from behind and rammed his legs. Mack swung at him with the iron, sending the yuppie crumbling to the ground, and then the dirty dog raised the bar above his head and lunged at Auntie Madge. Another explosive boom ripped across the valley. Big Mack flew backwards, bounced off the trailer, and landed on his back. The bull had a hole the size of a watermelon in his stomach where he'd been gut shot.

"Don't say I didn't warn you, Mister."

"Auntie Madge, I'm so glad to see you." Kimi ran to her and embraced her.

"Me too, princess. Who's your friend?" she asked, pointing to David with the nose of the shotgun.

"That's David Knight, one of the criminals who's destroying our land. Maybe you should arrest him."

David sat up and propped his head in his hands. "She's just joking....I hope."

"I wouldn't be too sure," Auntie Madge said. "Better watch out or she'll be riggin' your car with explosives. She's a regular little terror, she is." She squeezed Kimi around the waist, and then ambled over and extended her hand to help David. "Can you stand?"

He stood up and wiped blood from his face. "Nothing broken. Mostly my ego that's bruised."

"I like him." Auntie Madge turned to Kimi. "You should snap him up."

"Oil barons and thieves are not my type." Kimi smiled.

"Well, you can't blame your old Auntie for tryin'. I want a tribe of grandbabies, and before you get yourself killed or I'm too old to enjoy 'em."

"Auntie, forget about match-making. Nadie's inside having withdrawals and we've got to get her to the hospital now."

"Nadie's here? Why the hell didn't you tell me?" Auntie Madge marched past her and boarded the trailer, with

Kimi following close behind. The girls were inside, huddled together, whimpering and moaning. One of them had vomited in front of the entrance.

"Let's get them back to my place," Auntie Madge said. She'd taken the last batch of girls to her house, where she had her "good for nothing" son, Rowdy, taking care of them. Rowdy was trained as a nurse by the army, but preferred "sitting around in his blessed underwear" playing video games and making "that cow manure he calls art." (Rowdy created a cobbled together "sculpture" of local wild animals—a buffalo, an eagle, and an elk—made entirely out of used car parts.) Auntie Madge had convinced Dr. Hightower from Blackfeet Community Hospital to check on the girls daily, even though the doctor insisted on "feeding them more blasted drugs than the blessed drug pushers."

"Oh no!" Kimi exclaimed. Someone had bolted the door from the outside. "It's that dirty weasel."

"JesusChrist Ala Mode, I thought he'd run away," Auntie Madge said, and then she planted herself in front of the door, pumped the shotgun, and fired. "Time to meet your maker, Butt-wipe."

The blast blew a crater through the metal door. Thud. Through a jagged hole in the door, Kimi could see the weasel lying in a bloody heap next to the trailer. She reached through the hole and unlocked the door from the other side.

Auntie Madge called the local authorities from Sidney to come out and load up what was left of the "blessed dirty dogs." She explained what happened to a couple of very suspicious yokel deputies.

"Evening officers. I warned the good for nothings, but the blasted dirty dogs made me blow their guts out their a-holes. Believe me, they had it comin'. They were threatening me and my little princess here with deadly force."

One of the red-necked officers said, "the little Injun crack-whores should go back to the Reservation where they belong," as his partner lined them up against the trailer and cuffed them all.

CHAPTER THIRTY-THREE

KIMI REDFOX BIT her tongue as David recounted the "heroic" events that led to "two hardened criminals, scourge to humanity," lying in the dirt. He was wiping blood off his face with a starched white monogrammed handkerchief. To be fair, if David hadn't intervened, they'd probably all have gone to jail. In another of his windbag speeches, he commended Auntie Madge on her "fine police womanship, cracker-jack shooting, and brilliantly executed rescue." Maybe her grandmother was right, no one was all bad.

The redneck officer seemed satisfied, saying, "take those crack whores back where they belong and we don't want to see you around here again." The hick cops unlocked the handcuffs, bagged the bodies, tagged some evidence, took down their contact information and let them go. Kimi wanted to school the officers in racial profiling, but she was tired and hungry, and there was Nadie to consider.

When the hick cops were gone, Madge put her arm around Kimi's shoulders. "Say, what ever happened to your friend, Blondie?" she asked, kissing her on the cheek.

"Blondie? I don't know any...."

"That blonde girl who came looking for you. Long blonde hair. Big blue eyes. Dresses like a vagrant. Ring a bell? You know, the one you room with over there at the Park. What's her name?"

"Jessica James?"

"That's right. She came here looking for you. Then the little minx locked herself in my car and wouldn't get out, so I had to take her to Sidney with me. That's when we gathered up the first batch of girls. Blondie insisted she was staying in that skunk pit until she found you."

"She did? Jessica came looking for me?" Kimi smiled.

"She sure did. And, she was determined as dirt to find you. I sure-in-the-hell hope Blondie made it out of that stink-hole."

"I saw her last night at a poker game. She's fine." David said. "As feisty as ever." His swollen eyes lit up. "And she's a helluva poker player!"

Kimi's ugly pickup was right where she parked it, across the street from the barn where her kidnappers routinely left the trailer for the night. David crawled into the cab of her pickup, while Auntie Madge bundled the girls into the back of her patrol car. After driving all night, it was mid-morning by the time they reached Auntie's place in Browning. After Nadie and the girls were safely tucked into cots set up in the living room at Auntie's house-cum-drug-clinic for wayward girls, Kimi dropped David off at Enterprise to rent another car.

"My big bro wants me to give him an update on the new housing development he's building on the edge of town," David said as he got out of the truck.

She shook her head, "For a spoiled rich white pup, you're not so bad. But I really don't think you're cut out to work for the family business. Maybe you should quit before you get fired. Why don't you take a vacation?"

He just shook his head and hopped out of the truck. "Trying to redeem myself, Ms. RedFox, just trying to redeem myself," he called back to her as he bounded into the car rental office.

Before returning to the tribal police station to find out what "special assignment" Auntie Madge had waiting for her, Kimi drove to Two Medicine Gorge to clear her head. She liked that spot because the waterfalls were named for Pitamaken, Running Eagle, the only woman to lead Blackfeet war parties and to be given a man's name. Usually in the spring torrents of cascading water from the upper falls obscured the view of the lower falls, but to her surprise, she could see the edges of the lower falls too. The winter had been much milder than usual, so the spring runoff was down. If they didn't get more rain soon, the tender new ferns around the stream would curl up and die. A flock of ravens rose up squawking from the trees, followed by a bolt of lightning that hit so close to her the air sizzled and her skin tingled. Dry lightning was dangerous and bound to set off fires with this drought. Within seconds, a clap of thunder nearly knocked her off the bridge and into the water.

When she was a kid, her grandmother would tell her

stories about Thunder carrying off new brides. Only ravens had strong enough medicine to bring the brides back to life. Using raven feathers, one forlorn husband brought Thunder to his knees. Thunder promised to fly south with the ravens and come back only in spring to bring the rain to nourish the earth. Her grandmother said even the most thunderous tyrant could be brought to his knees by the right kind of feather. Kimi wasn't so sure.

The dry lightning was getting closer, so she sprinted back to her pick-up. Thunder was here, but where was the promised rain when they needed it? She ran as fast as her legs would carry her, which was pretty fast. When she was a senior in high school, she'd won the Montana state girl's championships in the 100-meter with twelve seconds flat. Kimi RedFox was good at running. She'd been doing it all her life.

CHAPTER THIRTY FOUR

BILL SILVERTON PACED back and forth, waiting for Dial and his men to show up. It had been a half hour since he called. That Russian gal's kick to the head had worn off, and Tom Dalton was awake lying in a pile of sawdust, tied up with a thick rope. Blood trickling from his split lip was forming a red exclamation point in the sawdust next to his mouth.

"What happened?" Tom asked in a hoarse voice. "Who was that badass chick?"

"I don't know," Bill said. He was standing next to Tom's head, gazing down at what used to be such a nice kid. *Poor shmuck.* "She's some amazon friend of Jesse's from back East."

"Ama-what? She sure done got the best of me."

"She sure did." Bill looked at his watch, pacing again. He stepped outside to call Dial again. "Where the hell are you?" he shouted into his phone. "I'm not a policeman. I can't guard Dalton."

"Calm down, Bill," Dial said. "Like I told you earlier, we've got a serious problem out here with these fires. It looks like we have an arsonist on our hands. We'll be there as soon as we can. Just keep him restrained until we get there." The line went dead.

Bill hurried back into the building. Tom hadn't moved. In fact, he wasn't moving at all. Bill's heart jumped into his throat. *Maybe he's dead.* He rushed over to Tom, and knelt down beside him. Maybe he should check his pulse or something. He stared down at his chest trying to assess whether or not he was breathing. He jerked back when Tom suddenly lifted his head.

"Can I ask you a question, Tom? What were you planning to do to Jesse? You weren't really going to kill her, were you?"

"She's so pretty and so smart. What do you call a smart blonde?" Tom asked, grinning up at Bill with his brown teeth. "A golden retriever."

"You wanted to kill Jesse because she's pretty and smart? Is that what you're saying?"

"I was actin' under orders," Tom said.

"Orders? From whom?" Bill stepped closer and stared down at the contorted face looking up from the muck.

"What the hell. It don't matter now. From that fancy lady." Tom tried to prop himself up but tipped back onto his side.

"What lady?"

"I was 'spose to do Jesse just like them others at the mill."

"What others?"

"Them accidents."

Bill's eyes widened and he stopped in his tracks. *Did*

Tom Dalton just confess to killing the mill workers? His mind was reeling. "Who ordered you to kill men at the mill?"

"Mr. Knight. I's 'spose to bust the machines and shut the mill. He give me hell for killing them men. But I done what he asked and shut the mill. That lady ask me to rig the debarker. I thought she just wanted the mill shut down, but she really musta wanted Mike dead. She knew he were the one in there and not that Injun. But I swear, Bill, I didn't know it were Mike. I really thought it were that injun in there."

"What lady, Tom? Tell me who."

"That Mrs. Knight lady."

"Mrs. Knight's involved too? I'm confused. Was it Mr. or Mrs. Knight that told you to shut the mill by causing those accidents?"

"Mr. Knight axe me to rig stuff and shut down the mill. He weren't happy that folks got kilt. Later the lady called and axe me to rig the debarker that morning. Billy, I swear I thought it were that dirty Injun in there not Mike."

"I can't believe what I'm hearing. Stay put. I'll be right back."

Bill stepped outside to call Dial again. He explained that Tom Dalton had just confessed to causing the mill accidents. He didn't mention that Richard Knight might be involved. He had to return the corrupt bastard's $100,000 check before anyone found out about any of this. Dalton was just a chip in a bigger game being played by Richard Knight, and apparently by Mrs. Knight too.

"Get your ass over here if you want Dalton. I can't wait any longer. I have work to do." This time Bill hung up, stomped back inside, and stared down at Tom, who was dozing off again. Bill tapped him on the shoulder and he jerked it away. "Dial Davies will be here soon to collect you," Bill said.

Tom swiveled his head so he could gape up at Bill. "Don't leave me here, Billy. Please. I'm scart. Come on, have a heart."

"Sorry dude, I've gotta go." A pang of guilt stopped him at the door. "Don't worry, Tom. They'll be here soon. They'll fix you up. Okay, buddy?" Torn between waiting for the police to arrive and getting rid of Knight's dirty money before any of this nasty mess hit the news, Bill took a few steps and hesitated again. As he stepped outside, he saw an unmarked patrol car followed by a squad car driving through the gate. He waved and waited as Dial pulled up beside him, stopped, and rolled down the tinted window of his black Charger.

"Sorry, Bill. We got here as fast as we could. This arson thing has thrown us for a loop. Half the valley is on fire."

"If this darned drought doesn't end soon, we'll all burn up." Bill stepped back inside and pointed toward the crumbled form lying in the sawdust. "Dalton's over there." On his way out, he heard Tom say, "she's the prettiest girl I ever saw." *Poor shmuck.* Then he realized he had it just as bad.

PART THREE

CHAPTER THIRTY-FIVE

WHEN KIMI REDFOX arrived at the rally, Leon was standing in the center of a small audience shouting into a bullhorn. About a dozen people carried signs and marched in a circle around the Chairman's beached yacht, marooned in a field across from his house.

Leon was leading a call and response chant:

"When the air we breathe is under attack, what do we do?" Leon shouted into the bullhorn.

"Stand up, fight back!" The crowd responded.

"When the water we drink is under attack, what do we do?"

The crowd chanted, "Stand up, fight back!"

"When the earth we need is under attack, what do we do?"

"Stand up, fight back!"

"What do we do?"

"Stand up, fight back!"

"What do we do?"

"Stand up, fight back!"

When the applause died down, someone in the audience started shouting, "Exxon-Mobil, BP, Shell, take your frack and go to hell!" More joined in. Some waved hand-made signs, others pumped their fists in the air.

When a light flickered on in Chairman Rowtag's house across the street, Kimi turned and saw two silhouettes clinging to each other, standing at the living room window. Caught between the past and the future, Kimi refused to accept big oil's exploitation of Blackfeet land, but she didn't want to betray Auntie Madge. She may not like the Chairman, but for some reason she couldn't fathom, Auntie Madge loved the old dog.

Kimi hung around the rally for another hour until the crowd dispersed and the sun was low in the sky. Leon was collecting signs, placards, and his soapbox and loading them into his vintage Volkswagen Vanagon.

"Hey Leon," she said, helping him load the van. "Too bad the media didn't show up to cover the protest."

"Hi there, stranger," Leon said over his shoulder as he piled stuff into the back of the van. "Long time no see."

"I've been busy at work." Kimi lied. "Do you think you could give me a lift? A friend dropped me here and now I can't find her. I think she left without me." Her heart was racing as she thought of her deal with Auntie Madge. It didn't feel right luring Leon into a trap.

"Not a very good friend, eh?" Leon closed the doors to the van. "Sure, hop in."

It wasn't until she was sitting in the passenger seat that Kimi realized there were people in the back seats. Startled, she gasped and swallowed hard.

"What's wrong?" Leon asked. "You look like you've seen a ghost. Don't you remember Karen and Matt?" He smiled and raised his eyebrows. "We're on our way to sabotage the new man-camp they're building on the Reservation. The tribal chairman may be a sell out, but we aren't going to let him sell us all up the river. We're going to fight back."

"You said it, brother," Matt said from the backseat. He grabbed a stick of dynamite from a box behind the seat, and snorted. "Kaboom!" Matt put the stick back in the box and made a mushroom cloud in the air with his hands, and then he pulled a joint from his shirt pocket, lit it, and took two long drags. He passed it to Leon, who grasped it between his thumb and forefinger and inhaled. Leon passed it to Kimi, who shook her head no. Choking back smoke, he shoved it at her again. She held up her hand and shook her head again. "No, thanks," she said. Leon shrugged and passed it back to Karen.

After drawing on the joint, Karen held her breath, let it out slowly, then began to sing a song about loving mother earth, and Matt joined in. Listening to their sweet voices and the truth of their song, the deal she'd made with Auntie Madge was beginning to feel like a deal with the devil.

"I'm glad you came back," Leon said. "Our people need to learn to stand up for themselves."

"Our people? I thought you were from the East Coast," Kimi said.

"Yeah, well I was born here on the Reservation but grew up in Boston. My mom's a nurse and my dad's a doctor. I didn't know what a Blackfoot was until someone at school called me a "chink." When I asked my mom what that meant, she told me I was adopted. Look in the mirror, Kimi RedFox, we could be related." He grinned, and turned the van onto the highway in the direction of the construction site.

Enraptured, Leon elucidated the dangers of hydraulic fracturing to extract shale oil from deep beneath the earth's crust. It was nothing Kimi hadn't heard before, but ever since he'd mention their resemblance, she'd been mesmerized by his face. She watched his lips move without really hearing his words. His face was animated and his voice was filled with passion as he talked about the oil companies poisoning the air and water on Blackfeet land. He swore he was going to stop them one way or another. "If not through peaceful protests, then through violent sabotage."

The word "violent" got her attention. Until Danny got hurt, she'd agreed with ELF, maybe violence was the only way to stop the exploitation of their natural resources, not to mention their girls. When money was involved, no one listened to protests. They didn't even listen to reason. Even Chairman Rowtag claimed their water was safe to drink. He drank a whole glass full at the last town hall meeting, even though flames had been coming from that very tap the day before. "See, it's safe," he'd said as he'd chugged the sluggish liquid. If someone had thrown a match at the right moment, he'd have drunk a flaming cocktail.

As they approached the construction site, a rush of adrenaline surged through her veins. Leon drove past giant pieces of heavy equipment parked around the development site spread out three city blocks in each direction—a monstrous hole in the earth on one end and row after row of concrete foundations on the other, some with wooden skeletons. Reflective signs read, "Rowtag Construction: Keep

Out." If the Chairman had a construction company, it was news to her.

"Wait! That sign says Rowtag Construction. That's the tribal chairman," Kimi said. "This isn't Exxon. Are we bombing Blackfeet owned companies now?"

"Dakota Rowtag is sleeping with the enemy," Leon said. "This is just a front for Knight Industries, so they can get permits to build on our land."

Fuming, Kimi crossed her arms across her chest. "Who do you think you are to tell me about *our* land?"

"I'm not going to stand back and do nothing while Dakota Rowtag sells us down the river. White people will take and take from us until we have nothing left. They put us on Reservations, and now they're trying to take those away from us, too. Well, I for one won't let them rape our land." Leon got out of the van and stomped around to the back.

Karen and Matt watched from inside, smoking another joint, holding hands, and humming another stupid song. Kimi hopped out of the van and darted after him.

"Our land!" Kimi shouted, catching up. "You come here from back East, from the privilege of your *white* family and your Ivy League education and tell us about our land!" Kimi stomped her foot. "You have no idea what it's like to grow up on the Reservation. I've lived here all my life. You don't know the Chairman or *our* people." Kimi stood, arms akimbo, staring at him.

Leon pulled a box of explosives out of the back of his van, and marched off towards the construction site. "To protect my people."

"Mr. College boy, coming back to protect us from ourselves. How arrogant. Is Running Wolf even your real name?"

Leon turned around and yelled back. "We're more alike than you know, Kimi RedFox." He disappeared between a row of concrete foundations into the shadows, and Kimi raced after him.

"What do you mean?" By the time she caught up, he was unspooling the fuse.

"Get back." He took out a pocketknife, cut the fuse, and then lit it. A spark sizzled along the wire on its journey to its final destination.

"Come on, let's go!" Leon grabbed her good hand and pulled her away from the explosives.

"Let go of me! I can out run you."

Pulling her along, Leon tripped over some rebar and fell hard onto the ground. She tried to lift him to his feet, but he was too heavy.

"Run!" Leon shouted. "It's going to blow."

"I'm not leaving you here," she said, tugging at his outstretched arms.

CHAPTER THIRTY-SIX

BILL SILVERTON DROVE straight to Glacier Bank to get there before closing and had the teller make out a cashier's check out to Knight Industries for $100,000. He tucked the check into his inside jacket pocket and dialed Richard Knight's private number. Knight said he was just finishing up eighteen holes and would meet him for a late lunch at the Whitefish Lake Golf Club restaurant in an hour. *Shit!* Not another three-hour meal.

The Whitefish Golf Club was on the edge of town at the southernmost tip of Whitefish Lake. When Bill arrived, Knight was waiting for him, sipping wine at a table on the patio. What should have been a stunning view across the smooth emerald fairway onto the rugged snow-tipped mountains was hidden behind a hazy mask.

"Thanks for meeting with me on such short notice." Bill extended his hand. Knight stood up, shook it, and motioned for him to sit.

"I hope you don't mind," Knight said. "I ordered for us."

"Fine." Bill shifted in his chair, troubling the

napkin between his thumb and forefinger. "But, Mr. Knight, you see...."

Knight interrupted. "Call me Richard, please."

"You see, Richard, I can't accept your check after all. I mean it's very generous and everything, but I really can't take it." Bill couldn't look him in the eye, so he was addressing the tablecloth.

"But why not, William? I thought we had it all settled." Knight motioned for the waiter. "Please bring a glass of champagne for my friend, the next Governor of Montana."

Bill blushed and shook his head, then reached into his jacket pocket, pulled out the check, and slid it across the tablecloth. Knight put his large dry hand on top of Bill's. Again, he had the sense they'd met before—something about the rich man's mannerisms, something in his sonorous voice, his light touch.

"Lunch first, business later." Knight held up his glass and peered into the golden bubbly wine. "Did you know this champagne is named after the widow of Francois Clicquot? She inherited the company when he died under suspicious circumstances." Knight chortled. "Its chalky minerality reflects its terroir, don't you think?"

"Its terror?" Bill was feeling some terror himself.

"Terroir, how the soil affects the taste. Like people, wine is the product of where it's raised. Regardless, some of us ripen into fine wine while others turn to vinegar." Knight lifted his glass again. "You, my friend, promise to become a fine wine. A toast to our partnership!"

"That's what I want to talk to you about," Bill said,

pointing to the check in the middle of the table, the one Knight was ignoring.

"See, we're already fast friends. Don't worry. You've made the right decision, Cannon."

"What did you say?"

"You've made the right decision."

"No after that. What did you call me?"

"William, of course. Or, do you prefer Bill?" Knight dabbed at his mouth with the corner of his napkin.

"No, you called me Cannon. Only my friends from junior high call me that." In a flash, it came to him. He knew why Knight was so familiar. His face went white. The voice. He was sure of it.

Stunned, Bill could hardly speak. "What the hell?" he whispered half to himself, then asked, "Do you know Arnold Specht?"

"No, why do you ask?" Knight shifted in his chair.

"He was my best friend when I was in high school. We were on the wrestling team together." Bill's voice was barely audible. "He was in the accident...."

Knight interrupted him. "Yes, I know. Sad story. But you survived. We're survivors, William, you and I."

Bill stared into Knight's face looking for clues. Everyone believed Arnold had died in The Accident. They never found his body. It wasn't until the snow melted that some hiker found his engraved silver watch. A reporter from the *Whitefish Pilot* speculated that some animal had dragged off his body and that eventually another unsuspecting hiker would stumble onto his bones somewhere in the woods. No one ever did.

"Maybe I did hear something. Wasn't there something about an engraved silver watch: To Arnold Jr., Love Arnold Sr." Knight nervously wiped his mouth with his napkin.

Bill looked at him in astonishment, and his stomach plunged into his loafers. "What the hell is going on? Arnold, why are you pretending to be Richard Knight? Why did you run away?" Bill's voice had risen, and he was now yelling, poking the air with his index finger. "Look, I know it's you, Arnold. So stop this fucking charade."

"Calm down, Cannon. You're making a scene. Calm down," Knight commanded. "Be quiet for a minute and I'll tell you. It's a long story."

Bill stared across the table, waiting.

He fought off a wave of nausea when Knight finally whispered, "I've missed you and our special wrestling moves." Bill remembered what he'd learned in a psychology class at college: most children's first sexual experiences were homosexual. As hormone filled teenagers, sweaty bodies sliding against each other, one thing led to another, and wrestling matches became desperate touching and lustful fondling, but never outright sex. He'd often wondered if his tousles with Arnold meant that he was gay.

Bill blushed. "That was a long time ago. A lot has changed."

CHAPTER THIRTY-SEVEN

"I HAVEN'T SEEN it this smoky since West Glacier burned up five years ago," Jessica James said, pointing towards the weathered barn. On their third round of vodka tonics, she and Lolita were sitting around her childhood table, trying to catch up with her mom, who had most likely been drinking all day.

"It's so dry the bushes are following the dogs around." Jessica drained her glass, slammed it on the rickety table with a bit too much force, and the table legs wobbled.

"Remember when you hit your head on this table and I had to take you to the emergency room for stitches?" her mom asked with a smile.

"Yeah, because you threw that spoon at me and I ducked."

"You flung it at me first, you little beast."

That chipped rubicund Formica table had witnessed her entire childhood, and its metal legs bowed under the weight of her juvenile lifetime. Every ding and scratch on it told the story of her youth. She thought of all the oversleezy eggs and mushy French toast she'd been forced to eat sitting there. At that table, she'd licked her first beater when her mom made whipped cream for Thanksgiving pumpkin pies; she'd done her math homework with her dad watching over her shoulder; she'd sewn badges for camping and horseback riding onto her girl scout sash; and on that ill fated blustery day in November, at that little red table, she'd heard the heart wrenching news from her aunt.

Jessica contemplated her mom, glassy eyed from a steady diet of vodka Collins, thin, leathery, and unbreakable.

"I heard on the news there are fires all around. This darned drought. Every time we have dry lightning, something catches fire," her mom said. "Wannaanother? I'm going to have one. I need one to cut through this darned smoke and clear my throat." Her mom mixed them another round of vodka Collins in her best cobalt cut-glass goblets, adding a slice of lime to each, and then lit another cigarette. "You girls want something to eat?" She opened a bag of BBQ potato chips and sat them in the middle of the table.

Lolita lifted her glass. "A toast: Let the tables break from abundance and the beds break from love."

Jessica dug into the chips, and then sucked the paprika and salt off of her fingers one by one. When her mom gave her a disapproving look, she chugged her drink, and held out her empty glass. "Another, bartender. I've had a traumatic day and I'm lucky to be alive."

"A toast," said Lolita. "To the survival of my Montana friend, Jessica James, cowgirl philosopher extraordinaire." They all raised their glasses and laughed.

Jessica surveyed the old doublewide where she'd grown

up caught between boisterous loggers with their practical jokes and horseplay in the living room and whispering homemakers squirreling away tasty bits of gossip in the kitchen. Drawn to both, but unwilling to commit to either, she used to stand in the hallway and watch. Years later, when she'd come home from college for Christmas vacation, it was painfully obvious she no longer fit in with her high school friends, girls who'd stayed behind to have babies and cook for their husbands or ex-boyfriends who'd gone to work at the lumber mill. Although she went to college in Missoula, just down the road by Montana standards, she felt light years away.

Now, getting her Ph.D. in philosophy "back East" in Chicago, she was practically an alien from another planet. Intelligent life, indeed. But she wasn't at home in graduate school either. When she'd gotten off the long stuffy plane ride almost a year ago, the Ivy League boys who drank without getting drunk and talked incessantly about Heidegger had been a stinging slap in the freckled-face. With their fancy pedigrees, silver spoons, and smooth talk, the prep school yuppies had been groomed for grad school since kindergarten. She hadn't been groomed at all, not unless a few good thrashings on the playground counted.

"I never told anyone, but I was pregnant when your dad died." Her mom's confession jolted her from her reveries, and she stared into those familiar bloodshot eyes, now filled with tears, wondering if she'd heard right.

"What?" Jessica asked. "When dad died…" She couldn't get the words out. Her mom's shoulders were shaking with sobs and she let out a squeak, just like that dreadful day eleven years ago when Jessica had come home from school early. The entire day had become a film clip playing over and over in her head: Earlier that morning, the snow had been up to her waist and she'd had to yank her legs up with her arms to get them to move through the thick vanilla ice cream covering the playground. At morning recess, she'd gotten in trouble for throwing snowballs at Tommy Dalton and had to write "I'm sorry" on the blackboard twenty times. When the teacher announced the buses were waiting outside to take them home early, at first she'd been disappointed, fascinated by the classroom discussion of her favorite novel, *The Giver*. Once back outside in the flurries, she'd been thrilled to get a snow day. By then, the entire world had gone white. Riding the school bus, she pictured living in a black and white world and suddenly seeing color for the first time. Sitting by herself in the front of the bus, she wondered if everyone saw the same things when they looked out the window. By the time she'd gotten home, the blizzard was worse. She dropped her book bag in a snow bank and went to fetch the horses. She needed to put them inside the barn to weather the storm. Mayhem had tiny icicles spiraling off his mane and frost crystallizing on his eyelashes. When she led them into the barn, even the horses were glistening in the winter wonderland. As she brushed snowflakes off her book bag, she hoped the snow would reach the top of the barn so she could slide off the roof later. She thought of Jonas from the novel *The Giver*, living in a climate controlled world without snow or sleds or horses. She tried to imagine she'd never seen snow or horses, that she was seeing them for the first time.

She marveled at the combination: snow and horses, two of her favorite things. She wished her dad would come home and hitch up the horses to the cutter so they could go for a sleigh ride. She loved the sound of the bells on the horses' harnesses, especially in the muffled depths of winter.

She'd been making a snow angel in the front yard when she heard a crippling sound. Scared stiff, she stopped mid-angel. The horrible noise was her mother screaming from inside the house. Jessica had never heard her mother wail before and the screeching terrified her. Instead of going inside to see what had happened, she scurried into the barn and hid in one of the stalls, where she stayed until it was pitch dark. Eventually hunger drove her into the house. Her heart was galloping as she turned the corner into the kitchen. By then, her mother's sobs had turned to whimpers. Her aunt, Mike's mom, was holding her mother's hand from across the table. Jessica studied a crack in the linoleum as her aunt explained that her dad had given hitchhikers a ride all the way across Marias pass when his truck jack-knifed on an icy patch and was hit head-on by a bus. For some reason, at that moment, Jessica had remembered she'd left her book bag in the barn. She turned to go back out, but her aunt stopped her with the brutal words, "He's dead." Her aunt's embrace felt colder than the icicles on Mayhem's coat. She struggled to get free, slammed the trailer door on the way out, and ran back to the barn, tears freezing on her wind burned face. Jessica felt abandoned and alone.

Now her mom was telling her she might have had a baby sister to keep her company all those years growing up without a father and a mother too emotionally damaged to count. Her mom wiped away a tear with her shirt cuff. "Yeah. I was pregnant and he didn't even know. I hadn't told him yet...." She put her head into the crook of an elbow and leaned on the table. Her thin shoulders rattled and heaved as she quietly wept.

"Mom, what happened? I always wanted a little sister."

"Jessica, I think you're tipsy," Lolita said, giving her a dirty look. "There, there, Mrs. James. It's okay." Lolita put her hand on the nearest sharp shoulder blade.

"Mrs. James was my mother-in-law. Call me Irene." She sniffled into her shirtsleeve.

Lolita nodded towards the small form folded over the kitchen table, and Jessica took the hint.

"Well, we drank an entire fifth of vodka." Jessica tipped the bottle into her mouth to get the last few drops. "We'd better go get another one. Not much else we can do but drink, smoked-in like this." She got up from the table, stumbled, and laughed. "Maybe you're right. I'm a little drunk." She exhaled a wistful sigh. "I coulda had a little sister or brother." Her mother's sobs were getting louder.

"Is it my imagination, or is the smoke getting thicker?" Lolita asked. "I can smell it." She gave her friend a dry look.

"Sure that's not just my cigarette?" Her mom had stopped crying but was still sniffling. "Jesse always did complain the place smelled like an ashtray."

"Can I bum a cigarette?" Lolita asked. "I'll join you, if you don't mind." Without lifting her head, Jessica's mom slid her pack of Marlboro across the table.

"Thanks." As Lolita took the pack and tapped out a

cigarette, the lighter slid across the table and whizzed by onto the floor. Lolita stuck her motorcycle boot out to stop it skating along the linoleum and picked it up. "Fight fire with fire!" Lolita said as she lit her cigarette.

Jessica coughed. "Mom already smokes like a chimney. Don't encourage her."

"I don't think she needs any encouragement, right, Mrs. James? Right, Irene? Anyway, talk about kettles and pot, you smoke as much dope… "

Jessica gave her a stern look and put her finger to her lips.

"Don't start on my smoking," Jessica's mom said. "I can quit any time."

"A toast." Jessica raised her glass. "To cigarettes: fire on one end and a foul mouth on the other!"

"Giving me shit about smoking may be hazardous to your damned health!" her mom said and crushed her cigarette butt into the overflowing ashtray. "Should we go out for more booze and dinner, girls? My treat."

"Let's go to The Bulldog." Jessica zipped up her sweat-shirt, pulled on her cowboy boots, and grabbed her mom's car keys. "Saddle up. I'll drive." But as she staggered towards the door, she tripped over the cat and crashed to the floor. Laughing, she said, "Oh shit. I'm sorry, Stoli. Come back little guy. I'm sorry. I didn't mean to step on you." She was crawling on all fours after the cat when Stoli darted into the living room and hid under the coffee table.

"It's my car and I'll drive it." Her mom picked up the keys. "For Christ's sake, Jesse, get off the floor."

Jessica did a downward-facing-dog to get up off the

floor. She was the last one out the door, but she stopped short when she spotted her mom and Lolita standing stiff as statues on the front porch. Sirens wailing in the distance, Lolita was pointing towards the hay field to the north. A strong southerly wind carried an ominous crackling sound, and a deadly orange glow on the horizon could only mean one thing.

CHAPTER THIRTY-EIGHT

A COOL BREEZE WAS blowing down the valley across the golf course, so Bill Silverton put his jacket back on. Shrouded in a milky haze, the resort had fallen into a gloomy funk. He wished the wind would switch directions so the forest fire smoke would clear out. He looked across the table at his unrecognizable lunch companion and still couldn't believe the CEO of Knight Industries was really his high school buddy, Arnold.

"The lies we tell our friends are nothing compared to the lies we tell ourselves," Knight said.

"You seem to be an expert on both." Bill lobbed his napkin onto the table. "Maybe instead of learning to love my enemies, I need to learn to hate my friends," he said under his breath.

"Now, now, Cannon, hate is a pretty strong word." Knight shook his head. "When did you figure it out?"

"I've had an odd feeling ever since our lunch at Café Kandahar. I couldn't put my finger on it." Bill narrowed his brows and pursed his lips. "It wasn't until just now when you called me Cannon that I recognized you." He sighed and slumped in his chair. "Should I call you Arnold or Richard? This is all really confusing. Why did you run off after the accident? And, why did you come back? Tell me what the hell is going on?" The forest fire smoke was thickening, his eyes were burning and so was his throat. He took a long drink of water and wiped his face on his napkin.

"I'm sorry if I put you on the spot all those years ago, but you've been a true friend. You kept your promise and everyone thinks Arnold Specht Junior died in a bus accident fourteen years ago. And in a way, he did."

"They looked for your body for months, but with all the snow, eventually they gave up. It wasn't until the snow melted and that hiker found your watch folks thought coyotes must have eaten... sorry." Bill took an uneasy sip of wine.

"As I said, you're a true friend, Cannon." He reached across the table and patted Bill's hand. "I really appreciate it. I had to get away." Bill jerked his hand away. "My father was a complete bastard," Arnold continued. "Especially when he was drunk, which was most of the time. I really thought he'd kill me someday if I didn't get out of there. He treated the dog better than he did me, and my mom just watched. I couldn't take it anymore. When the bus exploded, something clicked and I knew I couldn't go back. I realized life is too precious to waste it on bastards. The accident seemed the perfect escape, and my death the perfect punishment for my mom's betrayal."

"Betrayal? Do you really hate your mom so much?" Bill asked. "She was such a mess at your funeral. I almost told her the truth so she'd stop wailing. Where the hell did you go anyway?"

"I hid behind the Snow Slip Inn and called my dad, my real father in Texas. He hired a taxi from Kalispell to pick me up, and paid the driver to take care of me and keep quiet. I nearly froze my ass off waiting for Snow Slip to close and that taxi to arrive. The driver took me to his house, cleaned me up, and drove me to the airport at dawn the next morning. I was probably in Dallas before anyone missed me."

"Your father? Isn't Arnold Specht your father?"

"He's my stepfather. My real father is, was, Richard Knight Sr. When I was six, he lost a brutal custody battle with my mother. He happily took back his first son and no one was the wiser. Even his new wife was eager to have another kid. After trying for a long time, she finally had my hit-witted half-brother, David. But the doctors told her she couldn't have any more children, so she was glad to have me in the house, silly cow."

"You've been in Dallas all these years?" Bill gulped the rest of his wine and followed it with a water chaser.

"Pretty much. My dad died last year and I took over Knight Industries. That's when I decided to come back up here and expand the business. Actually, it was my wife's idea. She's from Missoula." Knight refilled both of their glasses from the bottle chilling in a silver bucket standing next to the table.

"Your wife is from Missoula?"

"What's so surprising about that? She's a doctor. I met her in Dallas. Like you, I have a wife and a kid."

"What's she like?" Bill asked.

Knight gave him a quizzical look. "Maggie? She's the best wife and mother to our son, my stepson…"

Bill interrupted. "You have a stepson?"

"Yes, Ricky."

"You'd better watch out, Arnold. What goes around comes around."

"Ricky's a sweet kid." Knight lifted his glass. "Let's talk about business. A toast to our partnership!"

"Partnership? What partnership? You've got to be kidding."

"To Montana's next governor!" Knight lifted his glass even higher.

"Arnold, or Richard, or whatever the hell you call yourself now, I can't accept your money." The folded cashier's check was still sitting in the middle of the table, and Bill pushed it further across toward Knight.

"It would mean so much to me if you'd take it. After all, Cannon, I'm one of your oldest and closest friends. Consider it the smallest gesture of repayment for all you've done keeping my secret over the years." Knight's fake smile made him want to puke.

"You mean hush money. I can't do that." Bill held his fork in his fist and resisted pounding it on the table.

"No one need know. Anyway, you need the cash to jumpstart your campaign. You'll be a fine governor. Montana needs you."

"Montana needs me to be honest and forthright. I can't in good conscience accept your money because I have reason to believe you're involved in some questionable business dealings, and worse, much worse. I can't be associated with that kind of corruption." Bill stared down a fleck of lint left on his dark pants from the white napkin. "No, I can't afford to keep your money."

"The past isn't important, Cannon. Think of the future."

"That's what I'm afraid of, a future in prison." Bill glanced across the table.

"But even you didn't recognize me. My father made sure I had an expert plastic surgeon who did much more than fix my face after the accident." Knight ran his manicured fingers over his smooth chin and sneered.

"How can you joke about that night? Your face may be fixed, and my hip may be bolted back together, but my soul is scarred forever." He leaned his elbows on the table and put his head in his hands. The smoke was getting thicker and his head was starting to hurt.

"Look, I've got to ask, did you hire Tom Dalton to kill Jesse?" Bill blurted out.

"What? That's ridiculous. What? Why would you ask me that?"

"Because Dalton kidnapped Jesse, drove her to the old Specht mill... your mill, and was about to feed her to the boarding machine. We got there just in time to stop him, thank God." Bill's stomach did a flip when he realized that he'd just accused one of the most powerful and well-connected men in Montana (hell in the country) of attempted murder.

"That's the most insane thing I've ever heard. What did Dalton tell you?"

"He suggested that you and your wife ordered him to kill Jesse and Mike, that you ordered him to make those accidents happen. Did Tom Dalton cause those accidents at the mill? The one that killed Mike James? Was Dalton working for you?" Bill demanded, staring across the table.

"Cannon, buddy, come on. You know me. Would I do such a thing?" Knight smirked then threw his napkin into the middle of his plate. "That kind of talk is not only dangerous, it's offensive. I think I'd better go. I don't want to listen to any more of this nonsense." Knight retrieved his wallet from his jacket pocket and tossed a couple of hundred-dollar bills on the table.

"This should cover lunch. Keep your damned cashier's check. There's a lot more at stake here than you realize." He stood up and peered down at Bill. "Anyway, you cashed my check and deposited it in your bank account. Let's face it, your hands are already dirty." Knight strutted away, but then turned back towards the table, "Remember Cannon, if I turn to vinegar, so will you. If I'm ruined, I'm taking you down with me."

CHAPTER THIRTY-NINE

"FIRE!" JESSICA JAMES jumped off the porch of her mom's trailer, pointing towards the Whitefish Mountains, and shouted, "Oh my god. Fire! We'd better get out of here. Mom, go with Lolita and drive towards town. Now! Holy Shit! Look how fast that fire is moving." She dashed toward the barn. "We've gotta go. Now! Move!"

"Where are you going?" her mom called after her.

"I can't leave the horses. You guys go ahead. I'll meet you in town. GO!" Coughing and squinting, Jessica made her way to the barn. Eyes stinging, she could barely see through the smoke. Luckily, she knew the place by heart. She grabbed halters and a can of oats and then dashed toward the pasture. She couldn't see the two horses, so she banged the metal loop on one of the halters against the oats can. She caught a whinny. "Mischief, Mayhem, come here boys," she called. When she saw two soft noses appear over the fence, she opened the gate and quickly slid the halter over Mayhem's nose, knowing Mischief would follow him anywhere, even if he jumped off a cliff. Sure enough, Mischief followed. She slipped a halter over his head and attached the lead rope.

She grabbed Mayhem's long black mane and pitched her leg over his back. It'd been years since she'd ridden a horse, but once she was on his back, it felt like only yesterday; it felt like home. There was nothing as thrilling as sitting astride a thousand pounds of warm flesh.

The fire had already reached the barn, and flames were licking up at its backside. She dug her heels into Mayhem's haunches and he took off at a gallop. Just at the driveway, she remembered Stoli inside the trailer. She turned back, slid off the horse, wrapped the lead rope around the porch rail, and darted inside. "Stoli, here kitty, kitty. Where are you? Cursed cat, get out here." She zipped through the house looking under furniture and calling his name. The smoke was getting so thick she could hardly breathe, so she grabbed the biggest dishtowel from a kitchen drawer, soaked it with water, wrung it out, and then tied it around her face. She spotted Stoli cowering in a corner behind the sofa. She hurried over to him, and just as she was about to snatch him up, he scooted under the coffee table. Every time she got close, the cat would run. He was heading for the kitchen. Aha! Jessica had him cornered. She lunged at him and grabbed him by the tail. The cat backed up and hissed at her. She dropped to the floor and gently caught Stoli between her knees. As calmly as she could, she cajoled him, saying "Good boy," and "It's okay little guy." When Jessica picked him up, he curled up like a furry little caterpillar. She stuffed him inside her sweatshirt, tucked the hem into her jeans, and zipped it up to her neck. Holding her cat-belly, she jogged back outside. Flames had engulfed the barn and the fire was blazing toward her across the dead grass.

She untied the horses, clicked her tongue to get Mayhem to move closer to the railing, then stepping up onto the rail with one foot, holding her cat-belly, she grabbed Mayhem's mane with her free hand and threw her leg over his back. Holding the reins in her right hand, gripping her cat-belly with her left, she couldn't hold Mischief's lead rope, so she had to trust he'd follow. She gave Mayhem a brisk kick, and they took off flying, fire chasing them all the way to the county road.

She squeezed her thighs as tightly as she could around Mayhem's round belly. God, he'd gotten fat. The horse was wheezing, from lack of exercise or the smoke, she didn't know. He was working up a lather of white suds on his neck. She glanced back and Mischief was right behind them. She galloped away from the fire and towards the slow moving Whitefish River. If necessary, they could take refuge in the water. She rode along the river toward town. Determined to keep ahold of the cat and the two horses and find her mom and Lolita, she rode on through the apocalyptic scene of charred, smoldering landscape. Stoli had his claws embedded in her stomach flesh and was holding on for dear life through the bumpy ride. At the city beach, she pulled up the reins to stop Mayhem. Sure enough, Mischief came up along side them. She restrained her cat-belly with one hand and bent down to reach the lead rope with the other. But every time she extended her arm, she'd start to slide off Mayhem's sweaty back. She gripped with her knees as hard as she could and caught hold of Mischief's halter without falling off. She followed the leather with her fingers until she got ahold of the lead rope. Still holding onto Stoli with her right hand, she grasped the reins and the lead rope in her left and gently tapped Mayhem's midsection with her heels.

When she reached downtown, heads turned, but then no one gave her a second look. With a rag around her mouth, and the cat bulging in her sweatshirt, she looked like a pregnant bandit. Smoky haze clawed at her throat. The furious orange blaze was swallowing the horizon, and baleful sirens cut the sultry air, creating a waking nightmare. She was living her recurring dream of fire and ash.

She kept the horse at a slow trot as they made their way through the streets of Whitefish. Arm wrapped around her cat-belly, she was white-knuckling the reins. Her hand burned from gripping the leather and coarse rope, and she could barely hold both with her small hand, but come hell or high water, she was getting them to safety. As they trotted up Main Street, Jessica remembered when she was just a toddler and her dad used to ride his horse to town with her in front of him on the saddle. He'd held her around the middle while she waved to folks on the street like she was in a parade. Every year as a kid, she and her dad rode horses in the Fourth of July parade. She hoped to hell Mischief and Mayhem remembered those days too and wouldn't freak out at the traffic.

She stopped in front of the Bulldog Tavern. Sure enough, there were her mom's old Subaru and Lolita's Harley. She slid the lead rope through both horses' halters and tied them to a parking meter. She had to deposit Stoli somewhere soon. Her stomach was stinging from his claws and he was now thrashing and yowling. With her free hand, she carefully opened the door to the saloon, taking care to keep a tight grip on the squirming cat. When they were safely inside, she unzipped her sweatshirt and one by one removed Stoli's claws from her stomach. As soon as she put the cat on the floor, he zipped behind the bar and slinked into a cardboard liquor box.

Her mom and Lolita were at the bar with a bottle of vodka between them.

"You brought Stoli. I was so worried about him." Her mom hugged her and poured her a shot of vodka.

"What about me?" Jessica wailed through the rag bandana tied around her face.

"You too, my little bandit." Streaks of mascara trickled down her mom's cheeks.

Jessica ripped the dirty dishtowel from her face, drained the shot glass, and slammed it on the counter. She called to the bartender, "Jack Daniels. No more rotgut vodka. I want a real drink." With trembling fingers, she reached into her mom's shirt pocket and pulled out a pack of Marlboros. "I need a smoke."

"Fight fire with fire," Lolita said. She tipped her head back and poured the chilled vodka into her mouth. "If only we had some Salo."

Jessica laughed until she started to cough. "Cured pork fat, Russian delicacy my arse. Out here, real men eat real food, elk blood-sausage, moose smokies, and venison jerky."

"Bring it on." Lolita raised her glass.

"The horses? The house?" Her mom looked at her with pleading eyes.

"Horses, yes. House, no." Panting, Jessica shook her head and then downed her whiskey.

CHAPTER FORTY

J UST AS RICHARD Knight aka Arnold Specht was getting into his Cadillac Escalade, two uniformed officers intercepted him. Bill Silverton watched while one of the policemen handcuffed Knight and led him to a patrol car. The officer put his hand on Knight's head as he ducked into the backseat. The two officers got into the front seat and then drove away. Detective Dial Davies strolled across the parking lot towards the Club House, and when he saw Bill sitting on the patio, he waved and picked up his pace.

"Annie told me I'd find you here," Dial said. "What's this? Champagne?" He sat in the seat recently vacated by Knight and picked up the glass.

"Only the finest for Mr. Knight, no doubt." He tasted it. "Blaaah. I hate champagne. I'll stick to Moose Drool Brown Ale."

Bill smiled. "It all tastes the same to me. I'm happy with my Budweiser."

"Even Buttwiper is better than this pisswater." Dial put the glass back on the table. "Good thing we got here when we did. Looks like your friend was about to take off. If he'd gotten wind that Dalton's confessed to kidnapping Jessica on Knight's orders, we'd never have seen him again. With all his dough, he could disappear anywhere in the world."

"You can say that again. He's a master at disappearing. You wouldn't believe me if I told you."

"Told me what?" Dial asked.

Bill troubled the edge of his napkin. "You won't believe me, Dude."

"Try me." Dial took another drink of the wine and made another sour face.

Bill took a deep breath, started coughing, and reached for his water. When the coughing fit stopped, he began his long story. He told the detective Arnold had faked his death, but he didn't tell him he'd seen Arnold flee the night of The Accident. He told him Arnold had gone to Dallas to live with his real father and had come back to get even with his stepfather by putting him out of business, but he didn't say anything about Arnold's wrestling moves or children's first sexual encounters. Finally, he confessed that Knight had given him a check for $100,000 as a campaign donation and then refused to take it back.

"Just rip it up, Dude," Dial said.

"Too late. I already cashed it and deposited it in my bank account."

"What? Why'd you do that? You should've known better than to take money from that crook."

"Well, when I took it, I didn't know he was a crook! Anyway, Annie was so excited when I got the big *donation*." He made air quotes. "Truth be told, I started having delusions of grandeur, imagining myself in the Governor's office. At the time, it seemed legit." Bill poured himself another glass of champagne. "Want some?"

"I'm not drinking anymore of that pisswater, especially if it's paid for by that crooked psycho! I mean, who fakes their own death to punish their parents? That's just sick." Dial shook his head.

Bill put the champagne down and drank water instead.

"If Knight is convicted, and it comes out I accepted a donation from that criminal, I'm not going anywhere but jail. What should I do?"

"You could donate the money to the Whitefish Police Protection Fund." Dial snickered.

A smile slowly spread across Bill's face. "Dial Down Davies, that's genius!"

"I was just joking."

"No, I mean if Knight refuses to take it back, I can give the money to charity. Brilliant!" Bill sat up on the edge of his chair. "But what charity? What's the most popular charity in Montana?"

"You're a politician alright."

"That's what Annie thinks, but I'm not so sure."

"Go home to Annie," Dial said. "She'll know what to do. She always does. She's the one who should've been a politician."

"You got that right. But instead, she's got me doing it. She's the mastermind and I'm just her puppet."

"Puppet, my ass. You need Annie. Remember that when you go chasing down memory lane after pretty ghosts."

"Jesse's not a ghost."

"She might as well be, Pal." Dial downed the rest of the

champagne and grimaced. "She lives in another world, one neither of us will ever be able to enter."

"I guess you're right."

"Man-up dude, and go home. My sister may not be perfect, but she's pretty darn close. Anyway, she's devoted to you. You've been through a lot together. Really, Bill, I'd hate to think where you'd be without her. You're lucky to have her and the girls."

"Yeah, you're right. If it weren't for Annie, I'd still be sweeping floors at Home Depot, weeping over lost loves, and drowning my sorrows in cheap beer. Hell, the way I was going after The Accident, maybe I'd be dead by now. I guess Annie saved my life."

CHAPTER FORTY-ONE

WHEN SHE REGAINED consciousness, Kimi RedFox was in the Blackfeet Community Hospital. As she absently stared out the window at Rowdy Blackthorn's hideous sculpture, suddenly the goofy metal forest animals came to life and started dancing. A loud beeping noise interrupted the funny scene and alerted her to a machine on wheels next to her bed. It was screaming and flashing. She struggled against the tubes stemming from the red-eyed monster that were yanking at the back of her hand. That must be why her hand hurt. When she tried to touch her head—it hurt even worse, the tubes resisted and her hand snapped back to her side. Her whole body hurt, but the pain in her head was excruciating and something was wrapped around it, almost covering her eyes. She felt queasy and the room was spinning.

A whirlwind of matching baby-blue cotton blew into the room, efficiently jabbed several buttons to placate the machine, and finally the monster stopped screaming.

"Don't pull on those tubes," the nurse ordered. "That's

your IV. You need to leave that alone. I'll tell the doctor you're awake. Quit fussing now or you'll hurt yourself."

She figured she must be hurt bad if she was hooked up to an IV in the hospital. She tried to remember what had happened and how she got there, but she couldn't. The only thing she knew for sure was that Rowdy Blackthorn's sculpture was doing a jig in the hospital courtyard. The buffalo and elk did a do-si-do, while the mountain goat and the sheep did the can-can. Kimi giggled. But when coyotes started pirouetting through the windows and boogying up the walls of her hospital room, she got scared.

A woman appeared in a long white coat. "Hello, I'm Doctor Hightower. How are you feeling Ms. RedFox? Please try to be still. You've been in an accident."

"What about the coyotes?"

"Coyotes?" The doctor examined the beeping machine and flipped through some pages on a clipboard. "I'll be right back." She went to the door, and then called, "Nurse, can you come here a minute."

The blue clad woman popped her head into the room. "Yes, Dr. Hightower."

"I ordered 5 milligrams of morphine, not 15. Someone has given her too much. No more pain medication today."

Kimi recognized the words but she didn't understand what they meant. She considered asking the coyotes.

The next time she opened her eyes, a fuzzy face came into view, and then a familiar voice whispered, "Princess, how do you feel? Can I get you some pudding or juice? They have lots of it down the hall in the refrigerator."

Her mouth was so dry, when she tried to answer, her tongue stuck to her lips. She nodded weakly.

"Here, have a sip of water." Auntie Madge lifted a pink plastic cup with a striped straw to her mouth and then adjusted the straw between Kimi's lips so she could drink.

"What happened?" she asked when she could speak.

"That blasted ELF kid blew you to kingdom-come and back. By the time Dakota and I got there, that blessed terrorist had already set off the explosion. We found you both under a pile of dirt. Thank God you're okay. I'd never forgive myself if you…" Her voice trailed off into tears, and she caressed Kimi's hand. "My poor little princess."

"Is Leon okay?"

"ELF-boy deserves what he got. Yes, he's fine. He's got a room down the hall with a deputy outside to make sure he doesn't get any ideas about blowing up the hospital. That boy's a public menace. Where did you say he came from?"

"Back East. Yale, I think. But he was born here, adopted by a white doctor."

"Just because a dog's born in a stable doesn't make him a horse. Why'd he bother coming back if he's just going to blow us up?"

Kimi stared out the window at Rowdy's reassuring statue. Even though it had quit dancing, it still looked silly. The mountain animals had wild metal springs for hair going and roly-poly hubcaps for bodies.

"How about a nice chocolate pudding? I have a couple in my purse." Auntie Madge reached into her mammoth purse and retrieved a cup of pudding and a small spoon. Auntie Madge was feeding her pudding one spoonful at a time when a knock at the door interrupted her. Auntie Madge raised her eyebrows at her patient, and Kimi nodded in response. "Come in," Auntie Madge called, and the visitors entered the room.

"Why if it isn't Blondie," Auntie Madge said. "Where have you been young lady? And who's that long tall glass of cool water with you?"

"More like tall glass of vodka." Jessica smirked.

"My guardian angel." Kimi's face lit up. "I thought I'd never see you again. I still have your jacket." She'd been dreaming about meeting the beautiful Russian again.

"You know each other?" Auntie Madge and Jessica asked in unison.

"We've met," Lolita said with a sly smile. She leaned down and kissed Kimi full on the lips. "Payment for my jacket," she said with a wink. Surprised, Kimi's cheeks bronzed and she was beaming in spite of herself.

"You gals want some chocolate pudding?" Auntie Madge asked in confusion. "They got a whole fridge full of the stuff. It's free."

"We just rode over the pass from Whitefish on Lolita's bike," Jessica said. "That tall glass of vodka gets up at the crack of dawn. I need some caffeine, or I'm going to have to push Kimi out of that hospital bed and crawl in myself."

"Don't you dare," Lolita said with a sexy wink.

"I need coffee. Is there a place to get coffee around here?" Jessica whined.

"There's a Dunkin Donuts next door. That's as good as it gets," Auntie Madge said. "As long as you're going, I'll take a black coffee and a jelly-filled donut."

"Anyone else?" Jessica asked. "Three coffees and one donut. Kimi, you want anything? Or are you on a strict pudding diet?"

"Make hers a hot chocolate," Auntie Madge said.

"Auntie, I'm going to overdose on chocolate."

"No such thing as an overdose of chocolate, Princess."

"Princess?" Lolita laughed.

Kimi scowled and gave Auntie Madge the evil eye.

"*Moya printcessa dorogaya.*" Lolita caressed Kimi's greasy hair.

"What language is that?" Auntie Madge asked.

"Russian." Lolita bent down and whispered, "My sweet princess," into Kimi's ear. The resonant vibration sent a tremor down Kimi's spine and made her whole body tingle.

Distracted by the sonorous whisper resonating in her ear, Kimi only half paid attention as Auntie Madge and Lolita swapped stories about their recent adventures. Kimi snapped out of her daydream when her guardian angel was saying something about Jessica saving two horses and a cat from a fire. Just as Auntie Madge was recounting the ELF rally and subsequent explosion that landed "my princess, that good looking David Knight fella, and the blessed tree-hugger" in the hospital, Jessica stumbled back into the room, barely managing to balance the coffees, as she held the door open with one foot.

"Did I hear something about David Knight?" Jessica put a cardboard tray loaded with coffees on the side table, then handed a small paper bag to Auntie Madge. She yanked it opened, pulled out the donut, and sunk her teeth into it. "Ummmmm. Anyone want a bite?" Auntie Madge mumbled, her mouth full.

"He's in the hospital too," Kimi said. "After the goofy pup tried to rescue us, he told me he was on an errand for his evil brother. Now, he's in the hospital too."

"David's in the hospital?" Jessica asked. "What happened?"

Red jelly on her lips, Auntie Madge retold the story of the rally and explosion. David Knight was napping in his rental car out at the construction site when the makeshift bomb exploded. Debris from the blast had buried the car and pinned David inside. Auntie Madge only found him because his cell phone alarm was going off. He must have set it before he fell asleep.

"Why was David at the construction site?" Jessica asked.

"No idea," Auntie Madge said. "Told Kimi he had to check on something for his brother. Near as I can tell, he was an innocent by-stander."

"I don't know about David, but his brother is far from innocent, Auntie," Kimi said. "Richard Knight is using the Chairman and his bogus construction company as a front to get access to Blackfeet land. Why do you think they could drill without getting all the permits from the Federal government? The Chairman is selling us out to big oil for the price of his own comfortable life and that idiotic whale of a yacht beached across from his house. Leon is right, the Chairman sold us up the river, and now that river is full of toxic wastewater from their fracking."

"That may be, Princess. But blowing people up isn't the answer."

"I agree," Jessica said. "Whoever fights monsters

shouldn't become a monster himself in the process. Speaking of monsters, did you hear I was kidnapped and almost offed? I swear if Cannon and Lolita hadn't shown up, that lunatic, Tommy Dalton, was going to kill me. Luckily for me, he's so stupid he couldn't track a bed wagon through a bog hole. Scared the shit out me though. If that wasn't enough, I barely escaped a forest fire that destroyed my mom's place. I've used up two of my nine lives in the last week!"

"Those dirty *Imitáá* are capable of kidnapping and murder. They'll stop at nothing to fill their bellies at our expense." When Kimi gritted her teeth, her head hurt even worse.

CHAPTER FORTY-TWO

WHEN VISITING HOURS were over and everyone had gone, Kimi RedFox wrapped a blanket around her shoulders and padded down the hall looking for Leon Running Wolf. Peeking into rooms, she saw all sorts of misery covered in thin hospital sheets. When she turned the corner, she realized Leon's must be the room with Deputy Ahanu Green standing guard outside. She'd known Wolfe Greene since she was a kid. He worked for Aunt Madge. Sometimes, when they were kids, he used to babysit her and her sisters.

"Hey Ahanu," she said approaching the door, suddenly self-conscious about walking around in just a hospital gown and paper-thin robe, crowned with a big bandage wrapped around her head.

"Hey Kimi. How are you?" he asked. "Poor little thing. Your poor little head." His eyes filled with tears. The Deputy cried at the drop of a hat, funny since his name meant laughter.

"I'm okay. It looks a lot worse than it is."

A tear rolled down his cheek, and with her one good

arm, she hugged him around his lean waist. "Don't worry, it'll be okay. Don't cry, Ahanu. Really, I'm okay. How's Leon? Can I visit him?"

"I don't know. Madge said no visitors." He blew his beaklike nose on his handkerchief.

"I don't think she'd mind, do you?" Kimi asked, smiling sweetly up at the deputy. "I won't tell if you don't. It's kind of important that I talk to him. Just for a couple of minutes."

"Okay, but only for a few minutes. We don't want to get in trouble with Auntie Madge." His thin lips parted, he gave her a conspiratorial grin, and then opened the door to Leon's room.

The window shades were pulled, the room was dark, and Leon was asleep. Various monitors were blinking in the dimness. Kimi crept to the side of his bed and peered down at his peaceful face. She studied his high cheekbones and heart shaped face, his full lower lip and long dark lashes, his arched brows and prominent collarbone. She could have been looking in the mirror.

"Leon?" she whispered close to his small almost round ear. "Leon, are you asleep?" She put her hand on his bare shoulder just above the bandages wrapped around his ribs and the bed sheets tucked under his armpits. "Leon, wake up. It's Kimi."

He slowly opened his eyes, turned his head towards her, his full lips chapped and dry. "Water, can I have some water?"

Kimi retrieved a pink plastic water pitcher from the side table and filled it at the little sink in the corner of the room. When she held the tiny plastic cup to his lips, he lifted his head, but winced, and then allowed his head to fall back onto the pillow.

"Are you okay?"

"I have two broken ribs," Leon said. "I shouldn't have taken you along. Look at your head. Are you okay?"

"I'm fine. Just a bump. Don't worry about me. Leon, can I ask you something?"

"Sure. Anything."

"What did you mean when you said we're alike?" The monitor on the machine next to Leon's bed beeped signaling time for another dose of morphine, so she pushed the red button to administer more pain medicine.

"Look in the mirror, Kimi. You'll take from them when it suits your purposes and then bite their hands when it doesn't," he said. "You're just like me. You take their fracking allotment checks and I take their affirmative action scholarships."

"I'm not following." Kimi scowled.

"I'll make it clear. I took from that rich bastard because it was the only way to fund our chapter of ELF. He wanted me to sabotage everyone else's rigs except his to monopolize fracking on the Reservation. But I knew I'd eventually bite his hand, too." Leon's cutting stare startled her. "We've got to use the master's tools to dismantle the master's house."

"What are you talking about? Did you learn that at Yale?" she asked.

"Richard Knight of Knight Industries, Kimi," he said. "Don't be so naive. He paid me to sabotage Chairman Rowtag's operations. But I wasn't going to stop there. I planned all along to ruin Richard Knight, using his own money to buy the explosives."

"Maybe you're the one who should look in the mirror. I may be naïve, but at least I'm not a hypocrite. I don't bomb my own people." She grimaced remembering Danny and the explosion that almost killed him.

Kimi slid down the hallway to her room, crawled back in bed, and waited. The doctor had promised she'd be discharged that afternoon. She watched the second-hand ticking on the clock on the wall next to the big boxy television that was hanging from a giant metal arm. Its worn-out support was ready to peel off the wall and crash to the floor. The hospital gave her the creeps so she'd had the TV on all night to keep her company. Nearly noon and she still hadn't seen a single doctor or nurse all morning. They hadn't even brought her the slop that passed for breakfast. She got out of bed, tightened the hospital gown around her waist, and peeked out into the hallway. To her surprise, her guardian angel was leaning on the wall across from her room.

"What are you doing here, Lolita?"

"I'm waiting for you. I'm here to spring you from this joint." Flexing her long red nailed fingers, Lolita pushed herself off the wall and ambled across the hall. "Mind if I come in?" She brushed past Kimi and strolled into the room. On the way by, the Russian beauty's hand touched hers and the electricity made her arm hairs stand on end.

Kimi followed her inside, shutting the door behind her.

Lolita leaned back against the concrete wall and put a booted foot on it for support. "When are they letting you out?"

"I thought I'd be out by now. It's nice of you to come get me."

"Someone's got to look after you, *Moya printcessa dorogaya.*"

Kimi was astonished. She hated it when Auntie Madge called her "Princess," but it sounded so much sweeter in Russian. Gazing at her guardian angel's broad smile, she felt as if she were being sucked into the tiny gap between Lolita's front teeth, a powerful energy vortex drawing her into a magical shadowy future.

CHAPTER FORTY-THREE

KIMI REDFOX'S HEART was skipping to keep time with the crazy animal sculpture dancing outside her window, but this time it wasn't from too much morphine. Afraid her face would betray her feelings, she looked out the window and the sun's golden rays flowed through her, golden honey bringing sweetness to life. Her hospital room had been aglow ever since her guardian angel's arrival.

"You might want to put on some clothes before we leave. Although you do look pretty cute in that gown." Lolita winked and then went to the closet and grabbed a huge plastic bag stuffed with dirty clothes. "Put these on." Lolita tossed the bag in her direction and then slinked into the bathroom. Kimi struggled to free herself from bed sheets, first-aid tape, and plastic tubes, and then tugged on her crusty jeans and buttoned her ripped and bloodstained blouse. She wished she'd asked Auntie Madge to bring her a change of clothes. She slid her feet into her Hushpuppies. "It's safe. You can come out now."

"You know, I could see you in the bathroom mirror." Lolita gave her a sly smile.

"You're the candle, I'm just the mirror reflecting your glow."

"A mirror can start a fire by reflecting sunlight. A candle can't do that." Lolita purred, taking her hand and caressing it. "Someone has to ignite it first."

The warmth of her touch radiated up Kimi's arm and exploded in her chest. She intertwined her fingers with Lolita's and stood gazing up into those brilliant sage-green eyes. They cut right through her. There was something severe and feline about the Russian beauty. A sharp claw seized Kimi's heart, tugged, and wouldn't let go. She was a keen hostage to this mysterious woman who had dropped from the clouds to save her.

She heard a knock at the door and released Lolita's hand.

"Can I come in?" Jessica intruded without waiting for an answer. Kimi's cheeks were on fire, and she put her cool hands to her burning face.

"Are you okay? You look flushed."

Kimi glanced at Lolita and smiled.

"What's going on?" Jessica asked.

"Not much thanks to you," Lolita said with a wink. "How's your mom and Stoli? Are they still at the Holiday Inn? Does she have insurance to cover the fire damage?"

"No. Are you joking? My mom have insurance! She's moving into Cannon and Annie's place until her new mobile home arrives. Can you believe it? Cannon Silverton insisted on buying a new doublewide for her. I wonder where he got all that money. He's way too generous. Makes me think of my dad. I mean..." Jessica's voice trailed off when she glanced up at the clunky television anchored to the hospital wall.

Kimi had forgotten the TV was on until Jessica pointed at it and gasped. Kimi glanced up at the screen just in time to see a grim faced man standing with his hands knotted in front of his fly. Rolling text at the bottom of the screen confirmed that several recent forest fires were the result of arson.

"Turn up the volume!" Jessica shouted, and then rifled through the bedcovers searching for the remote. When she found it, she jabbed at the volume control, and a voice blared from the set: "Thank you, Mr. Dalton. That was Frank Dalton of Hungry Horse, who just turned his younger brother James Dalton in to the police. James is believed to be responsible for at least three recent arson fires in the area."

Dumfounded, Kimi stared at the screen. "I don't believe it. I don't believe it. That's him! That's the filthy pig. That's him!"

"Who?" Lolita asked.

Pointing at the TV, hand shaking, Kimi just kept repeating, "That's him. That's the pig. That's him."

"*Lyubov moya.*" Lolita wrapped her long arms around Kimi's narrow waist and squeezed her in a tight embrace. "Please, Sweetie, who is it?" But Kimi was devastated and inconsolable.

"That's Frank Dalton," Jessica said. "He's Jimmy and Tommy's older brother. The three of 'em live out at Hungry Horse. Tommy's the little creep that kidnapped me. And apparently Jimmy's been busy setting those fires burning up the entire county. Kimi, do you know him? Do you know Frank Dalton?"

Kimi freed herself from the constricting embrace. "That man is my father!" She fell back onto the hospital bed and pounded her fist into the mattress. "I hoped the pig was dead."

"Your father?" Jessica asked, her face contorting. "That's impossible. Come on, Frank's only thirty. He can't be your father. What are you talking about?"

"My father's name is Frank Dalton. He looks just like that guy, also named Frank Dalton!" Jessica's incredulous face was infuriating. Kimi stomped her hushpuppied foot, making a black skid mark pointing right at the television appear on the floor.

"Kimi, be reasonable. That man isn't old enough to be your father. You must be mistaken." Jessica started pacing back and forth in from the TV.

"Don't tell me to be reasonable, Ms. Naïve. I'll never forget the face of my rapist, even if it was twelve years ago. That's him! Frank-the-pig-Dalton, my mother's filthy husband." Kimi flung the water pitcher and pink plastic cup across the room. They hit the grimy cracked window and bounced onto the grim blistered linoleum.

"Wait, Frank Dalton's your mother's husband?" Jessica stopped pacing and stared at Kimi with her buggy blue eyes. "I'm confused."

"I'll personally kick the shit out of that asshole," Lolita said. "Let's go find him."

"Hold your horses. Just calm down a minute." Jessica

retrieved her cell phone from the back pocket of her baggy jeans and started tapping on the screen.

"Kimi, is this man your father?" she asked, pointing to a picture of Frank Dalton Sr. from an obituary in the *Whitefish Herald* from eleven years ago, printed just after the accident that had killed him, along with all of the others. Kimi snatched the phone out from under Jessica's chewed up fingernails and then stared down at the picture on the screen. She zoomed in on the text and read the column aloud, "Frank Dalton is survived by his three sons, Frank Jr., James and Thomas, all of Hungry Horse." She put the phone on the bed table. "He's dead. My father's dead." She collapsed back onto the bed and fell back into Lolita's outstretched arms.

"Kimi, are you sure that's your dad? How can that be? His family lives across the mountains in Hungry Horse and…."

"Across the mountains might as well be Mars as far as the Reservation is concerned." Kimi interrupted, then sat up and kicked the side table across the room.

"Apparently," Lolita said, "Mr. Frank the-fucker-Dalton had a second family in Browning."

"But how could you not know your own father had died?" Jessica asked.

"He only came around a couple times a month, and then when my mom died, he stopped coming. How the hell should I know what happened to him? Are you naïve enough to think that shit like this doesn't happen? That evil men can't live double lives."

"Are you sure Frank Dalton is your father?" Jessica asked.

"Yes! I'm telling you, that's our father. My sisters and baby Apisi and me."

"Apisi?"

"It means Coyote in Blackfeet," Lolita said, and Kimi looked at her in surprise. "I like to do my homework." She smiled and cocked her head.

"Who's baby Coyote?" Jessica sat down on a corner of the bed and tilted her head. Suddenly, she jumped up, covered her mouth with her hands, and stared wide-eyed at Kimi. "Oh my god. The baby from the accident. That's what Mike was talking about. She took the baby! Holy shit. Mother of God."

"What is it?" Lolita asked. "What's wrong?"

"I know why Mike was killed. I've gotta go!" Jessica dashed out of the hospital room.

CHAPTER FORTY-FOUR

AFTER THE SHOCK of seeing the spitting image of her missing father on television, and then learning he was dead, Kimi RedFox buried her face in the pillow and sobbed.

"*Lyubov moya.*" Lolita rubbed Kimi's back and continued to whisper soothing Russian phrases into her ear. When Kimi had cried herself dry, her guardian angel retrieved the cup from the floor, went to the sink to fill it, and then, caressing Kimi's hair, encouraged her to sit up.

"Here, have a drink, sweetie."

Kimi grasped the plastic cup in both hands, sipped from a straw, and looked up at Lolita with her red-rimmed almond eyes. When she was finished, Lolita took the cup and sat it back on the bed table.

"I have something important to tell you." Lolita sat on the edge of the bed and stroked Kimi's cheek with long cool fingers. "*Lyubov moya*, I know where to find your sister Hurit." The color drained from Kimi's wet face and her guardian angel brushed the sticky hair off it.

"You know where to find my sister Hurit?"

"Yes."

"Where is she?"

"She's at the CCV compound, a couple of hours south of here." As Lolita stroked her hair, Kimi gazed into the Russian beauty's magnificent chameleon eyes.

"CCV compound? You mean those crazy people down south?"

"Church Complete and Victorious. It's a new-age cult founded by Clare and Earnest Firinne."

"Who?" Kimi asked.

"They got in trouble with the FBI a few years back for stockpiling weapons. They also stockpile food in case of a nuclear holocaust. Their church, if you can call it that, is the Pinnacle Beacon, and that's where someone saw Hurit."

"Who saw Hurit?"

"Let's just say an acquaintance of mine."

"How did you know about my sister?"

"I told you. I like to do my homework." Lolita put her arm around Kimi's trembling shoulders. "And, I have a knack for convincing people to talk, especially when my boots do the persuading. Come on. I'll take you to your sister." Lolita stood up and extended her hand.

"Where exactly is this Victory Church?"

"On a huge ranch outside of Yellowstone. Let's go."

"I'm not supposed to leave until I'm discharged from the hospital."

"You go first and I'll follow, *lyubov moya.*"

Kimi started for the door, and then turned around. "What does that mean, *lyubov moya?*"

"It means…" Lolita glided toward her, grasped her

hand, and kissed it gently. "It means." She looked Kimi squarely in the eyes and she said, "my love."

Kimi floated out the door on tiptoe. Even in the midst of her panic at recognizing her evil father, she couldn't shake the silly grin off her face. She glanced both ways down the hall. The nurse at the desk was on the telephone. Staring straight ahead, she held her breath as she strolled past and slid toward the elevator. She jabbed the down button and waited, her heart racing. The elevator doors opened and Dr. Hightower got out.

"Ms. RedFox, you've been discharged already? That was quick. I just wrote the orders an hour ago. Usually it takes them half a day. Be careful with that bandage. Remember to change it like the nurse showed you. And if your head hurts, take Tylenol. If it reaches an eight on a scale of one to ten, call me right away."

Kimi had forgotten about the bandage on her head and reached for it with her good hand. "Yes, thank you Dr. Hightower."

"Is someone picking you up?"

"Yes, I am," said a silky voice from the hallway. Lolita put her hand on the small of Kimi's back, then led her past the doctor and into the elevator.

"Call if you need anything," the doctor said as the elevator doors shut.

Alone in the elevator, Kimi gazed at her guardian angel, as tough and brilliant as a rare diamond. She entwined her brown fingers with Lolita's ivory ones.

"Nice nails," Kimi whispered, admiring their blood red intensity.

Lolita gently lifted Kimi's chin, and bent down, and kissed her on the mouth. Her lips were soft, fragrant, caressing rose petals. All at once, something inside broke free and Kimi kissed her back like her life depended on it. Lolita pinned her up against the back of the elevator, and they were still kissing when the elevator reached the basement. Kimi wished the hospital had five-hundred floors.

"Follow me. My bike is outside. I know a back way out."

Kimi followed her through a long cavernous hallway to the other side of the building and out a back door into a parking garage. When they came to her motorcycle, Lolita tucked her jet-black hair into a helmet, unlocked a compartment on her bike and handed another helmet to Kimi, who stared at it as she turned it over in her hands. Lolita reached over, brushed Kimi's slack hair away from her face, and then helped her put on the helmet. Kimi struggled to get her leg over the Harley. Once on the thundering machine, she held fast to her angel.

"Hold on, *lyubov moya*." No one had ever called her "my love."

Kimi tightened her grip around Lolita's waist. She was still wearing her leather jacket, protective armor, security blanket, and jasmine mist. It made her feel safe and happy. Since the day her guardian appeared and saved her from that horrible bastard in Whispers Tavern, she'd hardly taken it off. She leaned her head against Lolita's shoulder.

"Can you take me to get my little sister now?"

"I'll take you to the ends of the earth. All you have to do is ask."

Kimi buried her face further into the back of Lolita's

shirt and inhaled the heady scent of sweet jasmine and spicy Marlboros. She squeezed her eyes shut and held on for hours, wishing she could live there clinging to her love forever.

CHAPTER FORTY-FIVE

WHEN JESSICA JAMES barged into his hospital room, David was spooning red Jell-O cubes into his mouth as a nurse's aid combed his damp wavy hair.

"Ah, if it isn't the outlaw, Jesse James," he said. "Have you come to break me out of prison?"

"It depends."

"On what?"

"Whether or not you're a criminal." She walked over to the bed and glared down at him.

"Hmmm...now that's a trick question. Will Jesse James break me out if I *am* a criminal or if I'm *not* a criminal?" When David smiled, his boyish face took on a devilish gleam.

She put her hands on her hips and stared him in the face. "Does your sister-in-law have a son?"

"What? You mean Maggie?" He narrowed his brows.

"Is he Blackfoot?"

"How'd you know that?" He looked surprised.

"Where did your brother meet her?"

"Why the interrogation?" He dropped a spoonful of Jello-O onto the bed table and sat up.

"Just answer the question. How did they meet?"

David gave her a quizzical look. "They met in Dallas at a fundraiser for the hospital. Maggie's a doctor. And you know, come to think of it, she grew up around here in a town called Missoula."

"Can you take me to her?"

"You want to meet Maggie? Why?" David pushed the bed table away.

Jessica narrowed her lips and awaited, arms akimbo.

"I'd be happy to introduce you to Maggie," he said. "But tell me why you want to meet her."

Jessica's cowboy boots clapped on the scuffed industrial floor as she paced back and forth in front of the bed. She stopped pacing, stared at him, and blurted out, "Tommy Dalton kidnapped me, and tried to kill me, and he said Mr. Knight ordered him to do it."

"What are you talking about? You think it was me?" He cast off his blankets and leaped out of bed. "I would never hurt you. I'd never hurt anyone! You were kidnapped? What happened?" When he put his hands on her shoulders, she noticed he was wearing only a thin hospital gown, untied and sliding down his arms. She looked away.

"What? You think I had something to do with it? Believe me, Jessica. Truly. I was never even in a fight at school. I've never hurt anyone, except maybe if I accidently hit 'em with my snowboard or ran over them with my skateboard. I'm harmless...or as my brother says, worthless," he said under his breath. "Richard. Oh my god. That must be what it's about. He's a mean son-of-a-bitch, but kidnapping? Murder? No way. I don't believe it."

"Believe it," she said. "I've got the rope burns to prove it."

"That must be why I got a call from the accountant at Knight Industries this morning. Apparently, my big brother has been arrested. If you're looking for a criminal, you might try him." David sat back on the bed and combed his fingers through his wet hair. "Our accountant says I have to take over as Chief Executive Officer because of the scandal. That's what she called it, a "scandal.""

"What's the charge?"

"I don't know all the details, but seems he was involved in fraud on the Blackfeet deal and some shady business with the new lumber mill he acquired."

"And you didn't know anything about it?" she asked.

"Are you kidding? Up until now, all I've done is surf, snowboard, drink, and have a good time. I told you before, this is my first business trip. After our father died, and Richard inherited Knight Industries he decided it was time for me to grow up or get out."

"How could you not know what your own brother was doing? You're working with him." She tried to pull away, but he tightened his grip on her shoulders.

"Look into my eyes and I'll show you I'm telling the truth."

She hesitated, turned her face toward his but averted his gaze.

"I like you, Jessica. I really like you. I'd never do anything to hurt you. Please believe me? But my brother, Richard…" his voice trailed off.

She stared into his hazel eyes, searching for the truth. Her gut told her he was innocent. "I believe you. And you are not worthless. That's rich coming from your brother."

"Rich is an understatement. I've never understood him. All he cares about is money and he's ruthless. Return of the prodigal son. I still rue the day…"

"What about your sister-in-law?" Jessica interrupted.

"Maggie? What about her?"

"Could she be involved in all of this?" Jessica asked. "My cousin Mike had an argument with her at the picnic the day before he was killed. He recognized her from the bus accident."

"Maggie? Involved in murder? That's crazy. She has her hands full with her whiny son. He's a regular little emo. But I guess that's what it's like to be an eleven year old these days."

"Take me to her." Jessica insisted.

"To my brother's house? Right now?"

Jessica nodded towards his nearly naked body. "After you put on some clothes."

David glanced down at the hospital gown and tied its strings behind him.

"Right," he said, turning bright red. "Oops." He backed up to the closet, retrieved his clothes, and ducked into the bathroom.

"That was quick," she said when he opened the door in his khaki pants, button down plaid shirt, and designer hiking boots.

"Only one problem. Apparently, I'm not allowed to go

until they check me out, like a library book or something." He sat back down on the side of the bed.

"I've spent the last five years in philosophy libraries, and believe me, you aren't as hard to crack as those books." She sat down on the bed next to him. "And you're a lot cuter. Every time I see you, you're so nice and so sweet, but I hear such terrible things about you when I leave." She tried to imagine what it must be like to be an incredibly rich, good-looking, businessman. What was it like to be a bag lady, grubby hands wrapped in rags begging for quarters? Or, a smartly dressed businessman, walking briskly toward a revolving door swinging an umbrella? Or, a sad-eyed German Shepard tied to a parking meter, waiting impatiently for his master's return? Philosophy was her way of escaping her own life and inhabiting the skin of other mammals.

"That's proof," he said.

"Proof of what?" His voice brought her back from her daydreams.

"Proof that you shouldn't leave." He brushed her bangs out of her eyes. "When they finally let me out of here, will you have a proper dinner with me?"

"You mean like a date?"

"Yes, like a date, just the two of us?"

A knock on the door startled her and she stood up.

A perky nurse bounced into the room. "Here are your discharge papers. Could you sign them? Then you're free to go, David. Come back any time if you need your bandages changed. It can be tricky to change the ones on your back by yourself. So, if you need a hand, let us know. We'd be happy to help." The pert nurse smiled at David, and returned to sorting through paperwork, but didn't leave the room.

"Sounds like you have a fan-club lining up to change the dressings on your back," Jessica said, wishing the nosey nurse would leave.

"It's always best to stay on the good side of your nurse. Lucky for me, I was asleep in the backseat, and most of the glass and debris landed on the hood or went through the front windshield or I'd be spending more time with these kind nurses. That's what I get for following my brother's orders. He should have gone out there himself." He shuddered and managed a half smile.

"You always look on the bright side, don't you? Eternal optimist."

"Does that mean you'll have dinner with me? After all, I did try to rescue your roommate and her sister. That counts for something. Maybe an 'A' for effort, professor?" David stared down at his lap. "Okay, I botched the rescue. And if Madge Blackthorn hadn't shown up, I'd be in a lot worse shape than I am now. But I did it to prove myself to you. I didn't want you to think I'm worthless, too. I have a confession. I've always been more interested in surfing and snow boarding than girls. Growing up with the country club set, my mom pushed lots of girls my way, but they were silly bores only interested in my family's money. You're different. You just say whatever comes into your mind. I like that. "

"David, look!" Jessica pointed to the television. She was only half paying attention, as she watched the scrolling news bar at the bottom of the TV screen.

"They're evacuating East Glacier because of the forest fire. My stuff is still in the bunkhouse (All she really cared about fetching was her one prized possession, the silver belt-buckle she'd won just before her dad died). I need to get Lolita to take me over there and fetch it before they close the roads." When she retrieved her phone from the back pocket of her jeans, swiped it on, and tapped a text message from Lolita: "Left w/ K," her face fell.

"I have a driver waiting outside." David glanced up at her. "After my brother was arrested this morning, the main office sent him to me. Given my injuries, I accepted. I'm happy to take you to retrieve your things. We probably should go right away, don't you think?"

"Well, okay since Lolita's not answering. Thanks. But then can we go see your sister-in-law? It's urgent I talk to her." Jessica followed him out of the hospital and into his waiting limo, a shiny black sedan flanked by a driver dressed in freshly pressed livery.

On the road to the lodge, cars lined the narrow highway in and out of East Glacier. Tourists and workers alike were heeding the evacuation warning and taking to the roads. The air was thick with smoke, and when they reached the lodge, the mountains were obscured by haze. Without its panorama of jagged peaks to give it life, the lodge was reduced to a dying log house, its charm erased along with the view. The sky bled into the pool water, forming a billowing shroud that drained away the red rose bushes along with the vistas. The Ruby Buses were overflowing, and a long queue of people lugging suitcases wrapped around the train station was hemorrhaging into the parking lot. When the Amtrak train pulled into the station, tourists started shoving and shouting, jostling to board, and the air was electrified by sheer panic.

CHAPTER FORTY-SIX

WHEN THEY REACHED Rightway Ranch, using a bolt cutter, Lolita snapped the padlock off the gate at the entrance. Her girlfriend's resourcefulness was amazing and she beamed with pride. After over five hours on the bike, Kimi RedFox couldn't wait to get off. Her butt hurt and she needed to stretch her legs. They had to ride another full mile on a dirt road surrounded by farmland before they came to the central compound of the Church Complete and Victorious. In the distance, the sun-bleached tower of Pinnacle Beacon jutted violently from the verdant earthy landscape, an unholy zenith ascending out of the bowels of the planet. The spired temple towered over the middle of a square of charming brick houses. Beyond the square, a grand three-story mansion with manicured lawns, white fences, and horses grazing in lush pastures stood on a hill overlooking the bucolic town.

"You're sure my sister's here?" Kimi scanned the idyllic scene. It could have come from a futuristic sci-fi movie where genetically engineered people live in identically engineered houses. Fit young men and women wearing yoga pants strolled the spotless sidewalks carrying yoga mats and green drinks.

"I'm sure." Lolita parked the bike, swung her long limber leg over the handlebars, and turned to face her. "But not for long." Her wink melted Kimi's broken heart.

"Do you believe in love at first sight?" Kimi whispered, almost to herself.

"Depends." A sly smile spread across her lips.

"On what?"

"The lighting in the bar." Lolita winked again.

When Kimi frowned, the Russian beauty kissed her cheek. "I'm just joking, *lyubov moya*. If a star fell from the sky every time I've thought of you, the moon would be lonely."

Healthful new-agers stopped to stare. "Can we help you?" asked one thin blonde haired, blue-eyed woman wearing paisley tights. Her bright copper bracelet winked in the sunlight.

"We're looking for my friend's sister."

"Her name is Hurit." Kimi awkwardly slid off the back of the bike. "She's fourteen with black hair, brown eyes, about 5 feet tall."

"You mean Harmony. We take new names when we join the Pinnacle Beacon. She's in the garden planting peas and carrots. I'll go get her." The fit young woman handed her green juice to her equally healthy friend and jogged around the corner to a huge community garden. She returned with a nearly unrecognizable Hurit in tow. No longer wan and wasted, she'd gained weight and her rosy cheeks glistened in the sunshine. She wiped long strands of black hair off her face with the back of her gardening gloved hand. When she did, she smeared dirt all across her forehead, and the overly helpful woman pulled a Kleenex from her yoga jacket pocket to wipe it off.

"Hello sister," Hurit said in the voice of an automaton.

Kimi rushed to hug her, but her sister stood immobile, refusing to hug her. "Huri, baby bunny, I was so worried about you."

"As you can see, sister, I am well. My name is Harmony now and I've given up a past full of negative energy and moved into a place of peaceful love. My brothers and sisters in Church Complete and Victorious have saved me from the wickedness and abuse that was my life until now." Hurit's emotionless words sounded rehearsed and stiff. High on new-aged religion, she had an unnerving placid smile on her face that was almost worse than her spaced-out look when she'd been high on drugs. She'd gone from one form of opiate to another.

"Huri, bunbun, we're here to take you home." Kimi gently grasped her sister's hand.

"This is my home, Sister."

"She's happy here," the helpful woman said. "We found her naked and sick crouched on the side of the highway. We brought her here and gave her the physical and spiritual nourishment she needs to heal. She's our sister now."

"It's no use. They've got her brainwashed. Come on, Kimi, let's go." Lolita remounted her bike, turned the ignition, and revved the Harley.

"But I can't leave her...."

"Get on the bike. We're going," Lolita commanded.

Kimi narrowed her brows and gave her guardian angel a questioning look, but she complied. Once Kimi was seated on the motorcycle, Lolita turned and whispered, "Keep your feet firmly on the ground."

The Russian beauty jumped off the bike, grabbed Hurit around the waist, and whisked her over the handlebars onto the front of the motorcycle. Before Hurit could free herself, Lolita jumped back on the bike and held onto the struggling girl with one hand as she gunned the Harley with the other. When she peeled out of the square, Kimi nearly fell off the back.

"Hold on!" Lolita shouted. "We've got to get out of here fast. These religious zealots are armed to the teeth and more dangerous than the Russian mafia."

Kimi grasped her guardian angel around the waist and held on for dear life. Once they'd escaped the compound, and now that both of her sisters were safe, all she could think about was baby Apisi, on the long drive home. If he didn't die in the accident, he'd be eleven next week. She knew he had to be alive. She could feel it.

CHAPTER FORTY-SEVEN

"I'LL JUST BE a minute." Jessica James jumped out of David's sedan and dashed across the lawn to the bunkhouse to fetch her few belongings. She would have left her junk behind if it weren't for the championship silver buckle she'd won barrel racing just before her dad died. As she skidded to a stop at the entrance, she remembered how he'd beamed with pride and insisted her mom take their picture.

Inside the lodge, pandemonium greeted her as staff escorted elderly guests out to the Ruby Buses waiting in the parking lot. She weaved her way through the crowds all the way to the back building that housed the bunkhouse, then rushed into her room to gather her things and stuffed them in her backpack. She paused before she wrapped the framed photograph into a dirty shirt: hair pulled back into a ponytail, she was wearing a black hat, black boots, and a little red fringe jacket. Her dad was grinning from ear to ear, holding the belt-buckle above her head, and Mayhem was nuzzling her shoulder. Back then they were both in their prime, the horse and her dad. She swathed the silver belt-buckle in a wad of underwear, crammed it in the bag, scooted out the rear door and back around the grounds, and then hoofed it back around the grounds to the parking lot. When she got back to the limo, David was arguing with the driver. She would have given them some time alone, but sirens and cops meant it was time to go.

"Sorry to interrupt," she said as she settled into the back seat next to David.

"Is that all you have?" he asked.

"This is it."

"You travel light. The smoke's getting thicker, so we'd better get going."

"Where to, Sir?" the driver asked.

"Look, McQuin, I want to know every place Richard's been in the last week and who he's talked to?" David leaned forward and put his hand on the back of the front seat.

"McQuin, spill the beans. Would you rather tell me or the prosecutor? Out with it! My brother's in jail and you're driving for me now."

"Mr. Knight had me make several trips to Browning for business meetings, but I don't know who...."

"When?"

"Usually late in the evening," the driver said.

"Who did he see?"

"I can't say, Sir."

"Why not?"

"I don't know, Sir."

"Fine, just take me to them then," David said.

"Right now?" McQuin asked.

"Yes, right now. Let's go. Take me to the same places

you took Richard for these late night business meetings. I want to see who we're up against."

"Do you mind?" David turned to Jessica. "I'd like to get some things cleared up as soon as possible. Then we can have a nice leisurely dinner."

"David, I really do need to talk to your sister-in-law as soon as possible. It's about my cousin's death."

"Your cousin's death? All right, we'll go to Dallas to see Maggie, but one stop first."

"Dallas! How the hell are we going to get to Dallas?"

"Trust me. This time I know what I'm doing."

They sat in tense silence as McQuin drove back across the plains to the outskirts of Browning. The sign alongside the highway saying, "Entering Blackfeet Reservation" was unnecessary. It was obvious from the way the landscape had changed from uplifting green to depressing brown. As the Reservation got closer, the mountains got further. After nearly half hour on the highway, McQuin stopped in front of a sprawling ranch house with a monstrous yacht dry-docked in a field across the street.

"Time to find out what my dear big brother has been up to. Are you coming?"

"Me?"

"Why not? You can give me moral support and the courage to face whoever answers that door. Come on. Think of it as an adventure."

A large Indian man with a potbelly wearing tight pressed Wranglers, fancy cowboy boots, and a tan leather vest answered the door. "Can I help you?" His baritone voice boomed.

"I hope so. I'm David Knight. You know my brother Richard. If I'm not mistaken, we're in business together."

"That's right," the man said, extending his hand. "Tribal Chairman Dakota Rowtag. Nice to meet you."

"Good to meet you, Tribal Chairman Dakota Rowtag. May we come in?"

"Sure. Terrible news about the explosion at the construction site. I was sorry to hear you were injured."

"Yes, it was unfortunate," David said. "You may have heard that Richard is....He's out of commission for the time being, so, I'm taking over where he left off. Trouble is, I'm not sure where that is, you see. I was hoping you could help."

"Out of commission? I hope it's nothing serious. Is he sick?"

"That remains to be seen," David said. "Might you fill me in on the details of our business together? Remind me, what are your dealings with Knight Industries?"

Chairman Rowtag narrowed his brows and tightened his lips into a thin line. He opened the door wide and gestured them inside. "You might as well come on in and have a seat. Would you like a cup of coffee?"

"No thanks," David said.

"What about you, Miss?" he turned to Jessica.

"Apologies. How rude. I should have introduced you. Chairman Rowtag, this is my friend Jessica James."

"Coffee, Miss Jessica?" He pointed to the couch in his sprawling living room, and they all sat down.

"No thanks." Surveying the living room, Jessica was taken aback by two stuffed cougars, mouths open, fangs bared, staring down at her from a log perch high above her head. In the center of the polished wooden floor was a bear-skin rug that repeated the theme of beastly maws growling for all eternity. The far wall sported various mounted antlers, moose, elk, deer, and one colossal mountain sheep head. Obviously, Chairman Rowtag preferred dead things to living beings. He was into trophies, thing he could master and control. When she surveyed the room, she noticed photographs of Chairman Rowtag with various beautiful women.... More trophies.

"So what business were you conducting with my brother, Mr. Rowtag?" David asked again.

"This and that."

"This and that by the book, or this and that in a gray area?"

"I'm not sure what you mean, Mr. Knight. Are you making accusations?"

"No, Sir. Let's just say your dealings with Knight Industries have come to a close. We won't be pursuing any more drilling on Blackfoot land. I'm closing all the wells and pulling out of Montana altogether. This country's too beautiful to ruin with crude oil and fracking."

"I'm not sure I follow, Mr. Knight. You're shutting down your fracking operations on the Reservation? All of them?"

"That's right."

"But I gave Knight Industries exclusive rights to drill. You have the sole leases. That was the deal. Your brother and I were partners. You can't just pull out and close up shop. What about me?" Chairman Rowtag crossed his burly arms over his chest.

301

"What about you? Do we owe you money?"

Chairman Rowtag glared at David.

"Well, do we owe you money, Mr. Rowtag?" David asked.

"You'll owe me plenty if you close those wells. I'm counting on that income. I've invested my own cash in the housing development. What about that?" Rowtag pounded his big fist into his knee.

"I don't know what to say. I'm sorry." David stood up. "If we owe you for services rendered, please send a bill and I'll make sure you're paid. I would like to stay and chat, but we have a dinner date. It was nice meeting you Tribal Chairman Dakota Rowtag. I wish you well, but without Knight Industries." David extended his hand to Chairman Rowtag, who just looked away and huffed. When David offered his hand to Jessica on the way out the door, she didn't' have the heart to refuse. He looked so pleased that she took it, and he led her back outside to the limo.

"That was terrifying…and sort of fun!" David said once inside the sedan. His countenance had changed from stormy back to sunny. He'd been so authoritative inside with Chairman Rowtag and now he was downright giddy. Was it just an act? Which was real? The mean David or the nice one? Fortunately, neither David, the cute empty-headed surfer dude or the arrogant cut throat businessman was her type. She preferred sexy nerds. Although it was tempting, she'd sworn off men for the summer so she could concentrate on revising her Master's thesis. Still, David had his charm….and it had been a while.

"No more hydraulic fracturing on Blackfoot land, at

least not on my watch. This calls for a celebration!" he said. "We should tell Kimi. Call her and see if she wants to join us for a celebratory drink. Then you and I can sneak off to dinner alone!"

"What about Mrs. Richard Knight?" Jessica dropped his hand. "How can I get to Dallas, and where can I find her?"

"On my brother's private jet." He smiled and shrugged.

"Private jet! Well if that's what it takes." Jessica flung open the limo door and turned back to him. "She may be responsible for my cousin's death. And, I think she stole a baby."

CHAPTER FORTY-EIGHT

JESSICA JAMES FELT like James Bond when the smartly dressed flight attendant brought out a silver shaker and poured her martini into a chilled triangular glasses, *My name is James, Jessica James.* Even in her childhood spy fantasies, she'd never imagined herself on a private jet. Instead of rows of seats crammed into a flying school bus, Knight Industries' Boeing 737 was a posh one-bedroom apartment with four custom-made leather easy chairs, wood paneling, and a full bar. The crew consisted of a flight attendant and an ex-Air Force fighter pilot.

Whispering and holding hands, Kimi and Lolita were sitting across from her and David in their leather easy chairs, Orient Express luxury train style. Jessica eyed her best friend and realized why she hadn't planned another high stakes poker game. Usually, the poker Tsarina didn't pass up an opportunity to relieve rich gentlemen, or not-so-gentle men, of their spare change. The sexual tension between her roommate and her friend gave her a contact high.

David laughed and rubbed his hands together. "Believe

it or not, this is my first time on this plane. My brother will be so pissed when he finds out I'm using it."

Out of the corner of her eye, Jessica glimpsed her best friend kissing Kimi's hand. Come to think of it, she'd never seen Lolita kiss anyone. She'd seen plenty of men—and an occasional woman—put the moves on Lolita, but her friend never reciprocated. Lolita played with men like a kitten playing with a stunned mouse. Usually, she batted them around for a while, and then abandoned them, stunned, alone, and shivering. Given her friend's glowing countenance, she suspected Lolita was feeling the claw this time. She hoped to hell her friend knew what she was doing getting involved with such a prickly pear.

David was rambling on about his adventures in Glacier Park, gushing about how much he'd fallen in love with the place. He practically swooned talking about speeding along the Going-To-The-Sun road in his rented mustang. Munching on warm nuts, he proudly announced, "Ms. Redfox, you'll be glad to know, Knight Industries is closing all its wells and packing up."

Dropping Lolita's hand, Kimi smirked at him. "You have two dogs fighting inside you, good and evil. While you're throwing a bone to the good one in front of everybody, you're feeding the evil one behind our backs. Which wins depends on which you feed."

"Actually, I'm more of a cat person," David said. "I've always been afraid of dogs."

"Well, even cats scratch," Kimi said with a smile.

Jessica asked the flight attendant for a Jack-'n-Coke. The martini was tasty, but nothing beat the combination of whiskey and caffeine to achieve the sweet-spot of a relaxed buzz.

"I'll try to feed the good dog and to keep my claws retracted. For starters, I'll let you keep your job at Glacier Lodge, even though you run off every chance you get. Both of you!" Pleased with himself, he glanced from Kimi to Jessica and back.

"Just because you're rich doesn't mean you control everyone and everything, especially not Glacier Park Lodge," Kimi said.

"Actually, I do. I bid the contract to run the concessions in the Park and I won! While my brother was defrauding your people and hiring thugs to do his dirty work, I was falling in love with this place." He gazed into Jessica eyes, and she turned away to look out the window. "I plan to spend as much of the rest of my life here as possible," he said. "As a bonus, I'm reinstating you both."

"Are you joking?" Jessica jerked her head around.

"Dead serious," David said with a gleaming toothy smile.

"Oh goodie, I get to keep my crappy summer job." Jessica clapped her hands together and fluttered her eyelashes.

"After your botched rescue attempt, I'm surprised you're not dead period," Kimi said. "*Knight* in shining armor. Ha!"

"Very funny," he said.

"*Lyubov moya*," Lolita said. "David is flying us all the way to Dallas to look for the baby."

"I hate to admit it," Kimi said. "But I'm grateful to you, David. Not just for trying to rescue us, but for helping me find baby Apisi."

"How do you know Margaret Knight took the baby, Jessica?" Lolita asked.

"Well, the day before he died, Mike was arguing with her at the company picnic. He insisted he knew her and she insisted he didn't. He hauled me off in a huff. Later he told me he knew her from the Snow Slip Inn. He was there on the night of my dad's accident and saw a woman with a baby." Fighting back tears, she wiped her nose on her sleeve, and continued. "Mike mentioned records at North Valley hospital. So, yesterday, I went to the hospital and confirmed that a Margaret Wyatt worked as a nurse for a year; and she was on duty with the EMT the night of the bus accident."

"So she was a nurse on the scene. What does that have to do with my baby?" Kimi asked.

"At first," Jessica explained, "I thought Mike meant the hitchhiker woman with the baby, your mom's baby... that is, your baby...the ones who died in my dad's truck." She stared down at her boots to avoid Kimi's piercing gaze. "But when I realized the hitchhikers were Blackfeet, and Richard Knight's stepson is Indian, and his wife is from Montana, I put two and two together."

"Maggie always said her first husband was Native American," David said.

"Well, her baby is eleven years old, right?" Jessica asked.

"Right," he answered. "What does that prove?"

"Nothing in itself. But think about it. She was at the scene of the accident. The baby's body was never found. And now she has an eleven-year old son? In the chaos, she could have taken the baby..."

"Baby Apisi. His name's Apisi," Kimi interrupted.

"So you think Margaret Knight stole Kimi's baby brother, Coyote, the night of the accident?" Lolita asked.

"He's my son, too. Go ahead and say it." Kimi pounded her fist onto the armrest. "I've known all along my baby was still alive. I could feel it."

"I think Margaret Wyatt, now Richard Knight's wife, kidnapped your baby and then reported him dead," Jessica said. "She left town right after the bus accident. And now she shows up again a decade later pretending to be someone else. Come on. Something's up."

"Didn't anyone wonder why they didn't find the baby's body?" David asked.

"No one cares about a missing Indian baby," Kimi said. "All the news was about the tragedy of all those white teenagers cut down in their prime. Nobody mentioned my mother or my son."

"This morning, I checked with the hospital and they have a death certificate for an unnamed Native American baby dated the night of the accident. I'm betting Margaret Wyatt forged it, then left town with your baby," Jessica said. "The question is why? Why would she steal a baby?"

"And would she kill to keep him?" Lolita asked.

"That's what we're going to find out," Jessica said.

CHAPTER FORTY-NINE

JESSICA JAMES THOUGHT of Nietzsche as she stared out the window of the private jet into the puffy clouds, "The higher we soar the smaller we appear to those who cannot fly." She and her friends had been flying for an hour already, and in spite of three cocktails, the roar of the engine combined with the silence of her seatmates made her nervous.

"If only we'd found Hurit." David finally broke the silence. "I'm so sorry Kimi, I tried."

"Didn't you hear? We found her." Lolita reached over and caressed Kimi's arm.

"How is she?" he asked. "Is she hooked on drugs, too?"

"At least you can fight drugs with other drugs," Lolita responded. "But, religious brainwashing is a hell of a lot harder to treat than heroin addiction."

"Pure undiluted religion is as controlling as a drug, more potent than heroin," said Jessica. "Whenever I come in contact with a religious man, I feel the need to wash my hands."

"Let me guess," Lolita said. "Your main man, Nietzsche."

"How well you know me," Jessica said.

"Know Thyself." Lolita winked.

"That's Socrates." Jessica stuck her tongue out.

When they landed in Dallas, a driver from Knight Industries picked them up in a black Lincoln Town Car. Overwhelmed by the oppressive humidity, Jessica could barely catch her breath. The three girls squeezed into the back of the limo and David sat up front. Thank God the Town Car was air-conditioned. The driver delivered them to a posh neighborhood on the outskirts of town. The Knights lived on Armstrong Parkway in Highland Park, the most exclusive part of Dallas. Their fake antique stone castle stood in the middle of its brand new landscaping like it had sprouted overnight, and the huge house was aglow, every room illuminated. Their electric bill was probably more than Jessica's fellowship.

A maid in a white apron and cap answered the door, opened it a crack, and eyed the girls suspiciously, but when she saw David, she opened it wide and welcomed him with a hug. They waited in the library for Dr. Margaret Wyatt Knight.

Surrounded by books, Jessica was comforted by the familiar musty smell of an old library. She wandered around the bookshelves looking at titles on spines. In addition to books about finance and oil, the shelves were filled with row after row of novels—the best of contemporary American fiction, Hemingway, Chandler, Carver, and Roth. All macho men writing about manliness as the art of bullet-biting in the face of life's complexities. Philosophy had taught her it was better to tread water in the mire of indecision and ambiguity than to dive head first into an unknown abyss and risk doing evil, even unintentionally.... She hadn't always heeded that lesson and sometimes took a nosedive or did a face-plant as a result.

An elegant thirtyish woman with brunette hair in a neat bob, wearing a navy pencil skirt and a creamy silk blouse, floated into the library. The tense energy in the room became as unforgiving as a North wind in the dead of winter. The hairs on Jessica's arms stood on end, and shivering, she wrapped her arms around herself.

"Maggie," David said. "These are my friends." He introduced them and they took turns politely shaking hands with her. When Mrs. Knight extended her hand to Kimi, she scowled and folded her arms across her chest.

"What can I do for you, David?" she asked. "Would you and your friends like some tea or coffee? Please, sit down." Mrs. Knight gestured a sitting area, then rang a little bell sitting on a marble side table, and the mute servant appeared again. "Bring us some tea and sandwiches, please, Maria."

Jessica followed her friends to the sitting area, and took a seat on the edge of a fancy antique chair, then steeled her nerves. "Mrs. Knight, can I ask you a question?" She inhaled deeply. "Is it true that eleven years ago you were a nurse at North Valley hospital in Whitefish, Montana and your maiden name was Wyatt?"

Margaret Knight's face paled. She sat down in a high backed, carved wooden chair and smoothed her navy blue skirt with both hands. "You've got my attention. I'm listening."

"You were at the Snow Slip Inn that night, weren't you?" Jessica asked.

"You stole my baby Apisi and left my mother to die." Kimi broke down and started sobbing. Lolita moved over onto the white leather sofa, put her arm around Kimi, then started ripping tissues from a golden box on the end table.

"This interview is over." Mrs. Knight stood up and headed for the door. On her way out, she crashed into the tray the maid was carrying into the library, and the giant silver platter clattered onto the marble floor, sandwiches flying in all directions, teacups shattering. Mrs. Knight made a shrill shrieking sound and fell to the floor.

"Mom," a boy screamed and scurried over to the crumbled woman lying on the floor. "Mom, are you okay? I heard a crash." He knelt down to stroke her hair. "Mommy," he cried, his bronze cheeks flushed, and his almond eyes narrowed. "Who did this to you? I'll make them pay." His accusatory gaze cut through Jessica's soul.

"I'm okay," his mother said, gasping.

David jumped to his feet. "We need to get you to a doctor. You've been scalded." Her silk shirt was soaked with steaming tea and the skin on her neck was bright red.

"Uncle David, who are these people?" The boy's shiny ebony bangs fell over his forehead.

"These are our friends," David answered.

"Friends? Then why haven't I seen them before?" The boy stood up and put his hands on his hips and eyed Jessica with suspicion.

"Don't be frightened, Ricky. They won't hurt you." The boy's mother looked up at Jessica with steely eyes.

"But I might hurt them," the boy said, hitting the palm of his hand with his balled up fist. "If they did this to you, Mom, I'll get even."

Still lying on the floor, Mrs. Knight glanced at Kimi and then at the boy, no doubt as stunned as Jessica by the remarkable resemblance between them. Sitting up, Mrs. Knight embraced the boy around the waist, then looked straight at Kimi. "I knew his mother had already…passed away. There was nothing I could do for her. But I wanted… When he looked up at me with those forever eyes, I needed to do everything a mother could do for him. He was just a helpless baby. He needed me. And, even more, I needed him… and I still need him, now more than ever." Tears rolled down her pink cheeks. "I was young and foolish. But I'd do it again if it meant having Ricky in my life. I love him more than life."

"Mommy." The boy was fighting tears now, too. "What are you talking about? Who was already dead? Make these dirty dogs go away!" he yelled, glaring at Kimi through his tears.

"My heart hurts," Mrs. Knight was crying, too. "It's invisible. But each of your tears touches me here." She put her hand over her heart.

"Invisible threads are the strongest ties," Jessica said under her breath, nearly in tears herself.

Kimi stood up and took a step closer to her son. Frozen, she gazed down at the little boy with her shiny black hair, startled amber eyes, and perfect upturned lips. "Apisi," she whispered. "Coyote, my son, my brother, I've missed you every day of my life."

The boy shook his fist at her. "What did you call me? I'm no coyote, you are, you dirty dog."

"You're my son," Kimi repeated, gazing down at him.

"You're not my mother," he screamed, then kicked Kimi in the shin. Kimi reached down and stroked his hair. "Don't worry, Apisi. I won't hurt you."

"Quit calling me that!"

"Please, you're making Ricky upset. This is his home. The only home he's ever known." Mrs. Knight kneeled and buried her face in the boy's hair.

Kimi moved towards the boy. "My baby. Baby Apisi."

The boy kicked at her again. "Go away. I'm not your baby, you crazy snake lady."

"Please go and leave us alone. I'll pay you. I'll give you whatever you want, but please go," Mrs. Knight's beseeching eyes were trained on Kimi.

"I don't want your filthy money. What you've taken away from me can't be bought." Kimi knelt down by the boy.

"Want me to carry him?" Lolita reached down to lift the boy, but he kicked her and let out a piercing scream. "Tough little thing, like his mother." Lolita laughed.

Mrs. Knight stood up. Her neck and part of her face were scalded bright red, and her shirt was stained brown. "I'm begging you, let him stay. If you love him, then let him stay." She was sobbing. "If you love him as much as I do, you'll let him stay."

When Kimi caressed the boy's hair again, he glared at her and batted her hand away. She took him by the shoulders and gazed straight down into his suspicious amber eyes. "If you ever decide you want to come home, my heart is always open to you, my sweet little Apisi. I love you and always will." She released him, turned away, and covered her eyes with the crook of her arm. Shoulders shaking violently, she began sobbing again. Ricky punched her in the side, then hid behind his uncle.

"Warned you he was a little emo," David said, putting his arm around his nephew. "Don't hit the nice ladies, Ricky. It's not polite."

An elegant older woman wearing a lavender silk pantsuit entered the room. "David, dear, why didn't you tell me you were coming? What going on?" she asked as she surveyed the room. She embraced David and tousled the boy's hair.

"Mother," David said. "I didn't know you were home. I thought this was your evening for bridge." He kissed his mother on the cheek, and gestured toward Jessica. "Let me introduce you to my new friends from Montana."

"How do you do?" The silver-haired woman took Jessica's extended hand in her soft palm.

"Actually, Mother, we've found Ricky's biological mother. Isn't that wonderful?" A black cloud descended over his mother and she put her hand on Ricky's shoulders and held him to her.

"Grandma, should I chase these dirty dogs out of our house?" the boy asked, glowering at Kimi. She was still crouched nearby, face buried in her hands.

"No, Ricky," she said, approaching Kimi. "This is your biological mother. Remember we adopted you. You are a lucky boy. You have two mothers when most people only have one." She reached down and caressed Kimi's hair. "Perhaps we can adopt your biological mother, too. My dear girl, I can't begin to imagine what you've been through."

When Kimi looked up at the elder Mrs. Knight with a questioning look, Lolita swooped over and enveloped Kimi in a sung embrace. "Come on, *lyubov moya*, let's go."

As Lolita led her out of the room, Kimi turned back toward Margaret Knight. "You can give him expensive material things and I have only my love to give. I'll go, for his sake, not yours. When he's older, Apisi can decide for himself. His heart will lead him back to me, and his own people. I'll go, for now, on one condition. Promise, you won't let him forget me. Promise, when he's older you'll bring him to the Reservation to see for himself what it means to be Blackfoot."

Jessica followed Kimi and Lolita back into the hallway where the maid was waiting to show them out. No sooner had they gotten to the front door than the doorbell rang. The maid answered it and two uniformed policemen asked for Mrs. Knight. Kimi was shaking and sobbing as Lolita led her past them, back out into the rainy night to the waiting limo. Curious, Jessica stayed behind to watch.

The maid returned with Margaret Knight, followed by Ricky, David, and his mother.

"Margaret Knight, Mrs. Richard Knight, you are under arrest for your part in two deaths at the Specht Mill in Whitefish, Montana," one of the officers said. The other recited her rights.

Mrs. Knight bent down and kissed her son on the cheek. "Be a good boy and do what grandma tells you. I'll be back soon. Maria, bring me my raincoat." She turned back to the elder Mrs. Knight. "Call Richard's lawyer."

"What do you mean Maggie's under arrest for deaths at the mill?" David asked, looking at his sister-in-law and shaking his head.

"You have the right to remain silent..." Ignoring David, the cop recited her rights.

The maid scurried off, and then returned with a raincoat, hat, and umbrella and handed them to Mrs. Knight.

"Did you have something to do with my cousin's death at the mill?" Jessica asked, glaring at Mrs. Knight.

"Mrs. Knight. We need you to come with us now," the cop said, scowling at Jessica.

When one of the officers took her arm to lead her out the door, Ricky ran up and hit him with his little balled up fist. David pulled his nephew off the policeman, dragged him back into the house, and shut the door. Paralyzed by the realization that this woman may be responsible for Mike's death, Jessica stood motionless on the sidewalk in the pouring rain. By the time David returned, the officers had already led his sister-in-law outside to their cruiser, and helped her into the backseat. A shadowy figure, she looked back toward the house through the rain streaked window of the police car.

Chapter Fifty

THE HEAVY DALLAS sky opened wide and poured down sheets of rain. Jessica James was looking forward to getting back to Montana; at least there when it rained it was cool and fresh. When they arrived at the airport, the driver gave David an umbrella, so she huddled next to him, trying to stay dry as she sloshed through puddles and jumped over pools of water on the tarmac. David handed the umbrella to the flight attendant as he stepped into the airplane, and Jessica ducked in after him.

Kimi hadn't said a word since they'd left the boy behind. Silent tears streamed from her puffy red-rimmed eyes. Before takeoff, she'd whispered something to the flight attendant, who strode off and discretely returned with a barf-bag. As the plane ascended through the black clouds, Kimi quietly vomited into it. Once the plane leveled off above the storm, Lolita took Kimi's small hand and led her back to the bedroom.

Jessica pretended to be asleep but followed them with

her eyes as they went past, her best friend supporting her weepy roommate.

"Will it bother you if I turn on the television news?" David asked. "I can ask the attendant for headphones."

"No. I can't sleep anyway. I can't believe your sister-in-law had Mike killed. Why? Why didn't she just go away and leave us alone?" She leaned the seat all the way back and nestled her head into the headrest.

"I'm sorry about your cousin. I don't think Maggie would do that. I really don't. I'm sure there's some other explanation."

David tapped some buttons and a screen popped out of a compartment overhead. When she saw "Whitefish, Montana" scroll across the bottom of the screen, Jessica sat up. "Turn up the volume."

The news anchor reported: "There are strange things happening in the small mountain town of Whitefish, Montana. Two grisly mill accidents at a local lumber mill in the last two weeks have folks wondering." Tommy's high school graduation picture appeared in the corner of the screen. "The confession Mr. Thomas Dalton of Hungry Horse, a worker at the mill owned by Knight Industries, implicates Dallas businessman, Mr. Richard Knight, in the two accidents, which, it seems may, not be accidents after all, but murders." A video of David's brother getting out of a police car in front of the Whitefish jail, showed him handcuffed as the cops led him inside. The voiceover continued, "Mr. Richard Knight, CEO of Knight Industries, and owner of the largest hydraulic fracturing concessions in Western Montana is suspected of corruption and fraud involving the Blackfeet Indian Reservation across the mountains in Browning, Montana." A camera panned the streets of Browning, empty except for a pack of stray dogs and a beat-up old Chevy.

David punched a button and the television withdrew back into its hiding place above their heads.

"Why ruin a good evening?" He sighed and folded his hands in his lap. The sadness behind his eyes pricked at her heart.

"I'm sorry about your brother," she lied. "But he may be responsible for murdering my cousin!" The flight attendant delivered cocktails, and Jessica took a long drink of her whisky and Coke.

"He's an asshole, but it looks like he'll be going to jail for a long, long time. I guess if Margaret's involved, then maybe she will be, too. Little Ricky can count on me and my mother. We'll take good care of him until he gets used to the idea that Kimi Redfox is his mother. That may take a while, too. Imagine having Kimi Redfox as your mother." He forced a smile, then raised his wine glass. "To family— it is what it is, and that's the least of our troubles."

"To family." Jessica lifted her drink and smiled. "Family is like wallpaper—messy, clingy, and annoyingly repetitive."

She remembered her childhood wallpaper with its adorable baby forest animals. It had been on her bedroom walls since before she was born. At Alpine Vista last week, she'd spied its earth tones peeling from the walls, semi-hidden behind stacks of boxes. She was looking for the folding tables for the party before Mike's funeral and had gone rummaging around in her old bedroom. Her mom had it so crammed full of boxes, broken furniture, knick-knacks, Christmas ornaments, and other crap she'd accumulated over the last twenty-five years, Jessica hardly recognized the room. That is, except for the gaps where she could see her wallpaper: Flaking bear cubs peeked their furry round heads out of caves, shedding moose calves splashed in their own private lakes, peeling fawns nibbled at grass below a stand of fir trees, and cracking coyote cubs howled at skies full of stars, circled tiny buttery moons, halos hanging above their pointy little snouts, the whole forest connected by one faded meandering stream.

All those poor baby animals had been burnt to a crackling crisp in the fire, along with Jessica's childhood home. Now, she was going back to nothing but charred stumps, grim ashes, and melancholy revenants like those in her recurring nightmare. The remains of her Montana childhood was merely a skeletal remnant of where she'd come from, but hopefully not where she was going. Mike was dead and all of her dad's earthly belongings were now ashes. "Ashes to ashes, dust to dust," the preacher had said at the funeral, and as usual when in church, Nietzsche came to mind: "You must be ready to burn yourself in your own flame; how could you rise anew if you have not first become ashes?" After her father's death, she'd thrown herself into the fire—riding bucking broncos, hanging from rock cliffs, staying out all night, kicking the shit out of patriarchy. She'd become ashes, all right. She wondered if she'd ever rise anew.

Her childhood home might be nothing but blackened ruins, but Jessica was chompin' at the bit to get back for another sloppy reunion with her boozy mom. They'd been through a lot together, and even if her mom was an annoying mess, they were papered together for life. Those Ivy League educated brats may have had more pedigrees than she did, but they weren't forged out of tough Montana granite. Ducking flying pots and pans had prepared her for graduate school in ways those pansy-assed boys couldn't imagine when they ran back to their rich parents at the first sign of trouble. She'd like to see any one of them brave what she'd had to endure her first year away, not to mention her first homecoming. Maybe the blaze that destroyed her childhood home was a transformation by fire, sublimating even the darkest feelings into powerful resources to face whatever challenges were on the horizon.

After dinner, and a couple more whiskeys, David talked her into a glass of port. "You're not cut out for the business world. Face it, David, you'd rather be at the beach with your long board."

"How well you know me." He took her hand in his and looked at her with questioning eyes.

"Now, if only I knew myself," she said, withdrawing her hand.

She smiled at him, then turned to ask the flight attendant for a pillow and blanket. She leaned back in her recliner, and dozed off and on for the rest of the flight back to Glacier International Airport. The turbulent landing woke her from the recurring nightmare of fire and ash. Clutching her blanket, she gazed out the window at her favorite place in the world, and realized her dream had been transformed. In the dream, she was always riding a horse, surrounded by fire, gasping for air, looking for escape routes. But this time, instead of threatening her from the outside, she felt the fire inside her belly. Even if that fire in her gut was just heartburn from too much whiskey, she was determined to keep going until she rounded the last barrel, finished the race, and the next silver belt-buckle was in her sites.

ACKNOWLEDGMENTS

Thanks to my tireless editor, Lisa Mae Walsh. Without her encouragement, comments, and inspired editorial advice, I couldn't have written this novel. Thanks to everyone who read earlier drafts and gave me helpful feedback, especially Teri, Jason, Alison, and Rebecca. I really appreciate it! And, thanks to Beni, who not only cheered me on, but also gave me great ideas and insightful criticism all along the way. Finally, thanks to my furry friends and family who kept me company for hours on end, happily purring next to me or on me. It would be a lonely endeavor without them.

ABOUT KELLY OLIVER

WHEN SHE'S NOT writing Jessica James mystery novels, Kelly Oliver is a Distinguished Professor of Philosophy at Vanderbilt University. She earned her B.A. from Gonzaga University and her Ph.D. from Northwestern University. She is the author of fourteen nonfiction books, most recently, *Hunting Girls: Sexual Violence from The Hunger Games to Campus Rape* (Columbia University Press 2016), and over 100 articles on issues including campus rape, reproductive technologies, women and the media, film noir, animal ethics, environmental philosophy, and Alfred Hitchcock. Her work has been translated into seven languages, and she has published an op-ed on loving our pets in The New York Times. She has been interviewed on ABC television news, the Canadian Broadcasting Network, and various radio programs

Kelly lives in Nashville with her husband and her furry family, Hurricane, Yukiyu, and Mayhem.

For more information on Kelly, check out her website: kellyoliverbooks.com

COYOTE

Book Club Questions

How does the novel take up serious issues of Fracking, corruption, human trafficking, Eco-terrorism, and drug addiction? Did the novel make you more aware of these issues?

Did you like the way the novel moved between Glacier Park and the Blackfeet Indian Reservation? In what ways did the setting act as a kind of character in the novel?

The novel is told from three points of view, Jessica's, Kimi's, and Bill's. Who's point of view did you enjoy the most? Why?

All three main characters are affected by the bus accident. Did you like the way that the story is anchored by that one traumatic event?

What would Jessica's life have been like if she'd stayed in Montana? In what ways is Bill a sort of alter-ego for Jessica as someone who stayed?

Even though Jessica is from Montana, she doesn't seem to fit in. Yet, she doesn't fit in at graduate school in philosophy either. Discuss the ways in which Jessica is a misfit in both places, and why.

How is Jessica's life affected by others' expectations of her?

How does philosophy help her to cope with, escape, or navigate the world?

What did you think of Jessica's relationship with Kimi? How about Kimi's relationship with Lolita?

What was the biggest surprise in the novel?

Was Tommy a good bad guy? What about Richard Knight?

Did you like the double-identity subplot?

Did the novel do a good job of raising awareness of the poverty and hardship on the Blackfeet Indian Reservation?

CPSIA information can be obtained at www.ICGtesting.com
Printed in the USA
LVOW10s2329090616

491903LV00003B/30/P